JONATHAN D. VerHOEVEN

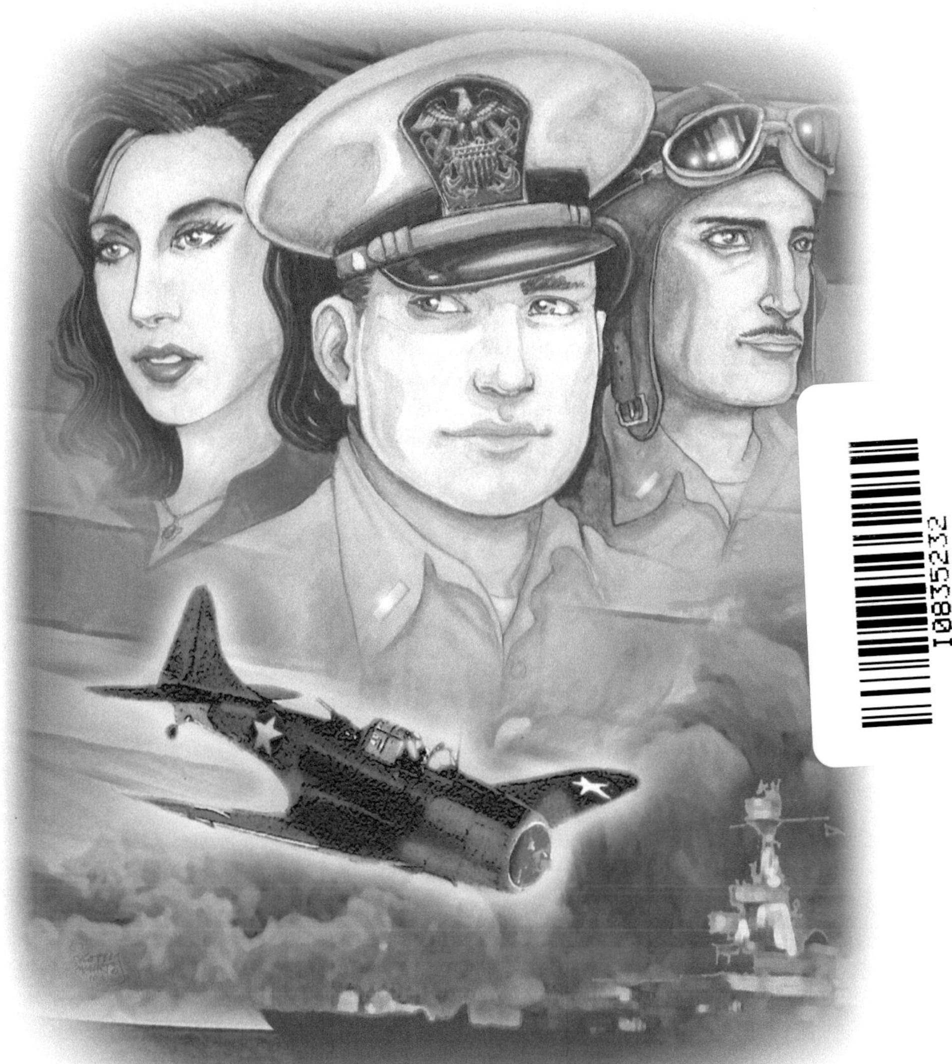

PERIL ON THE SEA

LIBERTY
UNIVERSITY
BOOKS

Peril On the Sea

by Jonathan D. VerHoeven

ISBN-13: 978-1-935986-02-7

Cover & Interior Design:

Megan Johnson
Johnson2Design
Johnson2Design.com

Cover Illustration:

Scott Roberts

A Division of Liberty University Press
Lynchburg, VA

For those who lived it.

This book is a work of fiction based on actual events.

Acknowledgments are due to the USS *Houston* (CA-30) Survivors Association for technical advice. Also, I relied on a number of published sources for historical data and occasional spoken lines uttered by non-fiction characters. Chief among these sources were the non-fiction books *Ship of Ghosts* by James D. Hornfischer (Bantam, 2006) and Volumes 3 and 4 of *History of United States Naval Operations in World War II* by Samuel Eliot Morison (Little, Brown, 1962).

Table of Contents

Prologue 1

Chapter One. 13

Chapter Two. 21

Chapter Three 37

Chapter Four 55

Chapter Five. 69

Chapter Six. 79

Chapter Seven 87

Chapter Eight. 95

Chapter Nine 107

Chapter Ten 117
Chapter Eleven 127
Chapter Twelve 137
Chapter Thirteen. 147
Chapter Fourteen 161
Chapter Fifteen 177
Chapter Sixteen. 187
Chapter Seventeen 195
Chapter Eighteen 203
Chapter Nineteen 213
Chapter Twenty. 223
Chapter Twenty-One 229
Chapter Twenty-Two 245
Chapter Twenty-Three. 253

Chapter Twenty-Four 267

Chapter Twenty-Five 275

Chapter Twenty-Six 285

PROLOGUE

Little Rock, Arkansas, 1926

Seven-year-old Preston Brown stood on the muddy banks of the Arkansas River alongside his father, Phillip, each of them holding a fishing pole with a line stretched out into the deceptively quick current. Both were barefoot, their pant legs rolled up to just below their knees. Their shirt sleeves were rolled up, too, a vain effort to provide relief from the June heat and humidity.

"River sure is big, Dad," Preston commented.

Phillip gazed across the surface of the brown water toward the north bank a good quarter-mile away. "Yes, son, it sure is."

"How many fish do you think are in it?"

"Oh ... I don't know. Thousands I'm sure."

Preston looked up at his father. "Why aren't they biting then?"

"Be patient. They might just not be hungry right now."

The boy turned his head back to the river. "Where does the river start?"

Here was a concrete question to which Phillip could give a concrete answer. "A town called Leadville, Colorado, way up in the Rocky Mountains."

Predictably, "How far away is Leadville, Colorado?" the boy asked.

"About 800 miles."

"Do the fish in the river here come all the way from Leadville, Colorado?"

"A few of them might."

"Where does the river end?"

"You know that," Phillip gently chided. "It empties into the Mississippi River down at Arkansas Post. You learned that in school, didn't you?"

"Yes, sir. I was just checking to make sure you knew."

"Oh, well," Phillip laughed. "Then you must know where the Mississippi ends."

"Yes, sir. At the Gulf of Mexico down in Louisiana."

"Good job."

There was a pause. "Did you ever see the Gulf of Mexico when you were in the Navy?" Preston asked.

"A couple of times."

"Did you ever fish in it?"

"Mmm-hmm," Phillip mumbled positive acknowledgment.

"What was the biggest fish you caught?"

Phillip smiled as he immediately recalled the epic struggle between him and that fish. "I caught a marlin once," he told his son. "It was about 6 feet long."

"Whoa!" Preston exclaimed. "No kidding?"

Phillip shook his head. "No kidding."

"Are any of those fish up here?"

Phillip shook his head and chuckled. "No."

There was another pause. Phillip looked down at the boy and could see the gears turning in his mind. Phillip could tell Preston's imagination was working by the way his son was absently staring across the river.

"What are you thinking about?" Phillip inquired.

"I want to be in the Navy like you," Preston replied decisively.

Phillip could not say that he was surprised, but this was the first time Preston had voiced this desire. As a reserve officer, Phillip still kept a set of uniforms in his closet at home, and Preston had been known to sneak in there while he was at the office and try on the various oversized jackets, coats, and hats. At least this was what Phillip's wife, Olivia, reported to him at night before they went to sleep.

"Don't let him get enamored with the Navy, Phil," she would implore him. "It's not all about wearing a fancy, white uniform and sailing the high seas," she would say. "It's about taking orders, about living according to someone else's wishes all of the time. Preston can be more than that. He can be a great man someday if he is allowed to be free."

Phillip would, of course, point out the contradictions inherent to her argument, but Olivia would always counter, telling him how she wished he would resign his reserve commission once and for all. And he had resisted, secretly relishing his son's interest in the life about which he had once been so passionate himself.

"You want to be like me, eh?" Phillip asked his son on the riverbank. "You know you don't have to be in the Navy to catch marlins."

"Yes, sir, I know. I want to have uniforms like you and sail on a battleship and see the world." There was a definite tone of adventure in the boy's voice.

"It's a lot harder than it sounds, Preston," Phillip warned. "You have to take orders from officers, and you have to excel in school. The Navy doesn't want boys who slouch at their schoolwork."

Preston was no slouch, but he did grumble occasionally.

"Oh, I know all of that, Dad!" Preston insisted. "I want to go to the Naval Academy like you did."

Doing his best to conceal his delight, Phillip replied, "Well, you'd best begin studying tonight. Only the smartest boys are allowed into the Academy."

Preston nodded firmly and confidently. "Don't worry. I can do it."

Phillip knew his son could indeed do it, though he did wonder if this sudden announcement was part of a youthful phase or some greater determination. Whatever it was, Olivia would probably try to put an end to it as soon as she heard of it. He would have to swear his son to secrecy, at least until he could determine if the desire was real. Phillip turned around and searched the edge of the bluff behind them. Somewhere up there Olivia and their five-year-old daughter, Carolyn, were setting up a picnic lunch, and Phillip's stomach told him they had to be almost ready.

Phillip slapped Preston on the shoulder. "I think it's about chow time, sailor. Let's go get something to eat."

"Aye-aye, Cap'n!" Preston replied formally and promptly began reeling in his line.

Phillip smiled in spite of himself and wondered if his son would indeed follow in his footsteps. That he even wanted to made Phillip proud enough for the time being.

Springdale, Arkansas, 1926

Five-year-old Elaine Wright finished securing her apron and turned toward the small table sitting in the center of the kitchen. The apron strings neither formed a knot nor had they actually been tied, for Elaine had simply twisted them together until they felt tight enough. By the time she dug her hands into the rough, wet dough on the tabletop, the red strings had worked themselves loose without her noticing. Across from her stood her mother, Antonia, a full-blooded Italian who took great pleasure in teaching her daughter the finer points of baking ciabatta bread.

"Mama, can I punch and turn the dough today?" Elaine asked.

"Absolutely, but you will have to remember to do it every thirty minutes for three whole hours," Antonia replied in that motherly tone intended for conveying the importance of grave responsibilities to children.

"That's six times!" Elaine declared perkily.

"Good, sweetheart! You're getting better at math all the time!" Antonia commended her daughter. "How are you with telling time?" She pointed up at the clock hanging above the window behind the sink. "Can you tell me when you'll need to punch the dough first?"

Elaine looked up to her right and squinted at the clock. "When the little hand is on the 11 and the big hand is on the 9."

"That's right. You're catching on."

"That was easy," Elaine assured her. "The next time I would need to do it is when the little hand is on the 12 and the big hand is on the 3, and after that when the little hand is on the 12 and the big hand is on the 9, and ..."

Antonia smiled as her little girl precisely rattled off four additional locations of both hands of the clock. Elaine was bright and precocious, always eager to learn, and usually excelling at whatever she did. "I can see that I can trust you with this task," Antonia told Elaine. "In fact, when your father comes home this evening, I'll tell him you made the bread."

Elaine flashed her mother a charming, bright-eyed smile. "Mama, how old were you when Nana taught you to bake ciabatta?"

"Mmm ... about your age. We'd stand in the kitchen just like you and I are doing now and she'd tell me stories about Italy and how much she wanted to take me there someday."

"But you didn't get to go, did you?"

Antonia shook her head sadly. "No, sweetie, not yet. I still hope to someday while your grandmother is still alive. I think she wants to go herself just as badly as she wants me to."

"Will you take me with you when you go?"

"Of course! I'll take your father and Danny and Nick, too."

Elaine's younger brothers, age three and two, respectively, were just outside the kitchen, making their usual racket that Elaine had learned to ignore but that Antonia keenly kept an ear to, ever listening for signs of trouble.

"I want to travel around the world when I grow up," Elaine announced.

Danny, pushing a toy truck on the wooden floor, crawled into the kitchen and began driving it between Elaine's feet. Nick hurried in behind him with a truck of his own. The room filled with the sounds of improvised engines. Elaine watched them with a perturbed look on her face that prompted Antonia to ask the boys to return to the living room. Danny, who had just sat down and parked his truck next to Elaine's left foot, struggled to stand, and used her long, dark-brown braid to help pull himself up.

"Owww! Dannyyyy!" Elaine protested as her head leaned back until Danny had gained his footing.

"Danny! Don't pull your sister's hair!" Antonia scolded the child, who quickly exited the kitchen with Nick.

Elaine rubbed her head as she watched them leave and adjusted the red bow in her hair that had been knocked askew.

"You were saying, honey?" Antonia prompted her daughter to continue speaking.

"I just want to see the world," Elaine explained. "I want to see Italy and Canada and England and Australia."

"You'll have to marry a rich man to be able to travel like that. Either that or you'll have to go to college and get a job that involves traveling."

"Can I do both?"

Antonia smiled. "Sure, but never marry a man because he's rich. Marry him because you love him." She thought of her own marriage to Douglas, a working-class, non-Catholic, non-Italian. Love had been the only reason she had married him, and she had certainly paid for her decision in regard to her family. Lack of time and money were not the only issues keeping her from traveling to Italy with her mother. "As long as you marry a Christian man who loves God and loves you, you can't go wrong. Just remember that when you're older."

"I will."

Antonia stood still for a moment and watched her daughter knead the dough vigorously. She tried to picture little Elaine all grown up and married, and frankly, Antonia could not do it. Though she knew adolescence, adulthood, and marriage were inevitable for her daughter, Antonia would always see a little girl when she looked at Elaine. It had to be a mother thing. Antonia smiled to herself and went back to work, hoping the years would not pass by too quickly.

Wichita, Kansas, 1926

Six-year-old Floyd Craven and his cousin Joey jostled their way through a maze of adults, ducking beneath elbows and squeezing between the occasional overweight bystanders. They emerged from the crowd directly in front of a rope cordon and gazed out at the field before them as two jungle adventurers might gaze upon a just-discovered Mayan temple. A pair of Curtiss JN-4 "Jenny" biplanes sat less than 30 yards away, a sandwich board stood facing the crowd with the straightforward, yet electrifying, message, *"Airplane Rides, $2!"* streaked across it in bright red paint.

Floyd turned and gave Joey's shoulder a light punch. "Two dollars! Look at that, will ya! Your dad would pay for that, wouldn't he?"

Joey responded, but did not take his eyes off the sign. "Yeah, I'll bet he would. Let's go!"

And with that the two adventurers plunged back into the human rainforest, hoping to find Floyd's uncle somewhere on the other side. An hour later, they were standing with him at the front of the line, ready to go for their rides. Floyd's uncle, an easygoing, easy spender, had agreed with hardly a second thought, remarking that he wouldn't mind flying either. Floyd's aunt, on the other hand, demonstrated grave reservations. She didn't relish the thought of her husband, her only son, and her brother's only son taking to the skies. Somehow she had formed in her worrying mind the twisted notion that the airplane ride would turn into an aerobatic demonstration of loops, dives, and rolls that the crowd had spent the morning observing with breathless fascination. What's more, she pictured the carefree pilots coaxing them into attempting wing-walking or some other entirely reckless feat, and she justified her fears not with her distrust of the barnstormers but with the absolute conviction that all three of her boys would try anything if asked. She relented, however, strangely developing an ironic trust in the wisdom of the daredevil pilots and convincing herself they would never let two six-year-olds into their airplanes.

Her trust could have been better placed. She watched in horror as her husband handed over four one-dollar bills and the two pilots took Floyd and Joey by their hands and happily led them to the biplanes. The helpless woman twice opened her mouth to call out her final objections, but gave up both times without uttering a word. She knew the jungle of human trees topped with fedoras and curly female hair would squelch an expression of her motherly instincts, and so she sank back, muttering a prayer and crossing herself, while her son and nephew prepared to do the one thing God had not designed the human body to do.

What happened next turned out to be one of the first — but by no means the last — defining moments of Floyd Craven's life. In 15 minutes of fairly level flying in a circle around the outskirts of Wichita, the boy fell in love with two things — speed and altitude. The takeoff had been both bone-jarring and thrilling, and though Kansas looks much the same from 1,600 feet as it does from six, Floyd became enthralled by the miniature-ness of all the familiar objects on the ground and by the realization that he was so far above it all thanks to a magical machine and an inspiringly cavalier aviator in leather and goggles. Thrust, drag, lift, and Bernoulli's principle were total unknowns to Floyd, and would have remained so had someone tried to explain them to him. All he knew was that he loved flying and wanted to learn how to fly. His uncle would certainly pay for Joey to take lessons, and Floyd, accustomed to getting whatever he wanted, was certain that his own father back home in Arkansas would pay for his lessons, too. Nowhere in his mind did the thought occur to him that he might have to grow a little older first, nor did the boy know that by the time he would be old enough a Depression would have interfered with his dream, and he would have to wait for a war to fulfill it.

"Yesterday, December 7, 1941, a date which will live in infamy—the United States of America was suddenly and deliberately attacked by naval and air forces of the Empire of Japan."

—President Franklin D. Roosevelt

December 8, 1941

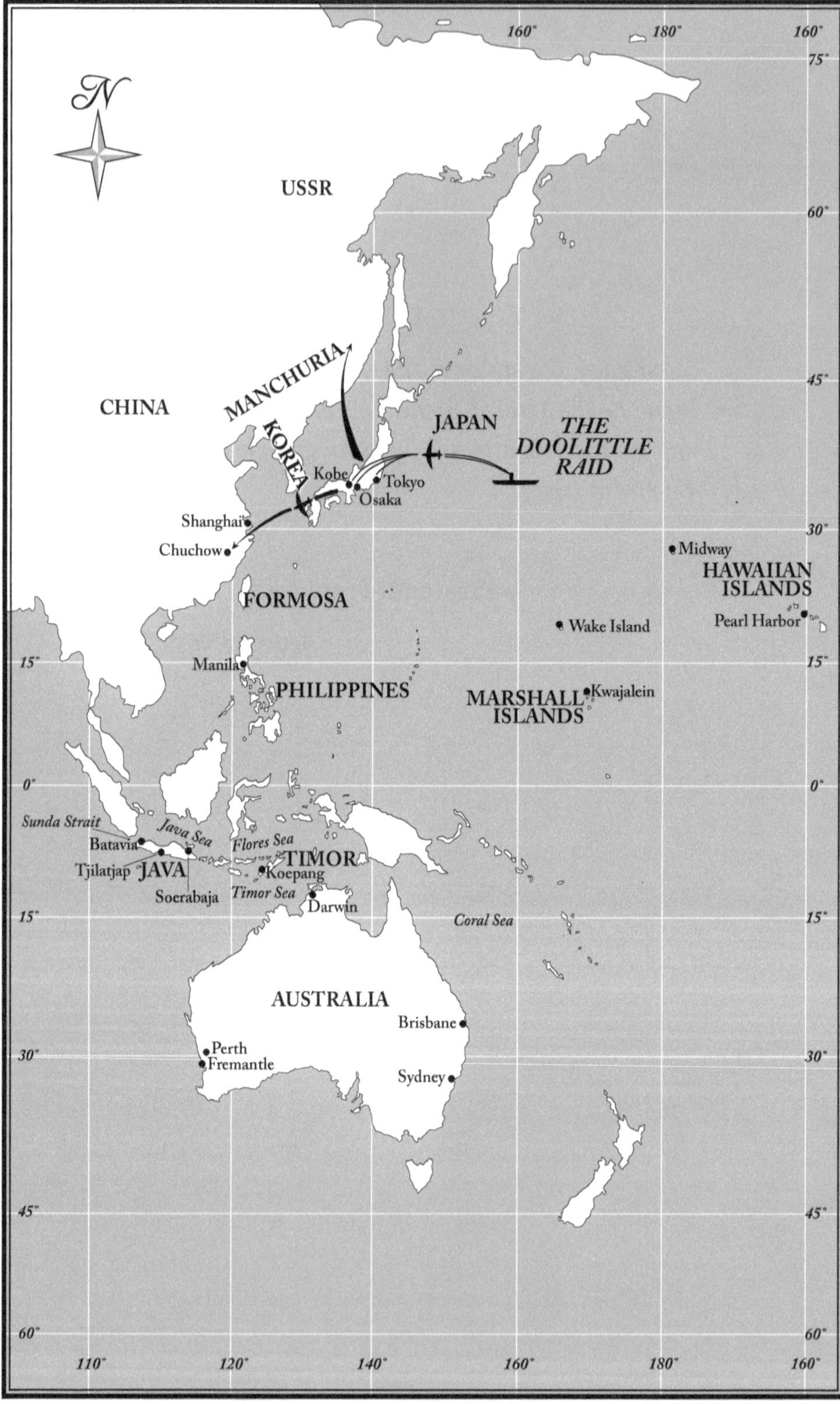

N
USSR
CHINA
MANCHURIA
KOREA
JAPAN
THE DOOLITTLE RAID
Kobe
Tokyo
Osaka
Shanghai
Chuchow
FORMOSA
Midway
HAWAIIAN ISLANDS
Pearl Harbor
Wake Island
Manila
PHILIPPINES
MARSHALL ISLANDS
Kwajalein
Sunda Strait
Java Sea
Flores Sea
Batavia
Tjilatjap
JAVA
Soerabaja
TIMOR
Koepang
Timor Sea
Darwin
Coral Sea
AUSTRALIA
Brisbane
Perth
Fremantle
Sydney

CHAPTER ONE

The Pacific Ocean, February 1942

The prow of the aircraft carrier pierced the glassy, tropical sea that seconds before had been reflecting a full moon and churned it into a swirling mass of white foam. Great waves tossed and rolled outward as the nearly 20,000 tons of steel that comprised the U.S.S. *Enterprise* plowed past with the power of 120,000 horses. For the few seconds it took the aircraft carrier to pass through that slice of the Pacific Ocean, the sea was anything but pacific. Aboard the great vessel, every hand was at his station, even though it was not yet 5 a.m. The most frantic activity was taking place far above the ocean's surface on the ship's flight deck, where khaki- and blue-clad sailors decorated with multi-colored vests scurried about wheeling the planes of Air Group Six into position for takeoff.

The flight deck was silent save for the clanking of metal against metal and the subdued voices of the deck crew. Occasionally a sharp, clear, invisible voice would address the crew over the loudspeakers mounted on the ship's island.

"Pilots, man your planes," was the latest command, at which signal doors at the base of the steel structure opened and pilots dressed in khaki flight suits and uninflated yellow life vests emerged from their ready rooms and trotted to their planes.

Floyd Craven was the last pilot in Bombing Squadron Six to step onto the flight deck. He paused just outside the hatchway to flop his leather flying helmet onto the top of his head. Pinching his clipboard between the last three fingers and the palm of his left hand, he tugged the helmet's flaps down over his ears with his left thumb and index finger and his right hand and then went to work buckling his chin strap as he started off toward his aircraft. Arriving alongside it, he walked around the folded right wing, tucked his clipboard underneath his right arm, reached for the fuselage with his left and with a one-footed hop climbed atop the wing. Never straightening out of his crouch, Craven deposited himself into the cockpit and settled into the seat as an enlisted deck crewman helped buckle him in. In the seat behind him, Craven's enlisted gunner/radioman was strapping in as well.

Craven was unusually focused and reflective as he went through his pre-flight checks. This was his first real combat mission since Pearl Harbor, and his first ever in which he was expected to drop a bomb on an enemy target. It was also his first takeoff in the dark. Known to his friends in the Navy and at home as a daredevil, Craven nonetheless balked at the notion of taking off virtually blind. He had never really had a vision of death before, but if he had, it would have been in a ball of fire after a spectacular racetrack collision or guiding a crippled dive bomber straight after its bomb into a Japanese target. He had little concern for his own life, but his greatest fear on the carrier was doing something to kill a fellow American. From the time Craven left the ready room to the time his aircraft left the flight deck, the reckless part-time race car driver, part-time collegian from Arkansas would be one of the most cautious men in the United States Navy.

Trying to adjust his eyes to the darkness, Craven looked ahead and up to his right at the island. Somewhere up there the ship's captain and his officers were leaning on the railing, waiting for the show to start. Some pilots would have thought those officers had it easy that morning, but not Craven. He knew most of them were former aviators, and that each one wanted to be in a cockpit that Sunday morning of February 1, 1942, the eighth Sunday morning since December 7, 1941. Not the least of those former aviators was Vice Adm. William Halsey, whom Craven could not see but knew was watching. Halsey was in command of the task force that included *Enterprise* and several cruisers and destroyers just as he had been on the day Pearl Harbor had been attacked, when the task force had been out at sea. Craven had been one of the "lucky" pilots to come winging into Pearl during the attack, unaware that a war had begun. Unlike some of his squadronmates, he had not been shot down or killed, either by the Japanese or by confused American gunners. But he had also not found the Japanese fleet in the succeeding days, and just like every other aviator or sailor, Craven had been deprived days later of the opportunity to bomb the Japanese at Wake Atoll and save the beleaguered Marines who had eventually been forced to surrender there.

Every disappointment Craven had felt had been felt by Admiral Halsey a thousand times over, however, and Craven knew it. The young pilot determined right then to go sink a ship for the admiral that morning. Craven wanted to do anything he could to end their mutual frustration and kick the Japs back for Pearl Harbor.

"Start engines!" the unseen voice blared.

A deck crewman hustled up to Craven's plane and shoved a small explosive cartridge into a compartment under the engine. When the sailor ran clear, Craven pushed the ignition button, which set off the charge and sparked the motor to life. The engine coughed a few times as the propeller made a few jerky, partial turns and then spun up to speed in a thin cloud of white smoke. The sound then multiplied by 80, abruptly ending the tense silence as the entire air group roared into action together.

"Launch aircraft!" barked the voice.

The tubby F4F Wildcat fighter planes ahead of Craven's bombing squadron took off first, one after another, rolling lazily down the flight deck toward the bow, dipping almost out of sight upon reaching the end, and then straining to gain altitude and reach their places in formation.

Craven's was the fifth plane to go in Bombing Six. The deck crew unfolded his wings and locked them in place just before he began his takeoff roll, and he checked the RPMs, his safety harness, and the wing and canopy locks as the bomber crept forward. With as much speed as the single engine could muster and as much headwind as the helmsman could create by steering the ship into the breeze, the Douglas SBD Dauntless roared off the front edge of the flight deck and rose into the pre-dawn Pacific sky.

Craven pulled back on the stick, gaining as much altitude as quickly as possible so he would not collide with other ships in the darkness. Bearing on his squadronmates' running lights, he steered his aircraft into formation and suddenly felt free. With the warm wind breezing across his face, he was now at liberty to focus on his mission. His and nine other SBDs, along with some of *Enterprise*'s torpedo bombers, would be targeting Kwajalein Island, a central Pacific outpost the Japanese had held ever since it had been given to them by the League of Nations after the last war. Kwajalein had once been German, but the Japanese had been on the right side of that war and had been rewarded for their efforts.

Craven had known that much even before the air combat intelligence officer had briefed the squadron the previous evening. Craven may have been a thrill-seeking slacker in civilian life, but he was smart, or else he would not have become a naval aviator. First, he had been smart enough to smell the draft coming for him, so he had dropped out of college in 1940 without a wistful thought and joined the Navy on his own accord. Second, he had decided to apply for midshipmen's school followed by pilot training, figuring that being an officer would give him as much personal freedom as possible and would also allow him to fulfill his lifelong dream of being a pilot. Racing had its thrills, but the boyhood joyride over Kansas had never faded from memory, and Floyd had never figured out how to make a car take off and land in one piece. Diving at high speed and a steep angle toward a firing enemy target and dropping a 1,000-pound bomb on said target just appealed to him, so he made his third brilliant decision to train for the SBD, which the Navy fliers boldly nicknamed "Slow But Deadly." Now all of those decisions were coming together into the most recent culminating moment of Ens. Floyd Craven's life.

Bombing Six and Torpedo Six arrived over Kwajalein just after dawn. Craven looked down and saw enemy ships languishing in the aquamarine lagoon and aircraft lined up on the ramp at the island's airstrip.

"Look down there, kid," Craven drawled in mock condescension to his gunner/radioman, who was not much younger than he. "Looks like they haven't even woken up yet."

The pilot of the lead plane briefed the others one last time over the radio before signaling for them to peel off into their attack. The pilots picked their targets and then, one at a time, pulled their goggles down over their eyes, rolled the planes over hard and pushed their noses into steep dives. Craven yanked a lever on the control panel in front of him, and four perforated metal panels — two on each wing, one on top, one on bottom — deployed, slowing the plane's airspeed to a manageable level. He leaned forward to place his right eye against the scope mounted on the cockpit's dashboard and lined up a small enemy vessel in the crosshairs. Craven was momentarily disappointed because the ship was tiny, not even as large as a destroyer. He figured it for a subchaser or a minesweeper at best, but it was a Jap, nonetheless, and in a few seconds it would be his first prize of the war.

The small vessel grew steadily larger in the bombsight as Craven held the plane in its shrieking dive. Finally, he jerked the bomb release, and pulled back on the stick as the nose rose automatically from the sudden lack of weight. He retracted the dive spoilers and climbed sharply.

"Whaddaya see down there?!" he radioed his gunner, who was now facing downward and could see the target past the plane's tail.

"Near miss," the Louisianan named Schumaker, from the German Coast upriver from New Orleans, called back a little dejectedly. He hastened to sweeten his report. "But it was so close, sir, da shock alone could sink dat little pirogue!"

The failure to land a direct hit disappointed Craven, but his aim generally satisfied him. He would have to sink a ship for Admiral Halsey another time. "That's all right, we'll have plenty of other bombs to drop in this war," he told Schumaker. "Tojo'd better hurry and skip town before the next time we come back." Craven's satisfaction would only last until he made it back to his ship.

Fortunately, Craven's groupmates sank or damaged several other ships at Kwajalein that morning, making the raid a success, albeit a modest one. A Japanese Pearl Harbor this certainly was not, though the pilots found out some time later that they had killed an admiral. The aircraft all returned safely to Enterprise and the pilots searched for the rest of their group, which had taken off toward a different target. Their attack had been a disaster. Four planes had been lost, but one of those losses bore particular significance to the men of Bombing Six.

Craven had not even made it back to the ready room when he heard voices from inside muttering something about "Hopping got it," and, "Scouting Six's skipper didn't make it back."

"What in the world are you fellas talking about?" Craven demanded to know as he ducked inside the hatch.

Several sweaty pilots standing and smoking amidst the tidy rows of leather-covered chairs turned to face him. One lieutenant (junior grade) pulled a cigarette out of his mouth and said, "Commander Hopping's dead, Floyd. We saw him go down over Roi just after he released his bomb." The lieutenant said it as if he was annoyed at Craven for making him repeat the solemn news.

Lt. Cdr. H.L. Hopping was the commander of Scouting Six, Air Group Six's other SBD squadron, and had been one of the first pilots to fly into Pearl Harbor during the attack two months earlier. Now he was dead, along with his crewman.

Craven cursed aloud and then, as if determining to put the death out of his mind, withdrew a cigarette from his pocket, stuck it in his mouth, and left the ready room through the opposite hatch. He didn't light the cigarette until he got back to his cabin, where he sat motionless for the rest of the morning, thinking about who else might die before this war came to an end.

CHAPTER TWO

Air conditioning made the wardroom aboard U.S.S. *Houston* one of the heavy cruiser's most popular compartments, at least for officers. Everyone from the baby-faced ensigns to the veteran executive officer ate, read, smoked, sang, and wrote in this floating officer's club. On this Saturday morning in the Timor Sea between the Dutch East Indies and Australia, breakfast had just ended, and the clatter of silverware and screeching of chairs across the deck filled the compartment as the officers headed to work. One junior officer stood from the main table holding a homemade, red greeting card. He did not notice the ship's chaplain standing just behind him with a cup of coffee in hand.

"What do you have there, Mr. Brown?" the chaplain asked.

Startled, Ens. Preston Brown awkwardly shuffled around to face the chaplain and waited for a couple of Chinese mess stewards to hurry past him before replying.

"It's a Valentine's Day card for my wife, sir," Preston responded. "I need some yarn to hold it together, and I heard there was some in the ship's office, so I brought the card with me to breakfast."

The chaplain's lower lip protruded in agreement and he offered a slight, sideways nod. Taking another sip of coffee, he replied, "Valentine's Day is today. It's a little late to be mailing that."

Preston grinned at the chaplain's raised eyebrows and half-serious, half-puzzled expression. "My wife's waiting for us in Darwin, sir."

Chaplain (Cdr.) George Rentz now smiled. "I know. I was just hassling you, Mr. Brown," explained the good-natured, mischievous Presbyterian minister. "There is a certain matter of commandeering Navy property for personal use, though."

"Oh, don't worry about that, sir. Reas gave me permission."

The chaplain, knowing that even the captain could hardly obtain any office supply without the enlisted yeoman's permission, nodded and gave Preston a wink and a pat on the shoulder.

"You might want to double-check with the captain regarding your liberty, though," the chaplain said as he headed for the door. "Scuttlebutt says we're only docking for a few hours this time."

Preston had heard the same rumor and was already a bit uneasy about it, but he agreed to check in with the captain when he reported to the bridge for his watch. The chaplain then wished Preston the best and headed toward his own office. It was good to see Chaplain Rentz smile, Preston thought. The past two weeks had been harrowing for everyone aboard this ship, particularly for the chaplain. Ten days prior, the *Houston* and several other American and Dutch warships had been steaming north through the Flores Sea on their way to attack a Japanese force in the Makassar Strait when they had run afoul of nearly 40 twin-engine Japanese bombers. Chaplain Rentz, instead of retiring belowdecks, spent the battle with an anti-aircraft crew, encouraging them as they tried valiantly to fight off the attackers. That was only the beginning of his ordeal, however; a Japanese bomb killed nearly 50 *Houston* sailors, and his duties as chaplain prevented him from avoiding contact with the mangled and burned bodies.

Preston tried now not to think of the tragedy as he finished preparing his wife's card. Obtaining a precisely measured six-inch length of brown yarn from Yeoman Reas, who conscientiously logged the transaction in his record book under the high-sounding designation "morale project," Preston finished the valentine and left for his room to pack the card in the briefcase he planned to take ashore with him. He then set off for the bridge to stand the 8 a.m.-to-noon watch.

Walking along the port-side upper deck and gazing out across the gently swelling Timor Sea, Preston had few fears of being denied his request. He had been allowed liberty to see Elaine on two prior occasions in December and January, and he was hopeful that the captain would give him another chance to see his wife, even if no one else was given liberty. After all, none of the other men had wives in Darwin. Capt. Albert Harold Rooks was a fine gentleman and a fair commanding officer, the kind that inspired the utmost loyalty in men like Ensign Brown. Preston had no qualms about going to war with Captain Rooks, and he would gladly die for him, if not, of course, for the pretty brunette waiting for him in Darwin.

The fact that Elaine was there at all was incredible. Preston knew few would believe the story behind it if they ever read it in a book. He and Elaine had only been married since September of 1941. In June 1940 he had just finished his third year at the United States Naval Academy in Annapolis, Maryland, when he returned to his hometown of Little

Rock and decided to drive to Fayetteville, Arkansas, to see his sister, Carolyn, who was living there after attending the University of Arkansas the previous school year. He met his sister's roommate, a sharp, witty girl from nearby Springdale named Elaine Wright. Elaine was smart and feisty, and although Preston didn't fall in love with her at once, she made such an impression on him that he decided to begin writing her on the off chance that a romance might develop. It did, and he found ways to get to Fayetteville every time he returned to Arkansas over the next year, eventually proposing to her in the summer of 1941, just after his graduation from the Academy.

Only two weeks after the wedding, however, Preston received an assignment to *Houston*. The Navy packed him on a passenger ship and dispatched him to the Philippines, where the cruiser served as the flagship for the U.S. Asiatic Fleet, leaving Elaine to figure out what to do next. Preston's wealthy parents stepped up to buy her passage to Manila, where she could live in their son's home port and the young couple could have some semblance of a married life.

Elaine's ship had been in the middle of the Pacific when the Japanese bombed Pearl Harbor on December 8th, local time, the same day the Japanese first bombed the Philippines. The ship diverted to Darwin, Australia, and after a few days it became apparent that Manila was the last place in the world any civilian captain would want to take his vessel. The ship left Darwin on the 17th and headed for Brisbane, a much more suitable port on Australia's eastern coast, but Elaine stayed behind to be closer to Preston. She found work in a restaurant and lived in a one-room cabin behind the establishment. She and Preston exchanged telegrams during this time, so he knew to look for her when *Houston* arrived in late December for a three-day port call. They had met again just a week later, but now more than a month had passed since that last visit, and Preston found it difficult to contain the excitement he felt at being able to spend Valentine's Day with his wife in Australia of all places.

Preston reached the ladder up to the bridge and quickly climbed it several decks to the top. He saluted the officer of the deck and spotted Captain Rooks standing across the bridge on the starboard wing. Preston wove his way past the sailors and officers standing watch in the enclosed pilothouse.

"Captain Rooks, sir, may I ask a question?" Preston said as he saluted *Houston*'s commanding officer.

Rooks turned, took a moment to recognize Preston, and replied, "Yes, you may, Mr. Brown."

"Sir, I've heard we will only be in Darwin for a few hours, and I am wondering if I still have your permission to go ashore in Darwin to see my wife?"

Rooks grinned slightly. "I gave you that permission two days ago, and you still have it. I just need you to be back aboard by midnight. I intend to have us underway escorting that convoy by 0300."

"Understood, sir," Preston replied obediently.

"Enjoy what little time you'll have with your wife, and don't forget that you're the envy of every married man aboard this ship. What we wouldn't give to have our wives waiting for us."

Preston nodded sympathetically. Deep inside, he felt a little awkward being so blessed, and he certainly did not intend to flaunt his blessings. God had been gracious, that was all. Elaine had simply not made it to the Philippines, and therefore, had not been evacuated or captured by the Japanese when they took Manila. And she had been brave and loyal enough to remain alone in an isolated, steaming hot, tropical port in order to see him once every month when his ship came in. He knew his shipmates were envious, and he would do his best not to add to their anguish.

"Aye-aye, sir. I will be back aboard by midnight," Preston announced confidently.

Rooks nodded his approval. "Good. You're dismissed."

With another exchange of salutes, Preston strolled into the pilothouse to assume his watch.

Elaine Brown stood at the dock later that day as the lone female among a handful of busy Australian military and civilian harbor workers, her clean green blouse and gray skirt subtly contrasting with the much dirtier khaki and blue outfits of the dock hands. She watched with pride and anticipation as *Houston*'s distinct gray shape came into sight. The American cruiser looked nothing like the small Australian warships that frequented the harbor. In contrast to their low outlines, *Houston*'s tripod foremast towered far above the rest of its superstructure and its twin, three-gun turrets mounted on the forecastle. The cruiser began a graceful right turn, revealing the mainmast, from which flew a modest-sized Stars and Stripes. Elaine's heart swelled with pride for a few minutes until the ship completed its turn and approached close enough for her to see Turret Three. What met her eyes puzzled her. A large canvas concealed the rectangular steel enclosure, something she immediately recognized as abnormal. That turret should have looked the same as the other two, and for the first time she felt fear. Something bad had happened to this ship, and she was desperate to know if it had involved Preston. Though she had heard tell around town of the ship's visit, she had not heard anything about a battle.

She glanced at her husband's battle station, Director Two — a fire control station mounted just aft of the cruiser's second stack and overlooking the boat deck, where the lifeboats and gigs hung from their davits. From there Preston would normally help call the turrets' shots in a battle against enemy ships. Elaine scanned the distance between Turret Three and Director Two and guessed it to be at least 60 feet, which was far enough to be safe, or at least that's what she surmised. Besides that, Preston's station, even to her untrained eye, appeared to be intact, and so a wave of relief swept over her, settling her rapidly pumping heart.

The level of activity on the dock increased as the 600-foot cruiser glided gently up to the pier. Under the watchful eye of a salty chief boatswain's mate, *Houston*'s sailors tossed thick rope lines from the deck to the Aussie "wharfies"' below, who hooked the great loops around bollards mounted on the dock. Down on the quarterdeck, surrounding the shrouded turret, other sailors hurried to secure the gangplank. Elaine immediately made her way over to it and waited at the bottom.

After a few minutes she saw Preston emerge from a hatch and begin walking toward her with a briefcase in hand. Their eyes met almost instantly, and she noticed that he had donned his gold-buttoned dress whites for the occasion, a charming gesture considering Darwin's uncomfortable climate. She waved and then gripped the railing of the gangplank as she watched him salute the officer of the deck and step off the ship.

Elaine and Preston embraced and kissed as several hundred jealous Americans and Australians watched. They were walking arm-in-arm away from the ship before either one spoke to the other.

"What are you doing here, Lainy?" Preston leaned close to ask her. "I thought I'd have to come to the restaurant and surprise you."

Elaine looked up at him and replied, "I've made friends around town, Press. These Aussie fellas will bend over backwards to help an American woman. They tell me everything, especially the enlisted men."

"Just so long as none of them get the wrong idea."

"Are you kidding?" Elaine cackled. "They know I'm untouchable. They treat me like I'm some kind of royalty, probably because I never stop talking about my wonderful, princely husband, Ensign Preston Phillip Brown, Annapolis Class of '41, an assistant gunnery officer aboard the flagship of the Asiatic Fleet, the U.S.S. *Houston*, President Roosevelt's favorite warship."

Preston smiled pleasantly with amusement. "That's quite a mouthful. I never realized I married a woman with so little humility."

"Being married to you is nothing to be humble about, darling." She leaned up to kiss him again. "Happy Valentine's Day, by the way."

Preston returned the greeting. "Happy Valentine's Day. I'm ashamed that I allowed you to say it first."

"You should be," she replied impudently.

"Where are we going anyway?"

"I borrowed a car from George," Elaine replied, referring to her boss, the restaurant owner and chef. "I told him I'd have it back to him around midnight."

"So you know I can only stay for a few hours?"

Elaine nodded. "Yes, but that's okay. We'll make the most of it. Tony's set our table for us at the restaurant. The food will be waiting for us when we get there, and we can do whatever we want after that until midnight when you have to go back to war."

"You sure have every detail covered, don't you?" Preston complimented her.

"I do my best."

"Well, listen, I think after this war's over, we deserve a second honeymoon. Where do you want to go?" he inquired with a twinkle in his eye. "Some place tropical?"

"Ha, no!" Elaine replied with a look of mock sternness. "Very funny. How about Canada?"

"It's up to you. You'll have awhile to figure it out."

"I'll start digging around town for some travel brochures tomorrow."

They had now reached the street outside the dockyard, and Elaine pointed to a gray sedan sitting by the curb.

"That's ours," Elaine announced.

"I'll drive," Preston offered.

She withdrew the keys from her purse and handed them to him. "As you wish, Mr. Brown."

Preston opened and shut Elaine's door for her and then walked around to the right side of the car to climb in himself. Once Preston had started the engine and pulled into traffic, he remarked, "It feels good to laugh again, Lainy."

"Why's that?" she wondered, already guessing that the answer had something to do with Turret Three.

"We've had a tough last couple of weeks."

"I saw the tarp over the after turret, Press. What happened to it?"

Preston gripped the steering wheel hard and took a deep breath. "The Japs bombed us last Wednesday, us and *Marblehead,* and a couple of Dutch cruisers. There were about three-dozen twin-engine "Nells." The bombs were falling all around us, but Captain Rooks steered us out from under them one right after another. It was amazing. He'd order a left turn, then a right one. He'd reverse one engine and keep the other one full ahead and then switch them. He'd order crashbacks — instantly going from full ahead to full astern. They're hard on the engines, but so are Jap bombs. I just kept waiting to get hit, but we never did."

"So how did you get hit?" Elaine asked.

"*Marblehead* had been badly hit and was taking water, so Captain Rooks was taking us over to help. The bomb must have been a stray. Some of the officers on the bridge told me that they and the captain never saw it. I heard it hit the searchlight platform on the mainmast, and then it bounced through the tripod legs before exploding just forward of the turret." Preston took a deep breath. "Are you sure you want to hear the rest of this?"

Elaine's gaze pierced straight through him. She nodded firmly and put her hand on his elbow.

"The shrapnel punched right through the turret armor and ignited some powder bags."

Elaine tensed. She had been a gunnery officer's wife long enough to know what was coming next.

"The bags flashed, and the fire gutted everything in the turret two decks down. If a couple of fellas in the magazine hadn't been alert, the flames could have gotten into the powder magazine and blown up the whole ship. We lost 46 men and buried them when we got back to Tjilatjap."

Elaine could only shake her head in horror. She had never been inside the ship before, so she could only vaguely picture what Preston had just described.

Preston, however, could see it all very clearly. He could still feel the ship swaying after the blast, hear the screams of his shipmates and see the blackened, melted interior of the turret and the rows of dead bodies lining the main deck as other sailors covered them with white sheets. He could also still hear the incessant hammering of nails as the crew constructed the coffins.

"I'm sorry, Press," Elaine finally said. "I'm sorry for you and the rest of the crew and for those boys who died."

Preston struggled to hold back tears and was helped by the right-hand turn that forced him to look away from Elaine for a few seconds. "We'll be all right, babe. *Marblehead* got it a lot worse than we did. She's headed back to San Francisco, and she's so old, I'm not sure they'll ever put her into a fight again."

"I'd rather they never put *you* into a fight again," Elaine commented.

"Not much chance of that happening."

"I know," she replied absently.

The couple rode in silence for a few more minutes until they reached the restaurant. Preston opened his door and climbed out to help Elaine. The doors shut with heavy metallic thuds that reminded him a bit too much of the bomb smashing through the searchlight platform. Together, Preston and Elaine walked inside the quaint, wooden structure with a wooden sign featuring a painted saltwater crocodile and the title "George's Saltwater Café." Tony, the teenaged waiter, greeted them stiffly and led them to their table in the back corner of the dining room. He was clearly sweating through his white tuxedo, which Preston had always thought oddly formal for a tropical-themed café, though to be honest, the entire place struck him as odd. He and Elaine were sweating, too, in the hot, heavy air. They sat down at a table for two decorated with two tall candles and a bouquet of tropical flowers.

"Tony, you did a beautiful job," Elaine commended her co-worker. "You followed my directions to a T."

"Thank you very much," the waiter replied. "I aim to please."

"Well, you certainly have pleased me. Thank you."

Tony bowed slightly, an elegant gesture that again seemed strange to Preston coming from a tanned, young Aussie who looked as if he would rather be wading the swamps hunting crocs. He said as much to Elaine once Tony had departed to get their food and drinks, which had already been prepared.

"Tony is George's grand-nephew, remember?" she said. "He's working here to pay off a debt to George."

"What kind of debt?" Preston wondered.

"George won't tell me exactly, just that 'Tony's a bloomin' idiot who has such poor judgment that he couldn't pick the winner in a cockroach race,'" she recounted her boss's exact words in a horrible, fake Australian accent.

Preston guffawed and looked at his wife with arched eyebrows. "So Tony's a gambler?"

"According to George, he's just a loser," Elaine deadpanned.

Tony returned shortly with their meal, and after he left again, Preston and Elaine joined hands as Preston asked the blessing. Then they set to eating.

"What's the latest news from home, Lainy? Have you heard from your folks lately?"

Elaine nodded as she chewed. She chased her food down with a swig of refreshingly cold water and replied, "I got a letter a few days after you left last month and a few more since then. Mom and Dad are both fine, but they're missing Danny. He left for the Navy boot camp near Chicago just before New Year's. Mom says Nick can't wait until he's old enough to go, too."

“The Navy needs good boys like your brothers,” Preston commented.

“Mom doesn’t think so. If she knew what you’ve just been through, she’d lock Nick up in his room and hop on the next train to Chicago to go grab Danny, too. And I can’t say I blame her. It’s bad enough that you’re out at sea all the time with Japs swarming over the East Indies like gnats. I don’t really want my little brothers out there, too.”

Preston looked down at his plate and shoved some rice around with his fork. “Me neither.”

“Do you remember the Mayfield twins?” Elaine asked.

Preston squinted off into the distance, straining to recall. “Matt and Mike, right? Danny’s best friends?”

“Mm, hmm. They both joined the Marines and are out in California for boot camp.”

“Anyone else I know from Springdale going to war?”

Elaine pondered the question and shook her head slowly. “No, I don’t think so.”

“What about that fella I heard had gone into naval aviation?”

Elaine suddenly looked perturbed. “Oh, you mean Floyd Craven?”

Preston’s face lit up with recognition. “Yeah, Craven. How’s he?”

“I don’t know, and I don’t really care, and I wish you hadn’t brought him up.”

“Why?” Preston asked in confusion.

“Because he’s a drunken ladies man, to put it politely,” she responded indignantly, “and he had the gall all the way through high school to think he could make me want to be his girlfriend! Of course, I knew his reputation, and I made it no secret that I didn’t like being in the same room with him.”

"Was he really that bad?" Preston asked a bit skeptically as he reached for his glass.

"And then some!" Elaine replied emphatically.

Preston drank and swallowed. "He was attracted to you. That speaks well of him," he said with a slight grin.

Elaine tilted her head forward and gave him a chastening look. "Darling, don't be naïve. Men with much less character than you have been attracted to me. Floyd tops the list."

"I didn't know any of this."

"Well, now you do, and if you ever see him, I expect you to tell him who you are and how glad you are that I married *you!* Anyway, all I heard was that he's flying dive bombers off a carrier."

"Oh, well, that's nothing," Preston remarked sarcastically.

The anger drained from Elaine's face within two seconds and was replaced by a twitching grin and a mischievous sparkle in her chocolate-brown eyes. Then she and Preston both started laughing softly.

Preston said, "Well, Lainy, just so you know, I was attracted to you as soon as you opened the front door at Carolyn's that day we met. Then I fell in love with your character soon afterward, and that cinched it. I decided I could never spend enough time with such a happy, confident, Godly girl, and I wouldn't be half the man I am today without you," Preston told her sincerely, reaching across the table to grip her hand. "I love you so much."

Elaine gripped his hand back. "I love you, too, Press."

He pulled his hand back and reached for his briefcase on the floor next to his chair. He had nearly forgotten the valentine. When he showed her the plain, handmade red card with a handwritten inscription, she fairly well melted and stood and walked over to him to give him a kiss. They happily finished their meal and left the restaurant.

At ten minutes until midnight, Preston pulled George's car up to the curb they had left several hours before. He and Elaine silently exited the vehicle and headed toward the dockyard gate.

"Lainy, stop," he said as he wrapped an arm around her. "I want to pray together before I leave."

She looked up at him with wide eyes and nodded. They always did this, knowing that each time he sailed might be the last time they ever saw each other.

"You start," she directed.

He placed his hands on her shoulders and bowed his head so that it touched her forehead. "Lord Jesus, I thank you for Elaine and for the time you've given us together tonight. I thank you for every second you've given me with this woman, and I ask you tonight for many more. Take care of her, Lord, and send your angels to keep her safe at all times. Strengthen her, Lord, and bless her life here in Darwin while I'm away. Thank you for dying for us, Jesus, and for saving us. We live to serve you. Amen."

It was now Elaine's turn. "Dear Father, I, too, want to thank you for this evening and for all of your blessings, especially Preston. You know how much I love him, Lord, and I pray that you will bring him back to me. Keep him and his shipmates strong and safe, and bless the U.S.S. *Houston*. Strengthen her so that she will protect the men who live aboard her and defeat the enemy. Give us victory in this war, Lord, and bring my husband back to me soon."

She paused for a second and whispered to Preston. "What is it that sailors say to each other when they say goodbye?

Preston opened his eyes, a smile playing on his lips. "Fair winds and following seas," he whispered back.

Elaine nodded, closed her eyes again, and continued her prayer. "Give him fair winds and following seas that will push him right back to me. I love you, Lord. Amen."

They embraced tightly and then walked slowly toward the ship, which loomed imposingly in the darkness, her decks alive with activity. They shared one more long kiss at the foot of the gangplank before Press climbed back aboard, sharply saluted the officer of the deck, and proceeded to his room to prepare for departure.

Elaine looked around the pier and found a wooden piling to sit on. She waited there for three hours before the ship and its convoy finally pulled away from the docks. Preston waved at her from the deck until the ship turned and she could see him no longer. Another ten minutes went by before *Houston* slipped out of sight around a bend in the harbor, and Elaine felt she could finally leave. She cried herself to sleep that morning unaware that Preston was still awake on deck, alone, staring at the blackness of the Timor Sea and trying his level best not to cry also.

CHAPTER THREE

Preston finally retired to his cabin for two hours of very restless sleep as *Houston* and the convoy steamed on toward their goal, the port of Koepang on the island of Timor. The convoy's transports were carrying several thousand Australian soldiers and an American field artillery regiment, all badly needed to shore up the island's defenses. The Japanese had already landed troops on Timor, as they had on many other islands in the Dutch East Indies.

The vast archipelago contained one of the world's greatest stores of petroleum and rubber, among many other profitable natural resources. The islands had made the Netherlands a rich empire for hundreds of years. Now, with their homeland occupied by Nazi Germany, the Dutch strained to hang on to their prized colonies at all costs.

The defense of the East Indies was being conducted by committee, however. An unwieldy chain of command included American, British, Dutch and Australian officers — "ABDA," as the coalition was known. The combined forces of this command had to fight language barriers and internal rivalries as well as the Japanese, but had managed thus far to deal tolerably with both. The Japanese onslaught showed no signs of abating, however, and the Allies' prospects of rolling it back appeared bleak to all.

Preston always tried to keep these considerations out of his mind, however. His sole task in battle was to help direct the fire of *Houston*'s nine 8-inch guns, and he would only get the chance if his boss, Cdr. Arthur Maher, became incapacitated or the main director mounted atop the forward mast became disabled. Preston would more than likely be a spectator to most surface engagements, especially since the only turret on the ship's rear half had been destroyed. The strengths and weaknesses of ABDA were for Captain Rooks to worry about, and after him, Rear Adm. Karel Doorman, the Dutchman in command of ABDA's naval striking force. Still, though, Preston could not shake the feeling that the Allies were doomed. Even in lonely Darwin he had the distinct impression of being backed up against a wall. What would happen if the East Indies fell entirely and the striking force had to retire to Darwin? It was the only major Australian port on hundreds of miles of coastline, and behind it lay thousands of square miles of seemingly limitless wilderness — the tropical bush of the coastline and the trackless deserts of the Outback. If the Japanese ever took the city, they could push the helpless ABDA survivors into a wilderness exile. It would be a bizarre outcome in the annals of war, but one that certainly seemed plausible from Preston's point of view. As far as he was concerned, Houston and her cohorts were far out on a limb that could snap at any moment.

The Japanese illustrated their omnipresence that morning when a four-engine flying boat appeared above the convoy. *Houston*'s bugler sounded the call for air defense, and the cruiser's gunners scurried to their battle stations. Preston dashed out onto the upper deck and climbed to his station. Locking himself inside the cramped metal director with some enlisted men, he could not hear Captain Rooks order the radio room to call Darwin for air support. Every man on the ship braced for another massive air assault.

Preston put his face to the eyepieces on the director's periscope and adjusted the knobs to bring the outdoors into focus. He rotated the compartment in order to scan the ship formation, but he could not adjust the rangefinder vertically to view the enemy plane. The men in the director waited anxiously for their shipmates outside to open fire.

Preston's talker, who would repeat all of Preston's orders and responses into a telephone headset, asked, "What's going on, sir?"

Preston pulled his face away from the periscope and looked at the man ("boy" would have been a more apt description). Seaman Second Class Madison was only 18, and he was sweating both from the stifling heat and from fear.

"I don't know, Madison. I can't see anything," Preston replied patiently. "But if that Jap flies low enough, the boys in Turret Three will ..." He suddenly realized what he was about to say. Turret Three would have blasted any low-flying Japanese plane to shreds if it had ever gotten the chance. Now Turrets One and Two and *Houston*'s assemblage of high-angle, five-inch anti-aircraft guns and smaller-caliber machine guns held sole responsibility for the ship's defense.

Outside, a P-40 Warhawk zipped in from Darwin, and the flying boat began to make a bombing run. No more Japanese planes were anywhere in sight. *Houston*'s five-inchers roared their dissent, lobbing their shells toward the enemy aircraft, where they exploded in great puffs of black smoke and sprayed the surrounding airspace with deadly shrapnel. The frightened Japanese pilot dropped his bombs early and turned away.

Preston caught a glimpse of the towering, white waterspouts tossed skyward by the explosions, but never saw the flying boat or the P-40, which had done nothing and soon flew back to Darwin.

The convoy sailed on.

At about 11 o'clock the next morning, the air defense alarm sounded again, and this time the incoming Japanese attack was the real McCoy. Preston lingered outside his battle station long enough to size up the threat. A swarm of over 40 aircraft droned high in the sky above the convoy. A group of them suddenly broke off into a dive aimed directly at the ships. Preston ducked inside the director turret as *Houston*'s anti-aircraft guns noisily threw up a curtain of flak.

Preston and his enlisted crew, blind except for his view of the sea surface outside, hung on to every fixed piece of metal they could grasp as the ship heeled one way and then the other. Again at the con, Captain Rooks raced the cruiser to and fro to protect the transports and avoid the Japanese bombs.

Preston could see the splashes, both of bombs and of stricken airplanes. The bombs created the best spectacle of the entire battle, as they spat enormous geysers hundreds of feet into the air. The splashes from near misses would reach their peaks, remain there momentarily, and then crash back to the surface, drenching the upper decks of the ships as they fell. He could also see the thick smoke screen being deployed by the smaller American and Australian escort ships but that was all he could see. If *Houston* took another bomb, Preston would again never know it was coming. The last one had come within yards of making Elaine a widow short of their four-month "anniversary." Where might the next one fall? His spine tingled as he pondered the possibilities. At least a direct hit would be relatively painless, he thought, but then again, he had never spoken to a man who had been killed by one. He prayed that the Japanese aim would be poor.

It was, and his worst fears were never realized. Stepping into the wardroom after the battle, he picked up the relieving news that no transports had been seriously damaged. There was other news as well.

"Koepang's fallen, gentlemen," Commander Maher announced. "And ABDA thinks we're too exposed to air attack, so they're sending us back to Darwin."

Those words electrified Preston, but he was shortly grounded by other, less positive news.

After another senior officer made some wisecrack about how "ABDA's really got the top brains working for it," Maher continued, "Also, Admiral Hart's been relieved of his command."

The men in the wardroom immediately rose in an uproar. Rear Adm. Thomas Hart, the much-beloved commander of the U.S. Asiatic Fleet, had been the ABDA coalition's naval commander, "Abdafloat."

"What?!" someone shouted. "Why?"

Maher replied, "Health problems," in a tone of voice that told everyone he didn't believe it himself.

"Health problems, my foot! We all saw him last week when he toured us and *Marblehead*. He was fine; he was all over this ship!"

Maher didn't want to preside over a verbal lynching of the high command, and he said so. "They've made their decision, and Admiral Helfrich has replaced Admiral Hart in operational command, and that's that. If any of you fellas has a problem with it, you can take it up with Churchill, or Roosevelt, or the Dutch queen after the war, understand?"

The officer corps mumbled their agreement, and the issue dropped to the deck, where it lay like a dead animal, untouched, but not unnoticed. It made the additional bombshell of British-owned Singapore's fall to the Japanese seem a distant concern. Meanwhile, Preston looked forward to possibly seeing Elaine again, though the loss of Timor and Singapore made him feel pressed just that much closer to the wall.

Preston should not have gotten his hopes up. *Houston* never docked in Darwin, just dropped anchor in the harbor and took on fuel from a barge. By 5:30 on February 18th, the cruiser was back at sea, on its way to Tjilatjap, which was more commonly pronounced as "Slapjack" by the sailors. As darkness fell, Preston and his roommate, another ensign named Terry Galloway, leaned on the starboard railing and gazed out over the sea, savoring the hot outdoor air because it was fresh compared with the hot air belowdecks.

"I'm sorry you didn't get to see your wife again today," Galloway told him. "I'm sure she missed seeing you, too. You think she knew we were back?"

Preston nodded and looked down at the foaming waves that streamed away from *Houston*'s sides. "She knew. She knows everyone in that town by now. She was probably at the pier waiting for us."

"You worry about her being all alone in Darwin?"

Preston bit his lip and replied, "No, she seems to have everyone's respect. Her boss is a sharp businessman who's glad to have the help in these times. He'll look after her."

"I can't believe that she'll stay in a dump like that, though," Galloway marveled. "I don't know any woman who would have stayed in Darwin and let that passenger ship leave without her."

"Lainy's a rugged country girl, Terry," Preston stated simply. "Her hometown's a few notches above Darwin, but she knows what it's like to have dirt under her toenails. She's also had two years of college, so I think, deep down, she's enjoying her chance to see the world."

"Well, and she loves you, right?"

"Of course," Preston chuckled. "I'll tell you, that gal is my greatest earthly treasure. Do I wish she were safe back in the States, absolutely? Does it make me a little bolder going off to battle knowing that she's over here with us? You bet."

Galloway could only shake his head. "I don't know what else to say except that I hope you two have many happy years ahead and that I can find a wife that loyal someday."

"You might ... you might. I hope I haven't bragged on her too much. God brought her into my life; I didn't have much to do with it at all."

Galloway paused in thought for a second and then just grunted softly. He turned to leave without commenting.

Preston's mind had already changed tracks. "They're closing in on us, Terry," he told Galloway, not realizing his friend was several feet away already.

Galloway turned around and came back. "Who? The Japs?"

"Yup ... the Japs. They're out there, and they're coming for us. And no one is going to come help us. I think we're on our own."

"Hmm ... I think you're right." Galloway paused and then said, "I can feel it, too."

"There's going to be a big fight somewhere up there," Preston said, referring to the East Indies, "and we'll rush headlong into it with only two-thirds of our main firepower, and those Japs are going to take us apart."

Galloway had never heard this sort of pessimism from his friend before, and it scared him. "Where's this coming from, Preston? I know what you're saying, but I've never heard you talk like this before. Why the change?"

"I'm just becoming attuned to reality," Preston said with a sigh. He glanced at Galloway. "I don't think we're ever going back to Darwin."

Galloway returned the glance and saw fear in Preston's eyes. That, too, was unfamiliar coming from him. After Preston left, Galloway realized that the look of fear was the look of a man who believed he might never see his wife again.

Thursday the 19th of February dawned hot and muggy like every other day during northern Australia's summer. Elaine awoke to sunlight filtering through the thin, ragged curtains that covered the windows of her one-room shack-apartment behind the restaurant, but she knew that clouds would roll in by the afternoon, and that rain would more than likely follow, setting up Friday the 20th to be just as sultry as the day before.

Elaine sat up in bed and reached for her Bible. As she did every morning, she read the Scriptures and then prayed for God's blessings upon the day, Preston, the men of *Houston*, and the Allied war effort in general. This morning, though, her spirits were sagging. She knew Preston's ship had been in the harbor the previous afternoon, and she had been miserable most of the day knowing he would remain beyond reach. If he had been able to go on liberty, he would have appeared on the pier early in the visit. When he had failed to come, Elaine had known that the visit was supposed to be a quick one. Two liberties in four days were too much to ask in wartime, even of a gentleman like Captain Rooks.

Elaine fought despair that morning as she walked about town, running a few routine errands at the handful of stores and checking for any stray travel brochures at the hotel before returning to her cabin to get ready for work. She allowed herself to wonder just what she was doing in muddy Darwin after all. How had she allowed herself to come here? The answer was simple; it was Preston. She loved him like she loved no other human being, but she wondered if it would not be easier to be just like every other Navy wife and live in Hawaii or San Francisco waiting for her husband to return from sea.

She returned to the cabin after about an hour, and as she stood in the doorway, her eyes drifted to the paper valentine standing upright on the nightstand next to her Bible. How many other Navy wives had experienced a Valentine's Day like she just had? She shut the door softly behind her and crossed the room. Sitting down on the edge of the bed, she picked up the card and then swung her legs on top of the bed. She leaned back against the headboard, closed her eyes, and smiled at the memories of Saturday evening. Those were memories she would cherish forever. She would tell her future daughters and granddaughters about the dinner and show them the valentine someday and tell them how she hoped that they might find such wonderful husbands themselves. Then, as she was prone to do in the silent solitude of her room, she prayed aloud.

"Thank you, God, for this place and for all the things that you are teaching me here. Amen."

She had scarcely uttered the "amen" when the sound of distant airplane engines penetrated the rickety walls of the little house. Elaine took a second's notice, but figured they were Australian or American planes from the nearby airfield. She climbed off the bed and started to change into her waitress's uniform. Standing in front of her small, wall-mounted mirror, she pinned her shoulder-length, dark brown hair up off her neck and put on a necklace. She was still locking the clasp when she heard an explosion come from the direction of the harbor. The mirror suddenly shifted on the wall. In fact, the entire building felt as if it had shifted.

The blast startled Elaine. It could not have come from farther than a mile away, and the drone of the airplanes was louder than normal. Much louder.

Another concussion rattled the cabin, causing the lamp on the nightstand to bounce. Then came another and another. Officially frightened now, Elaine rushed to the far window, which looked toward the harbor. Through a gap in some of Darwin's low-slung wood-and-tin buildings she caught a glimpse of the harbor, and above the buildings she could see a swarm of aircraft darting every which way in the distance. She watched as bombs fell in the turquoise water and threw skyward white towers of spray that dwarfed the Allied ships tied up at the docks. Another cluster of bombs struck the docks themselves, blowing crates, machinery, and buildings into oblivion. Those blasts severely jarred the window, alerting Elaine for the first time to the possibility that any closer hits might shatter the glass in her face. She dropped to her knees and curled up beneath the sill.

Even though she had not yet identified the planes for certain, no doubt remained in her mind that they were Japanese. Where they had come from, she did not know, and neither did she care. George, Tony, the military men in town, and Preston had all spoken of Japan's fearsome air forces that could strike seemingly anywhere and at any time. They could fly from land bases that were sprouting wherever the Japanese army went — which was just about *everywhere* — or from aircraft carriers that could bomb Pearl Harbor in December and strike targets in the East Indies two months later.

It made no difference to Elaine where these planes had originated. What she cared about was that they were bombing Darwin, which had been safe until then, and that Preston's ship was at sea somewhere between the Japanese planes and their base. Had they already attacked *Houston*, or were they in Darwin looking for her? Elaine knew the ship had been marked for destruction by the Japanese. On the first day of the war, they had bombed the remote Filipino anchorage where *Houston* had been just hours before. Tokyo Rose had boasted on Japanese radio that night that the American cruiser had been sunk, and she had done so on a few other occasions since then. "The Galloping Ghost of the Java Coast" — as her crew had taken to calling their ship because she had been reported sunk so many times — was the most powerful ship in the U.S. Asiatic Fleet, and by extension one of the most powerful ships in the ABDA navy. The Japanese desired very much to eliminate her as an obstacle to their plans.

So too did they apparently desire to eliminate Darwin. Elaine covered her head with her hands and prayed, shuddering along with the cabin at every explosion in the harbor. A roaring blast louder than all the others suddenly hammered Elaine's ears and, just as she feared, burst the window into shards. She restrained the urge to stand and bolt and lay motionless instead as the tiny pieces of crystalline gravel rained down on her back, neck, and hands, tickling her skin.

After a few seconds, she finally lifted her head to peek around the room. She would not have been surprised if the tin roof and wooden walls had been blown away, but they had not been. The only apparent damage was to the front window, which had been shattered as well.

She wasn't staying there any longer, though. Putting her hands to the floor — and immediately feeling sharp, pricking pains from the broken glass — she pushed herself upright, took a moment to brush herself off, and dashed out of the cabin. With the explosions and the sound of aircraft still assailing her from afar, she ran across a 15-foot dirt alley to the back door of the restaurant. She hurtled through the door and nearly ran into George.

"I was just coming to check on you!" her 60-ish boss announced. "That big one must have been an ammunition ship going up. Are you all right?"

Brushing a few strands of hair out of her face, Elaine checked herself over. Her skirt and blouse were dusty from being on the floor, but she did not seem any worse for wear until she looked at the palms of her hands. They were speckled with sparkling bits of glass and streaked by fresh red blood.

"Oh, for pity's sake!" she exclaimed. "I should have known there was glass all over the floor!"

"Here, let me take a look at that," George offered, taking her hand. He examined her wounds briefly and then made eye contact with her. "Get down and stay down," he ordered. "I have some iodine in my room."

Hunched over at the waist, and with knees slightly bent, George hustled out of the kitchen and into his own little apartment in the next room. In fact, the cabin out back had been his place of lodging until Elaine arrived, and he had traded her for it as a supplement to the meager wages he was able to offer. He returned a few moments later with a brown glass bottle and a rag. Gasping for breath as a man his age would be, he dropped to the floor next to her against the cabinets. He uncorked the bottle and poured some of the liquid onto the rag.

Elaine reached for it. "Here, I can do it."

George, ever impressed but no longer surprised by her self-sufficiency, handed her the rag. She pressed it to her wounds and cringed at the stinging pain. It was by no means the worst she had felt, however. The time she had tripped when she was nine and landed on an old piece of lumber that had a nail protruding from it held a solid place at the top of the list. She had been chasing then-seven-year-old Danny across the back yard next to the family's woodshed and had stuck the nail clean through her left hand. She had never cried harder in her life than she had at that moment, which was soon overtaken by the subsequent tetanus shot at the doctor's office. The memory of Danny crying for her still touched her, however. He had felt horrible about the accident because he had been fleeing the scene of a little-brother-on-big-sister prank at the time, and she had been pursuing him to exact retribution.

The round, white scar lay just to the left of the largest chunk of glass in either hand, a piece about the size of a dime. As George looked on, she closed her eyes, gritted her teeth, and pulled the piece out, releasing a fresh mini-gusher of blood, which she quickly stanched with the rag.

"They're not going to bomb the town, are they, George?" she asked.

"Who knows, Elaine," the old man responded. "The Japs could be landing troops at the mouth of the harbor as we speak."

His anger was palpable, and apparently so was her fear because he quickly backpedaled upon seeing her sudden, fearful glare.

"Don't worry, girlie. I spent two years in France during the last war, and I didn't come back as the only survivor from my old neighborhood just to have these bloomin', bucktoothed Jap lizards try to take my home away from me! Not to be critical of your General MacArthur up in the Philippines, but the Japs haven't even seen a fight like they'll see if they try to invade Australia."

Elaine wasn't certain if the speech was intended to comfort her or to make her more prepared to die. Whatever the case, the air raid still swirled outside over the harbor and began to spread throughout the area. George and Elaine could now hear explosions coming from the direction of the airfield, and then, even more terrifying, the sharp staccato of machine-gun fire. Bullets began ripping long gashes in the tin roof above them, exiting the room by punching through the east wall near its joint with the ceiling. Those sounds were immediately chased away by the deafening roar of an airplane buzzing the building. Elaine and George both ducked, understanding fully that they were now targets, albeit random ones.

The front door opened and shut across the dining room, and Tony rushed into the kitchen, panic gouged onto his face and sweat streaming down it.

"They're strafing the town now! Several buildings are catching on fire!" he announced. "They already got the docks and the airfield, and I just saw dive bombers getting ready to attack the ships in the harbor!"

"Any word of an invasion?" George wanted to know.

Tony shook his head. "No, I haven't heard anything yet. But it could happen."

"Have you heard anything about the *Houston*?" Elaine queried.

Again, Tony did not know. "It's a good thing she didn't hang around yesterday, though. The rest of that convoy stayed here, and they're getting it now!"

Houston's short stay. which had been such an annoyance the previous day now seemed to be a blessing, and she had plenty of time to give thanks. The attack lasted into the early hours of the afternoon, and when it ended, eight Australian and American ships lay sunk in the harbor, and nine others still floated but were damaged. Eighteen Allied aircraft, their airfield, and the harbor's supply stores had been destroyed. The town itself, not much to look at on a normal day, had been ravaged by the strafing, and now its citizens were packing their belongings and heading for the bush. Elaine, George, and Tony watched them leave. Talk of more attacks was rampant.

"Elaine, you can't stay here any longer," George insisted.

"What?" she responded incredulously.

"You have to go with them. They're headed for Adelaide River. It'll be much safer there."

Elaine's feistiness boldly manifested itself now. "George! I can't do that! I have to stay here for Preston!"

The old man was up to the challenge. "Listen! The docks and the harbor are completely wrecked, and if your husband's ship doesn't get sunk by the Jap fleet that launched those planes, it won't be coming back to Darwin, I can promise you that!"

Elaine rested her knuckles on her hips — still protecting her hands — and looked around in frustration, searching for more words. "Then where will it go?" she finally asked.

"Probably Fremantle."

"Where's that?"

"It's Perth's port city, on the southwestern coast, about 2,600 kilometers from here."

"Wonderful!" Elaine was beginning to feel overwhelmed, and she finally started to cry, something she had not done in public since her wedding day. "How am I supposed to get there?"

George softened. "I don't know," he replied more calmly, "but if you go to Adelaide River, I'm sure you can find someone to help you. Right now, you just have to get out of this town. If the Japs do land, it'll probably be here first, and I can't think of a greater tragedy than for you to get killed waiting here for your husband while he's at sea. You have to leave, and if you insist on staying, I'm afraid I'll have to fire you."

He paused and looked at her for a few seconds. "You remind me a lot of my granddaughter in Wollongong, you know? I have your best interests at heart."

"I know that, George, and I appreciate it," she replied quietly.

"Would it make you feel better if Tony went with you?"

Wiping the tears from her cheeks, Elaine looked at the short 18-year-old. She was a good two years older, and to be honest, wasn't sure who would wind up taking care of whom in such an arrangement. Still, the thought of having a trusted friend accompany her was reassuring.

"How will you manage the restaurant if we both leave?"

George snorted in disgust. "My business is ruined, and so is this town. I think I'll probably have to push a food cart around down on the waterfront to get any customers."

She nodded reluctantly. "Okay. I'll go, and Tony can come, too." She had arranged her words intentionally. Tony would be her protector, but would in no way be her commander, and she determined to assert herself as much as would be practical as soon as possible.

George looked at his nephew. "Tony?"

"Sure, Uncle George," the kid replied not too confidently. "Anything you say. But I won't be coming back."

"You won't?"

Tony shook his head. "No. I'm joining the Navy. I'm done waiting tables until the war's over."

George stepped forward and shook the young man's hand. "Well then, best of luck to you, mate. Go find a way to give it back to the Japs. You can finish repaying me for that money of mine you lost when you get back."

"I will, sir," Tony replied, returning the handshake.

"Then hurry and get moving. You need to be well on your way before dark."

"Yes, sir."

George turned to Elaine. "Elaine, cable me when you get to Fremantle. It's been a pleasure having you here because, like I said before, you remind me of Emily. Take care, will you?"

"I will, George. Thank you for everything."

"You're welcome."

Again overcome with emotion, she stepped forward to hug the man. "God bless you, sir."

"And you, too."

Elaine returned to her cabin, packed everything she owned into the trunk in which she had brought it, and waited for Tony, who loaded it onto his rickety pickup truck. She climbed in on the passenger side, and the two former coworkers set out east toward Adelaide River, not knowing who or what would be waiting for them.

CHAPTER FOUR

Dusk fell on the evening of the 23rd as Preston stood watch in *Houston*'s pilothouse as an assistant officer of the deck. Barely four months into his tour aboard the ship, the young ensign was already well on his way to qualifying as a full-fledged OOD, but for the time being his job was mainly to learn from the more senior officers. One of them, the navigator, Cdr. John Hollowell, stood bent at the waist in the chartroom behind the pilothouse, compass and ruler in hand, plotting *Houston*'s course. Preston quietly strolled through the door into the chartroom and observed Hollowell and the chart intently.

The ship had left Tjilatjap the previous morning and was now sailing west along bone-shaped Java's southern coast. At Java's western end, the Sunda Strait separated it from the larger island of Sumatra. From all appearances, *Houston* would be sailing into Sunda Strait.

Hollowell must have seen Preston out of the corner of his eye because he addressed the junior officer without looking up from the chart. "We're headed up into Sunda Strait, Mr. Brown. It's a ship handler's worst nightmare."

Hollowell straightened and strode past Preston into the pilothouse without making eye contact.

"Come right new course 010. Maintain speed," Hollowell ordered the OOD crisply and plainly.

"Come right new course 010. Maintain speed," the OOD repeated in like manner.

The helmsman echoed these same commands followed by a sharp, naval "aye" of acknowledgement.

Hollowell paused for a moment to gauge the ship's progress as it heeled slightly and swung north, then he returned to the chartroom. He picked up with Preston right where he had left off.

"The currents in the strait are strong, and they run south out of the Java Sea, toward us. An officer of the deck must maintain his focus at all times to maintain proper speed and heading. There are old volcanoes under this water, too, and they create eddies and riptides that can drag a ship under if her OOD isn't paying attention."

That bit of information raised Preston's eyebrows.

"Vigilance is the word of the day," Hollowell said.

Preston mumbled a "Yes, sir," and a few seconds passed silently before Hollowell spoke again.

"Ever heard of Krakatoa?"

Preston's face brightened with recognition. "The volcano? Yes, sir. It erupted in 1883 and killed 36,000 people."

Hollowell nodded approvingly. "It's been adding to that total since then. We'll be sailing over the top of what's left of it." The navigator returned to his crouch over the charts and gazed across the paper strait with a trained, concerned eye.

Preston stepped to the edge of the table and placed his hands on the edge. Submerged volcanoes bothered him but not as much as the Japanese did. "Sir, where are we going?" he asked.

Hollowell tightened his lips into a grim pucker before he looked up and locked gazes with Preston for the first time in the conversation. "Son," Hollowell replied, "we're going to hell, we're going to hell."

Even though Preston was sure of his own soul's security, he knew exactly what Hollowell meant, and no response could have startled Preston more. He had been holding similarly bleak sentiments for days, and hearing them from a senior officer did nothing to encourage him.

The ship was now completing its turn, and the voice of another junior officer, who could not have possibly heard the navigator's statement, floated in from the pilothouse. "Say, didn't I just hear a gate clang shut behind us?"

Preston heard a few nervous chuckles and turned away from the chart with a cautious parting glance at Sunda Strait.

Houston's destination, the port of Soerabaja, could have passed for hell the next night as the American sailors watched it burn. A cargo ship loaded with rubber had been bombed recently and belched a thick, churning tower of black smoke far into the sky. Ashore at the docks, several warehouses burned as well. The men were fully aware of all that was taking place in the region, and the news of the attack on Darwin — and Tokyo Rose's boasting that *Houston* had been sunk there — only darkened the mood. Now that they were in Soerabaja, more air attacks were imminent since no Japanese warplane within 50 miles could miss the pillar of smoke.

The fire continued to burn well into the night, and Preston and Terry Galloway were two of its most devoted spectators. The Dutch authorities were doing everything they could to extinguish the blaze, which in the darkness had become a pillar of fire that still beckoned the enemy. Preston absently watched as a Dutch torpedo boat attempted to scuttle the cargo ship, only to have the fresh explosion add to the inferno's intensity.

Galloway stood with him and kept silent. The Darwin raid had shocked all of them, but it had demoralized Preston more than anyone else. Galloway knew well that his shipmate's wife was familiar with the port facilities and was friends with many of the Australian naval personnel there. He knew that she often went wandering around the docks and the administration buildings, looking for someone to give her news of *Houston*'s movements. That was how she had known to meet Preston pierside on Valentine's Day. Galloway could picture her getting caught in the wrong place at the wrong time, and he was certain that Preston was thumbing through all the horrible scenarios in his mind as he stared into the fire.

Galloway finally had to turn and leave. He was loyal to his friend, but the anxiety was contagious, and Galloway himself couldn't let his mind dwell on what Preston's mind was dwelling upon.

Preston spent the rest of the night alone by the railing, wondering if this is what the rest of his life would be like if he lived long enough to see it.

Floyd Craven and his fellow naval aviators from *Enterprise* arrived over Wake Atoll two months and two days too late to help the Marine garrison that had surrendered on December 23. It was now the morning of February 25, and Floyd still simmered over having not been given a chance to hit the Japanese while their landing on the American territory might still have been preventable. Relief expeditions had put to sea but had been recalled because the admirals at Pearl Harbor feared risking their carriers too early in the war. Now the carriers were being used, but for minor strikes against lightly defended enemy islands.

The Japanese carriers were nowhere to be seen in the Central Pacific. They were, instead, plying the Southwestern Pacific and the Indian Ocean, bombing Australia, and generally making nuisances of themselves. Craven longed to join the action thousands of miles to the southwest, but the briefing officers told all the pilots that their missions were intended to distract the Japanese. If the island air strikes went as planned, they might just lure the Japanese carriers away from the Dutch East Indies and Australia and give the Allied forces there time to breathe. Floyd had his doubts, but he was too frustrated to analyze them. He flew airplanes and dropped bombs, and he finally determined that he had best focus on his job because that was all he could really do. If the admirals were wrong, it would be their careers on the line, not his.

Floyd looked down from the cockpit at the coral and sand atoll below. Its shape appeared to him to resemble a snake's head with its jaws open, the space in between being filled by a lagoon. As he prepared to roll his SBD over into its dive, the selection of targets arrayed below disappointed him. He could only see three enemy flying boats in the shallow water.

"Tojo's not giving us much to pick from today," he said over the intercom to his gunner. "Which one should we go for, the one on the left, the one on the right, or the one in the middle?" he asked sarcastically.

"Right," replied Schumaker.

"Okay, I'm going left," Floyd announced.

He eased the stick over to the left and peeled out of formation. Floyd pitched the plane forward, lined the flying boat up in his crosshairs, and held it there through the dive, as Japanese flak burst uncomfortably close. He released the bomb at the usual point, and pulled up steeply so his gunner could see the results.

"Got it!" Schumaker declared. "The bomb chopped off the right wing before it exploded."

Only marginally impressed, Floyd replied, "That's it? I didn't even hit the fuselage?"

"Sorry. Congratulations, though, sir. That was a tiny target, and with all due respect, it was closer than at Kwajalein."

Floyd sighed. "Thank you, Schumaker … I think."

"Uh ... you're welcome," the gunner replied a bit uncertainly.

As the SBD climbed back to altitude, another airman's voice shrieked through the radio. "We're hit, we're hit! This is Torrance, the gunner! My pilot's dead ... the engine's destroyed ... we're going down!"

Floyd bit his lip as he and Schumaker listened to the doomed man's screams. He looked over his shoulder and saw the stricken SBD trailing a stream of black smoke as it streaked toward the lagoon before it struck the surface and exploded in a great ball of orange flame surrounded by a cloud of water and smoke.

Floyd wouldn't trade a parked flying boat for an SBD and its crew any day. These missions were too dangerous for what they were accomplishing, and were not challenging him to perform to the level at which he knew he was capable. He had felt a greater sense of accomplishment each time he had simply landed his plane than he felt at this moment. It was a lousy, uninspiring way to fight a war.

On the other side of the International Date Line, it was already February 26. Elaine awoke that morning unsure of just where she was. She opened her eyes and stared up at a tin ceiling, and for a moment, she thought she was back in Darwin. But no, this room and this bed were both much smaller. The last thing she remembered was collapsing atop the bed after an exhausting day's drive. She propped herself up on one elbow and peeked out the window. Sure enough, she was no longer in the tropical port. Instead of dried mud, the ground here was red dirt, and she remembered she was in Alice Springs at Tony's parents' house.

They had made it safely to Adelaide River and had stayed there with the rest of the refugees for just one night before Tony decided to head home where his parents lived. She recalled asking him just where that might be, and he had replied by showing her a tattered and faded road map of the Northern Territory. One of the few roads on the map stretched 1,500 kilometers to the south to the only other noticeable island of civilization. She had quailed inside at the thought of driving that far across the desert, but she knew she had to get to Fremantle somehow, and there had to be people in Alice Springs who could help her do so.

They had not been the only ones on the road that week. Many of the other refugees struck out for "Alice" as well, including many of the military personnel from Darwin. Elaine knew some of them. She had previously thought them to be hard-working, dedicated patriots. She now thought of them as cowards. In fact, she would have thought of herself as a coward, too, had she not been forced to flee by George.

Elaine read her Bible, prayed, and left her room. She did not need to dress for she had fallen asleep the night before in her regular clothes. She found Tony's mother, Gladys Fraser, clearing the table of breakfast.

"Good morning, Mrs. Brown," Gladys announced cheerfully. "Don't worry, I'll fix you something to eat. My husband just left for work."

Elaine smiled. "That's fine, thank you. Where's Tony?"

"He had to run to the parts store to get something for the truck. He'll be back in a minute."

Elaine figured a complete overhaul would be in order after the trip the truck had just endured, if it was still fit to drive at all. She took a seat at the small table, and Gladys soon set a plate of bubbling, greasy meat and hash-brown potatoes in front of her. Never one to complain about the quality of food, Elaine ate quickly and unhesitatingly.

Gladys spoke from the sink as she dried dishes with a dirty towel. Everything in the house seemed to be permeated with desert sand.

"We discussed your plans last night after you went to bed, Elaine," Gladys announced.

"Oh?"

"Yes, you want to get out to Fremantle, right?"

"That's right," Elaine replied as she chewed her food, remembering only afterward that her mother would not have approved of such poor manners.

"The fastest way for you to do that would be by train. Do you have much money with you?"

Elaine hesitated, reluctant to divulge the true amount, which happened to be quite large. "I brought every bit I had with me from Darwin. It should be enough to cover any fares."

Gladys laid the towel on the counter and sat down across the table from Elaine. "Good," the lady in her late 30s said.

She placed her hands on the table and began tracing lines on it. Elaine's eyes followed Gladys's fingers closely as they blazed clean trails on the dusty surface.

"You can take the train from here down to Port Augusta in South Australia and then all the way out to Perth. From there, it's practically a long walk to Fremantle."

Elaine swallowed another bite of food. "How long will this take?"

"Three or four days, I suppose."

Elaine closed her eyes. She was already exhausted. The week since the Darwin raid had flown by in a blur, and she was ready for a rest. Still, though, the only place she could get news about Preston was Fremantle, or at least it seemed to be. She couldn't count on hearing anything in Alice Springs, that was certain. The only military personnel she had seen in town were the bunch of soldiers who had rounded up the Darwin deserters and pressed them back into service, and she figured they had already left.

At that moment, Tony came walking back inside. He saw Elaine sitting at the table and asked, "Did Mum tell you about our plan yet?"

Gladys answered for her guest. "Yes, I just told her. She hasn't made up her mind yet, though."

Elaine opened her eyes again and looked up at Tony. "Will you be going with me?"

Tony shook his head. "Don't have the money," he replied simply. "There's a place in town where I can enlist in the Navy, though, and then they'll pay for my ticket out."

Elaine nodded with approval. "That sounds like a good idea." She then returned to her previous thoughts about Gladys's proposal. Sighing with resignation, she finally announced, "Okay, Mrs. Fraser, I like your plan. I need to get to Fremantle as quickly as possible, so can you help me get to the train station?"

"You sure you don't mind traveling alone?" Gladys queried.

"I'll be fine. I sailed from the States all the way to Darwin by myself. I'm sure I can handle a couple of train rides, though I really don't know what I would have done without Tony's help this past week." She addressed him specifically. "Thank you, Tony. Your uncle will be proud of you when I tell him."

Tony waved her off. "Don't mention it."

After breakfast they all gathered Elaine's things together and put them back in the pickup truck. The three of them then drove to the train station, where Elaine purchased her ticket. Within a few hours, she left Alice Springs, bound for Port Augusta. She had not been in her seat for more than two minutes when she fell soundly asleep, not to awaken again until the end of the line.

The events of February 26 convinced Preston and his fellow crewmen it would truly be just a matter of time before the Japanese invaded Java. The only questions regarded when and where the invasion might take place. *Houston* had spent the previous night with two Dutch cruisers probing for the Japanese invasion fleet, but their search had turned up nothing. Would the invasion come near Soerabaja, which sat about five-sixths of the way to the eastern edge of the narrow island's northern coast, or would it fall closer to Batavia, the colonial capital of the Dutch East Indies, located about the same distance away from the western edge, also on the northern coast? If Preston had been asked for his opinion, he would have voted for Soerabaja simply because the Japanese pounded it from the air yet again that morning and early afternoon.

The all-clear siren sounded, and Preston opened the hatch to the director and stepped onto the platform outside. The ship was still maintaining general quarters, so no one could leave his battle station, but the respite did give Preston and his men a chance to breathe some fresh air. The ship's band assembled below them on the quarterdeck and began playing some light-hearted jazz rhythms. Chinese mess attendants circulated topside delivering ham sandwiches and coffee in Styrofoam cups to the sailors.

For a few fleeting moments, the music took him back to his family's occasional visits to Memphis from Little Rock during his childhood. Then awareness of the present slapped him back to reality, and he saw that, regardless of the music, he was still stuck in a smoldering, chaotic Dutch colonial harbor, halfway around the world from Arkansas, separated from his possibly-dead wife, waiting to be attacked by the most powerful army and navy in Asia. And there would be no reinforcements and no place to which to retreat. His level of despair became so great in that moment that all he could think to do was pray for help, but the tone of his supplication was such that he almost seemed not to believe even God could help him. It was the most faithless prayer he had ever uttered, and that made him feel all the worse.

What happened next stirred his hopes slightly and made him think that God had perhaps decided to answer his prayer in spite of its faithlessness. Sailors in the open anti-aircraft gun mounts began to point toward the harbor mouth and exclaim something about British ships.

Preston looked in the direction of their attention and saw three camouflaged destroyers steaming into the port, blowing smoke from their stacks, and flying the stark, white-and-red ensign of the Royal Navy from their mainmasts. Word spread that these were, indeed, reinforcements, and the fact that they had simply been relocated from the western end of Java did not dampen anyone's enthusiasm. Half an hour later, however, the Americans and Dutchmen received an even greater thrill when two cruisers entered the port. Again, word got around that one was the British heavy cruiser H.M.S. *Exeter*, and the other the Australian light cruiser H.M.A.S. *Perth*.

"I heard *Exeter* sank a battleship once," Seaman Madison noted to his crewmates in the director. "Isn't that right, sir?" he asked Preston.

Preston nodded. He knew *Exeter* by sight. He had been in his third year at Annapolis in 1939 when she and *Achilles* and *Ajax* had chased the German pocket battleship *Graf Spee* into the South American harbor of Montevideo, Uruguay. The German had tried to escape, but had been driven back inside by the gritty cruisers. Desperate to avoid capture, her captain ordered her set ablaze at anchor and then committed suicide in a hotel room. Preston and the other midshipmen had studied the battle in their classes and were well familiar with photographs and silhouettes of all three cruisers.

"She didn't exactly *sink* a battleship," Preston replied, "but she did beat one in combat." He proceeded to tell Madison and the others the story in as much detail as he could recall, which greatly enhanced their appreciation both of him and of *Exeter*.

The new arrivals signaled the end to the pensive waiting. That night, at around sunset, Admiral Doorman led his bolstered striking force out of Soerabaja and into the Java Sea to seek a decisive battle with the Japanese. The admiral himself, sailing in *De Ruyter*, led the way, followed by *Houston*, *Exeter*, *Perth*, the other Dutch cruiser *Java*, and nine Dutch, American, and British destroyers.

The mood in the harbor was festive in that unique martial sense. Civilians stood on the docks and waved as the buglers on *Exeter* and the Dutch destroyers played rousing tunes over the ships' loudspeakers, the tune on the British ship being "A-Hunting We Will Go" and the tune on the Dutch ships being a simple but inspiring call to close watertight doors. The setting sun tinged orange *Exeter*'s massive, white battle ensign as well as the Stars and Stripes rippling atop *Houston*'s mainmast. The only out-of-place event occurred when *De Ruyter*, rather clumsily, struck and sank two small harbor craft on the way out, but the striking force nonetheless took to sea with great optimism.

That optimism floated away gradually throughout a full night's fruitless searching. Shadowed by Japanese flying boats in the daylight hours of the 27th, Admiral Doorman's force found nothing, and turned around to sail back to Soerabaja.

The ships were proceeding past the minefield guarding the harbor when the men on *Houston* began chattering again. Signal lamps began blinking across the formation, and soon, *De Ruyter* began turning around yet again.

The word finally reached Preston in Director Two. The Japanese had been sighted nearby, and the striking force was finally heading into battle. Preston looked at his watch. It was about a quarter to three in the afternoon on February 27, 1942.

CHAPTER FIVE

Captain Rooks hastily called an officers' conference in the wardroom, and Preston climbed down from his battle station to attend. It was the first time in nearly 24 hours that he had left Director Two for more than a few minutes. When he arrived, Commander Maher was doing the talking with Captain Rooks and the ship's executive officer, Cdr. David Roberts, standing by him.

"Gunnery department officers especially, I want you men to listen up," Maher addressed Preston and a handful of other officers. "Our objective is to destroy the enemy invasion convoy, but don't get cocky and think we'll just be dashing in and shooting up a bunch of unarmed transports."

Preston wasn't sure about his comrades, but he was beyond the point of being cocky, despite his ship's excellent gunnery record.

"We're going to have to destroy their escorts, too," Maher continued, "and those could be anything from destroyers to cruisers to a couple of battleships that have been reported in the area."

Some of the junior officers exchanged nervous glances, while the senior ones kept their eyes on the gun boss. A fight against a battleship was no fight at all for a heavy cruiser. Battleship shells measured roughly twice the diameter of cruiser shells and the guns that fired them could reach several miles farther. Against a battleship, a heavy cruiser could be pounded to bits without ever having the chance to fire a shot.

"The invasion fleet itself is estimated to be about 35 to 40 troop transports, but we're not certain of its size because our aircraft have not been able to conduct a reconnaissance of it."

All of *Houston*'s catapult-launched floatplanes had either been destroyed in accidents or sent off to safe havens. In battle, they were typically used to fly over enemy fleets and spot for the gunnery officers aboard ship, but during air attacks they were liable to catch ablaze if hit and were usually flown to rear areas until the attacks ended. Two of the floatplanes had previously done so, and one was currently far away in Australia. Two others had been in the process of being launched when the concussions from the anti-aircraft guns had stripped the fabric off the wooden frames of their wings and fuselages. Their unharmed pilots stood silently in a corner of the wardroom. They would be nothing but spectators in this fight.

Commander Maher finished his briefing, and Captain Rooks dismissed the gathering. Preston spotted Terry Galloway across the room and started toward him. The two friends slapped each other on the back, exchanged best wishes, and headed off to their respective battle stations.

For the first time in over a week, Preston's anxieties began to depart him, giving way to an adrenaline-driven excitement that focused him on nothing but doing his part in fighting the battle. The moment of truth was at hand, so to speak. Every other thought in his mind could wait. He might die in the next few hours, and if that happened, he would no longer have any control over his distractions anyway.

He climbed back up to Director Two and stood outside the hatch for a few moments, surveying the Allied force assembled around *Houston.* About 900 yards ahead steamed *Exeter*, which followed *De Ruyter* by about the same distance. Several miles ahead of the Dutch flagship, Preston could see the British destroyers — *Jupiter, Electra,* and *Encounter* — plowing ahead side-by-side, scouting. Looking astern of *Houston,* he could see *Perth* at the customary interval, followed by *Java* and four American destroyers — *John D. Edwards, Alden, Paul Jones,* and *John D. Ford.* Preston was certain the powerful force could handle anything the Japanese hurled at it, except a battleship or two, of course. Confident of the Allies' chances for success, yet apprehensive about his first surface combat, Preston said a quick prayer as he entered the director and took his seat at the rangefinder.

"What's a sea battle like, sir?" Madison asked as Preston tried to get comfortable in his tractor-style seat.

"I wouldn't know," he replied. "I've never been in one."

"How do you picture it, though?"

Preston scanned the memories of his naval history lectures at Annapolis for an answer. Two pictures came to mind.

He responded, "I'm not exactly sure. The Battle of Jutland in the last war lasted for several hours. Twenty-five British and German ships were sunk, and over 8,000 men were killed. What we're taught nowadays, though, is that battles should only last a few minutes. Our weaponry is so much more efficient than what they had back then, most battles won't last very long before one fleet or the other is destroyed."

Madison had seemed nervous before, and he looked more so now. "What are our odds?"

"I don't do odds, Madison. We either live or we die, and God's already made up His mind which it's going to be, so let's just do our jobs. And if you need to make peace with God before you find out, I'd suggest you do it quickly."

With that, Preston busied himself preparing his machinery for combat. His small enlisted crew became very silent as they rode into battle.

It was a little after 4 p.m. when an electronic transmission of Commander Maher's talker's voice from Director One alerted the gun directors, the turrets, and the plotting room belowdecks of an approaching enemy fleet.

"We have smoke on the horizon off the starboard bow."

Preston activated the control that swiveled the director from side to side. The unarmed turret rotated automatically with a mechanical whir. He pressed his eyes to the binoculars mounted inside the rangefinder tube and turned the knobs to adjust his view. The stereoscopic rangefinder presented him with two halves of the same image, cut horizontally, gathered by two lenses at either end of the long tube, which extended for several feet on either side of the director. The proper adjustment of the knobs would align the two halves, at which point a mechanical display would give the range to the target. Preston soon saw the same thing as Maher. Across the gently swelling sea to the north, he could make out a smudge of funnel smoke at the base of the horizon.

Several minutes later came, *"I can see masts and superstructures."*

Within seconds, Preston could see the prickly upper works of enemy ships come into view.

Before long, Maher was passing along to his officers reports signaled by *Electra* and relayed by Admiral Doorman. *"One cruiser, large destroyers, number unknown, bearing 330, speed 18, course 220 degrees."* An amendment three minutes later: *"Two battleships, one cruiser, six destroyers."*

Madison sat bolt upright in his seat. "Battleships!" he exclaimed.

"Don't worry," Preston calmed him. "If they were battleships, they'd have fired by now."

The boy's expression calmed and his spine relaxed.

"Two heavy cruisers," came a sudden clarification.

"Now that's more like it," Preston commented.

Preston watched the Japanese fleet emerge bit by bit over the next few minutes. His eyes stayed locked on the heavy cruisers, though as more ships kept appearing, he began to fear being outnumbered. Had the ABDA task force stepped into a snake's den here? Whatever the size of the enemy force, this was the moment for which *Houston* had been built, and it was the moment for which he had trained for four years at the Naval Academy. Tension mounted inside his mind and body as he waited for the first shots.

The two heavy cruisers suddenly flashed dull orange and became cloaked momentarily by two large clouds of brown smoke. The sound of distant thunder joined the throbbing vibration of *Houston*'s turbines. Preston tightened at first, and then relaxed. The Japanese were well out of range; those shells would fall over a mile short. About a minute later, waterspouts rose from the sea off the starboard side of the Allied formation and dispersed harmlessly.

Preston recognized a new danger, however. The enemy force was steaming to the southwest; the Allied force was steaming to the northwest. The ships were on converging paths, and if the Japanese reached the intersection first, they would be able to fire every gun in their formation at Doorman's column, which would only be able to respond with its forward guns. This maneuver was known as "crossing the 'T,'" and Preston had learned it well at the Naval Academy. It had been made famous by the Japanese themselves, nearly 40 years earlier, when Admiral Togo had annihilated the Russian fleet at Tsushima in 1905. If the Japanese beat

Doorman to the intersection, the battle would be a very quick one indeed.

Admiral Doorman sensed the trap, however, and turned the column to parallel the enemy's. Preston watched as the British destroyers, confused by the sudden movement, scrambled through a forest of shell splashes to regain their proper stations. Meanwhile, a handful of Allied aircraft appeared over the Japanese force, dropped a few bombs, and flew off. Preston observed no hits.

A forceful roar emanated from the front of the column, and Preston saw a burst of cordite smoke in the extreme left of his viewfinder. *Exeter* had opened fire. In his headset he could hear the talkers for Commander Maher and his spotters feeding information to Lt. Cdr. Sidney Smith in the plotting room belowdecks near the waterline. They were apprising him of their target's range, course, and speed, as well as *Houston*'s, so that his team could calculate the angle from which to fire the cruiser's guns.

A few terse commands followed, capped by, *"Fire."*

The eyepieces of the binoculars shoved back into Preston's face. He bounced in his seat, and the entire director shuddered. A terrific *BOOM* erupted in their ears. Houston had fired her first salvo. Six 8-inch-wide, armor-piercing projectiles raced toward the Japanese cruisers less than five miles away. Inside the ship, picture frames, clothing, drawers, dishes — anything not held fast to a shelf or bulkhead — crashed to the deck into pieces or heaps. The ship's guns caused nearly as much destruction to domestic items as the enemy's shells could to the ship's structure.

Preston recovered his senses and peered through the binoculars to spot the salvo's fall. *Houston*'s shells had been loaded with a special dye that would make the misses easier to spot, so bright-red geysers appeared around the enemy ships when the shells hit the water.

Atop the foremast, the spotters in and around Director One called back the range of these misses, informing Commander Smith of the data changes that he needed to make in the ship's mechanical gunnery computer. For a quarter of an hour, the exchange continued — *Houston* and *Exeter* versus the two Japanese cruisers, with *De Ruyter, Perth,* and *Java* just waiting until the enemy came within range of their smaller six-inch guns.

"Straddle," the spotting officer at the top of the foremast reported.

Preston knew his ship's guns were getting close. The shells of the last salvo had just landed on either side of *Houston's* targeted cruiser, but had not scored a hit.

Four more thunderous salvos followed before Preston finally saw what he had been longing to see: some subdued flashes on the enemy ship followed by a burst of flame and a cloud of smoke too large to have come from her own guns.

"Yes!" he exclaimed. "We got a hit!"

Madison jumped up from his seat. "Let me see, let me see!"

Preston leaned back in his seat far enough for the enlisted men to catch a brief glimpse of the burning target. Normally, they could not see anything from their positions inside the director, but better they be there than below the waterline in the fire and engine rooms, where hits meant death by drowning or scalding. If an enemy shell happened to lop Director Two off *Houston*'s superstructure, they would be dead too quickly to feel anything.

Excited chatter jammed the intercom as spotters and talkers all over the ship watched the Japanese cruiser cease firing, pull out of column, and withdraw.

"Let's take that second Jap," Maher's talker repeated a directive to his boss's gun crews.

The earlier, professional, monotone communication of numbers and angles picked up where it had left off, and Turrets One and Two rotated to find the new target. It was not long, however, before puzzled curses began to make their ways through the wires.

"What's wrong with the deflection?" "Something's wrong with the range." "No, the range is fine, it's the deflection! That one fell too far to the left." "What the ... that one fell to the right!"

The crew of Director Two could only guess what all the fuss was about until they heard an electrician's report. The tremendous vibration of *Houston*'s main battery had shaken the fire control system's wiring so badly that the deflection readings, which controlled the fall of shot from side to side, had become skewed. The cruiser's gunners could no longer control the lateral aiming of their guns.

Meanwhile, *Houston* itself had become a target. Enemy shells splashed uncomfortably close to the ship as it forged ahead, keeping formation with the other cruisers. The waterspouts sometimes blocked Preston's view until the ship pulled clear of them. The ship took a hit through the starboard bow, but the shell entered and exited on the same side without exploding. A Japanese shell hit *Java* also, but not seriously.

At about eight minutes after 5 p.m. a Japanese shell smashed through a secondary gun emplacement on the deck of *Exeter* and penetrated through several decks to a fireroom, where it detonated within a boiler. The resulting explosion released plumes of superheated steam into the compartment, killing many of the crewmen stationed there. The steam sought any exit it could find and soon became visible to the stunned sailors aboard *Houston*. The British cruiser lost power for its main gun battery and had its speed cut by more than half. Crippled, it fell out of formation to port. Captain Rooks apparently believed that *Exeter*'s captain had been following Admiral Doorman in *De Ruyter*, which was concealed from view by the heavy smoke of battle, because he turned *Houston* to follow *Exeter*, and then steamed past the British ship. *Perth* followed suit, though her captain placed her on a course between *Exeter* and the Japanese and laid a smokescreen that would block the enemy's view of the stricken ship. Admiral Doorman, meanwhile, realized that his column was no longer behind him and swung *De Ruyter* around to catch up.

As he watched *Perth* gallantly complete her screening run with flags flying and guns blazing, Preston saw dozens of tiny white wakes come into view, which he recognized as the bubble trails of Japanese torpedoes. Many, having reached the limit of their range, popped to the surface, out of fuel. Others self-destructed, while still more plunged into the Allied column. One bounced noisily off of *Houston* without exploding. Another caught the Dutch destroyer *Kortenaer* on her starboard side and detonated. Preston watched as the explosion kicked up a remarkable geyser that crashed down upon the small vessel, almost seeming to sink it instantly. Once the spray cleared, *Kortenaer* could be seen sitting split in half, its bow and its stern both jutting skyward. Houston sailed past as survivors clung to *Kortenaer*'s hull, some of them waving to the American cruiser as their ship sank beneath them within minutes. There was no time to pick up the Dutch sailors; more torpedoes were sure to appear, and for that very reason, the Allied column was under strict orders to keep moving and to stop for nothing. A knot formed in Preston's stomach as his ship passed out of range of the survivors. He said a quick prayer for them, hoping that they might be rescued somehow before the sea claimed them along with their ship.

De Ruyter finally sailed back into sight and signaled *Houston* and *Perth* to follow. They cut a clockwise loop from the south to the east, while *Exeter* still sat nearly dead in the water, trying to get up enough steam to escape. *Perth*'s smokescreen still protected the British cruiser for the moment.

Admiral Doorman ordered the three British destroyers to launch their own torpedo attack, and the smaller vessels headed off individually toward the Japanese fleet that lay somewhere on the other side of the smokescreen. *Electra* emerged from the smoke and was immediately dismantled by a series of Japanese shells that destroyed a boiler room and literally knocked gun turrets and pieces of superstructure off the ship. Her captain ordered her abandoned, and she sank around 6 p.m. She never had a chance to launch her torpedoes. Neither *Encounter* nor *Jupiter* had any better fortune as far as their torpedo attacks were concerned, but both escaped damage.

The Allied cruisers had, by this time, targeted the Japanese ships and began dropping shells close enough that the Japanese admiral felt compelled to withdraw and cease their harassment of *Exeter,* which was now steaming at about 15 knots and soon withdrew to Soerabaja with the Dutch destroyer *Witte de With.* The rest of the striking force retreated to the east, covered by a futile torpedo attack by the four trailing American destroyers. These ships possibly achieved some shell hits on some Japanese destroyers with their four-inch guns and then raced to catch up with Doorman.

CHAPTER SIX

Preston had thought the battle was over when *Houston* and the other Allied ships turned back east, and he got a sinking feeling in his stomach when he felt *Houston* turn again to the north. Word was that Admiral Doorman wanted to take another stab at discovering the enemy troop convoys. What he found were the same two Japanese cruisers his warships had been fighting for three hours already.

Houston's gunnery department soon found itself back in action as darkness fell across the sea. This time, the Japanese cruisers were located off *Houston*'s port bow, and Preston swung the director around accordingly. *Perth* had leapfrogged *Houston* at some point and now sailed between her and *De Ruyter,* with *Java* still holding position as the trailing cruiser.

The Allied guns sounded forth again; *Houston*'s continued to jar Preston and his men with each salvo, while those of the other ships sounded somewhat muffled and distant. About ten minutes into this new duel, Preston thought he saw through the rangefinder a series of pinprick flashes along the enemy line. Knowing that ship-mounted torpedo tubes used light explosives to launch their weapons, he braced for another torpedo attack. *Perth*'s captain apparently saw the flashes, too, and pulled his cruiser out of line to starboard. Captain Rooks followed suit, as did the rest of the ships in the Allied battle line. *De Ruyter,* once again left out on a limb, quickly adjusted to the improvised maneuver, and all the Allied ships steamed away from danger.

Darkness did not deter Admiral Doorman from attempting to find the enemy convoy. Preston could no longer see anything through the rangefinder except the Java Sea's surface dimly illuminated by the moon. As the column turned again to the south he made out a distant lighthouse and some mountains, but that was all.

He leaned back from the binoculars and stretched the best he could. He had been sitting in the same place for over four hours.

"Open the hatch," he directed one of the enlisted men. A light gust of warm but fresh air breezed into the stuffy, humid director. Each one of the men was soaked in sweat, thirsty, and hungry. They were therefore very thankful when the mess attendants showed up with more coffee and sandwiches.

"Is it over?" one of the men asked Preston.

He shook his head and shrugged. "I don't know. We still haven't found the convoy, and I imagine the admiral won't take us back to Soerabaja until we do."

Madison muttered, "The old man's going to keep us out here until we die."

"What was that?" Preston replied sharply.

"Nothing, sir. I'm sorry. I meant no disrespect for the admiral, but just how much more luck can we have left?"

The young seaman was visibly exhausted and still scared.

"It has nothing to do with luck," Preston replied. "Like I said a few hours ago, God already knows how this battle is going to end."

The sailor asked no more questions, and the inside of the director fell quiet. Preston rose and moved toward the hatch, where he stood, looking forward, sipping his coffee out of a paper cup. His words had not particularly been intended to comfort or inspire; he was just saying what he believed. He was quite worried about dying himself. Of course, his faith assured him that he would spend eternity in heaven if that happened, but he still dreaded the pain of death, just as any other human would.

Death at sea bore many uncertainties. Preston never dwelt on the subject, but he occasionally wondered how he might die. Considering the location of his battle station, the most likely possibility would be for an enemy shell to strike the director, which would probably kill him instantly. If he had to abandon ship, the possibility existed that he might get dragged underwater by the suction of the sinking ship. If that didn't happen, he would have to find a raft or some wreckage to cling to and then wait to be rescued like the men of *Kortenaer* and *Electra* were likely still doing. And if rescue never came, then drowning would be the ultimate conclusion of his life on Earth, unless a shark got to him first. He gazed down at the water far below him and shuddered. If he had to die, he wanted to die quickly. He did not want to have time to think about what it would do to his parents, his sister, or Elaine.

He willed Elaine out of his mind. The suspense of not knowing if she had been hurt or killed in the Darwin raid threatened to drive him mad when he dwelt on it, and he could not bear to think about her until the battle was over. If anything happened to Commander Maher and the other officers manning the director high in the foremast, the ship's main source of protection would be in Preston's hands, and with it the lives of his 1,100 shipmates. Preston had to focus on his job and put his fear of death — both of his own and of his wife's — behind him.

The American destroyers, running low on fuel, turned east and headed back to Soerabaja at about 9 p.m. Admiral Doorman swung the rest of the column back to the west in an attempt to outflank the Japanese warships and finally locate the convoy. Intrigued by the new maneuver, Preston suddenly realized the battle was still afoot, and it helped him consolidate his thoughts. The mountains of Java were now visible as jagged shadows to the south off to port. Somewhere between them and the Allied column lay a Dutch minefield that Admiral Doorman was certainly taking great pains to avoid.

Preston had been slow to realize it, but unseen Japanese floatplanes were marking the column's path by dropping parachute flares into the ships' wakes. The yellow lamps bobbing in the foaming, white wakes lent to the evening's already eerie atmosphere. With there being no sounds but the steady rush of water against steel and the constant thrum of the engines, the lights added to a sense of doom, or at least a sense that there was more fighting ahead. Preston was absolutely convinced that the column's every movement was being watched, and he felt as if the Japanese were watching him personally. He felt exposed and vulnerable and was sure that he was not alone in having these thoughts. A distant explosion shattered the uneasy peace. It had taken place somewhere astern, and Preston soon learned it had originated from the British destroyer *Jupiter*, whose dying words conveyed by signal lamp to *Java* had been that she had been torpedoed. It was also a distinct possibility that *Jupiter* had hit one of those Dutch mines. At any rate, the column was reduced by yet one more destroyer, and now only *Encounter* remained of the original nine.

Preston prayed silently for a resolution to this battle. *"Lord, please end this battle quickly and help us to find the enemy convoy. Please protect us and prevent any more of our shipmates from dying."*

Shortly after *Jupiter*'s demise, the column turned north again. Preston suspected Admiral Doorman had caught the convoy's scent, but for nearly an hour, the ships steamed on without sighting anything but enemy floatplanes and more flares. At about a quarter after ten, voices from the water below reached the men in Director Two. Preston looked down from his perch to see the survivors of *Kortenaer* still bobbing in the sea, waving and calling for help. The column had by now looped around to the original field of battle. Per orders, *Houston* and the other cruisers sailed on, leaving the men to their fate.

Preston prayed again, *"Father, send someone else to rescue those poor fellas."*

He then looked astern and saw *Encounter* peel out of the column and into the crowd of Dutch sailors. Preston immediately breathed a prayer of thanksgiving.

Encounter would save 113 men and head back to Java, thereby missing the carnage to follow.

The Allied column stumbled upon the same two Japanese cruisers at approximately 10:30 p.m., and once again, both sides chose to fight. The Japanese reversed their southerly course and began steaming parallel to the Allies. Throughout all the ships, the exhausted gun crews pulled themselves together for yet another round of long-range shelling.

"How much more can our guns take, sir?" Madison asked Preston.

They both knew that the eight-inch gun barrels each had a life span of roughly 300 salvos. How many salvos had been fired that day, let alone since *Houston* had left Manila three months prior, was anybody's guess but the turret crews'.

"I don't have any idea, Madison. They have to be nearly spent, though. I lost count of the salvos hours ago, but I'm sure those barrels are too hot to touch even now."

The concern was not so much that the barrels would melt but that the rifled grooves lining them would strip out. Low ammunition levels in the magazines posed problems as well, and though *Houston*'s lack of a third turret had kept that situation tolerable throughout the afternoon and evening, it also meant that the shell handlers had been forced to haul the massive projectiles on bed sheets from the aft magazine through the passageways to the forward one. Preston and his men would not know this until after the battle, however.

Low on ammunition and with their crews sapped of energy and the darkness preventing effective spotting, the Allied cruisers opened fire almost reluctantly. Both sides fired star shells at each other, hoping that the phosphorous charges might illuminate the opposite column. The shells exploded short, however, failing to create silhouettes. *Houston*'s gunnery officers, and those on all the other cruisers, then decided to spot by moonlight. Neither side scored any hits, although some shells fell dangerously close to *Houston*.

De Ruyter this time sighted more torpedo-tube flashes and turned to starboard, away from the spread of underwater projectiles. The trailing cruisers followed. For the two Dutch cruisers, the effort was in vain. The explosions rocked the night in such rapid succession that Preston never was certain which had come first. It would later be determined that *Java* had been struck before *De Ruyter*, but in any case, both cruisers erupted in flames, pieces of them and their crews spinning off into the night and tumbling into the Java Sea.

The destruction was immediate and complete, as both ships soon became fully engulfed and began to settle. Had Preston been out on deck at the time, he would have been able to feel the heat from the blazes, especially *De Ruyter*'s, as *Houston* passed close aboard. The flagship's 40 mm anti-aircraft ammunition began to explode in its magazine, flinging burning pieces of metal through the darkness.

"Oh, boy, this is it!" Madison exclaimed, hearing but not seeing the blasts, which Preston could see all too well. "We're next!"

Preston said nothing. For all he knew, the kid might be right.

The end nearly came at the hands of a friendly ship. *Perth* suddenly filled his view as she and *Houston* struggled to form up in the chaos. He felt a jolt as *Houston*'s engines reversed and he leaned slightly with the ship as it turned. He imagined the near panic that must have been taking place on the bridge as the captain, the officer of the deck and the helmsman shouted orders, yanked the handle on the engine-room telegraph, and spun the ship's wheel in a desperate attempt to avoid the Australian vessel. Whatever they did worked, because *Houston* and *Perth* soon separated.

That danger past, the two cruisers scurried out of the battle zone. There would be no more chasing of the phantom convoy. *Java* had already sunk in eight minutes, and *De Ruyter* would eventually follow. Survival alone filled the minds of Captain Rooks and Capt. Hector Waller as they hastened to obey Admiral Doorman's last order to sail west to Batavia. At his own request, *Houston* and *Perth* left Admiral Doorman and his Dutchmen to die. Virtually all that remained to resist the Japanese invasion, the lives of those two unharmed ships and their sailors were now more valuable than the lives of the two Dutch ships and their crews.

Preston found himself praying once more for the safe rescue of the survivors as he sailed away from the scene of defeat. The echoes of secondary explosions from dying *De Ruyter* chased *Houston* and *Perth* over the horizon, haunting those who heard them.

CHAPTER SEVEN

The sun rose on February 28, 1942, and Preston could never have been more thankful to be alive. How *Houston* and *Perth* had escaped the previous night's holocaust was not up to him to explain. In some sense, it was another example of the randomness of war, but in another sense it was the deliverance of God. Either way, hundreds of Dutch and British sailors had perished as a result, and Preston's gratitude was tempered by a pronounced attitude of mourning.

Also present was a curious feeling of hope that had not been present before the battle. The two cruisers were now completely alone in the Java Sea, running from a superior enemy, and struggling to escape the Japanese noose, and Preston realized that their goal was no longer to seek battle but to get home. Home could be Darwin, Fremantle, Pearl Harbor, or San Francisco, but any of those places would do as long as they were safe and would afford him a chance to reestablish contact with Elaine. Such optimism was common on board *Houston*, though all hands were duly aware that severe trials might face them as they made their getaway.

The two cruisers pulled into Batavia early that afternoon. Preston returned to his room to find it a total wreck. The concussions of nearly 300 salvos had jarred every loose item in the compartment. Both his and Galloway's uniforms lay crumpled on the deck, and the glass in Preston's framed photo of Elaine had been cracked in several places as had the compartment's porthole. All of the light bulbs had burst, and Preston had to sweep the bits of glass off his bunk before he lay down to sleep for the first time in over 48 hours.

Galloway awakened him after a couple of hours. Preston's roommate had only been tidying his own bunk, but the rustling noise startled Preston, whose nerves were still on edge. Galloway quickly apologized.

Preston groaned and stretched. "Don't worry about it."

"Listen," Galloway said, "do you want to go ashore while we still have the chance? I don't think we're going to be staying in Batavia for more than a few hours. I hear we're supposed to sail directly through Sunda Strait to Slapjack to pick up our Army boys and then run like heck for Australia."

"Running never sounded so good to me," Preston quipped.

Galloway chuckled.

Preston dragged himself out of bed, grabbed his cap, and followed Galloway out onto the deck.

At the base of the gangplank they found the Batavia docks to be in a state of pandemonium. Burnt and sunken ships littered the harbor, and American, Australian, and Dutch sailors swarmed all over the wharf. Off in the background, Dutch engineers could be seen readying explosives to demolish the port's facilities, while the *Houston* and *Perth* sailors lined up at the port canteen to scoop up the cigarettes, liquor, and other products the Dutch were giving away before the demolition. Preston and Galloway saw Captains

Rooks and Waller some distance away examining a pile of life rafts. Crewmen from both ships stood by and were soon carrying the rafts aboard *Houston* and *Perth*.

"It doesn't look like anyone's planning to stay here very long," Preston observed. He began to feel hunted again, as if every second his feet stood on Javanese soil brought him closer to some sort of doom, though what sort of doom, he did not know for sure. He just knew he did not want to meet up with the Japanese again for a long time.

"Terry, I'm going back aboard to sleep some more," he told Galloway after just a few minutes.

"Well, okay," his friend replied. "Do you want anything from the canteen?"

"See if you can find me a Baby Ruth or two."

"Do the Dutch sell those?"

"I don't know. Just look for something chocolate."

"Sure thing."

Preston climbed the gangplank once again, saluted the officer of the deck, and headed toward his cabin, stepping over fuel hoses snaking across the deck and down hatches that led to the ship's oil bunkers. A sudden burst of nearby anti-aircraft fire distracted him, and he instinctively ran beneath Turret Three's guns over to the starboard railing to see what was the matter. At first fearing another Japanese air raid, he recognized the distinctive shape of *Houston*'s last floatplane returning from Soerabaja. The Dutch gunners were obviously jumpy and somehow managed to miss the plane, which landed in the harbor and taxied back to the cruiser under the escort of a Dutch torpedo boat. Preston didn't wait to greet the pilot, but from a distance he could clearly make out the lieutenant's annoyed expression.

As Preston napped the second time, the deck crew disconnected the fueling hoses and pushed them back over the side onto the dock. He awoke as *Houston* and *Perth* were weighing anchor and steaming out of the harbor, the Australian cruiser taking the lead. Preston was due to stand watch on the bridge beginning at 8 p.m., so he washed his face and hands and walked to the wardroom to eat a quick supper. It was the first sizable meal he had consumed since Soerabaja and might be the last until the ship cleared Sunda Strait, the only way out of Java.

Galloway would also be standing watch on the bridge that night. He sidled up to his cabinmate and the two ate dinner and chatted together.

"You think we might actually make it through there?" Galloway asked Preston, referring to Sunda Strait ahead.

"If the Dutch were right about the Japs not being there, yes," Preston replied quietly. "I think our chances are pretty good."

"I thought you didn't believe in chances?"

"Only as a figure of speech, Terry. Let's just say I feel better now than I did before the battle yesterday."

"How about before we got here from Darwin the last time? You were practically sulking then, talking about how you didn't think we'd ever go back there and all."

Preston looked at Galloway. "We're not going back there, are we?"

Galloway shrugged. "Probably not. But we're still headed for Australia."

"Well, there's more to Australia than Darwin, isn't there?"

"Am I supposed to trust all of your hunches from now on, is that it?" Galloway chuckled. "Has God given you some sort of revelation that we're going to survive?"

Preston shook his head. "No, He definitely hasn't. I know no more about our future than you do, my friend. In fact, as hopeful as I am now that I might see Lainy again in a few days — or at least know if she's still alive then — I have a feeling that it's not going to be as easy as simply rounding St. Nicholas Point and gliding down the strait. We may very well make it to Australia, or we may die trying."

There was also a third possibility that neither one considered or had ever before imagined.

Silence again fell over the two officers, and the only sounds that they heard were of the ship's engines, the soft tinkling of silverware on china, and the subdued conversations of the other exhausted officers.

"Well, now that I know how you feel," Galloway abruptly spoke again, "you may as well know that I'm scared to death. I feel like we're trailing by a run with a man on first and two strikes and two outs in the bottom of the ninth. The entire game — our entire lives — hinge on this pitch, and we basically need to hit a home run to win. It's nerve-racking."

"I understand perfectly," Preston commented. "I've felt that way since the last time we left Darwin, and it only got worse once we left Slapjack." Preston then recounted Commander Hollowell's chilling forecast of *Houston*'s destination.

Galloway shook his head and took a deep breath. "That would have taken the fighting spirit right out of me."

"I know, and it really haunted me because I realized immediately that it was true on two levels. Yes, we were figuratively headed for something like hell, but at the same time, many of the men on this ship are literally headed for hell if they get killed."

Galloway paused to ponder this thought. He was a Christian, too, and believed he was beyond hell's reach, so he had not thought of war in those terms before.

"Think of all the fellas who went down with those ships yesterday, or who died waiting to get rescued. What happened to all of them?"

Galloway was still silent. His only motion was to pick up his coffee cup and take a sip out of it.

"Listen, Terry, you've told me your beliefs before, and I take you at your word, but if you have any doubts about whether or not you will go to heaven when you die, set them straight with God right now because something could happen in the next few hours that will make every other part of your life inconsequential."

Galloway set the cup back down. "Well, thank you for your concern, but you have nothing to worry about. I settled all of that a long time ago, though I don't really believe in deathbed conversions ... or battlefield conversions in this case ... life raft conversions if you will."

Galloway had to stop himself before he let his gallows humor skew the conversation.

"I didn't trust Christ in order to save my own skin," he continued. "I did it because five years ago a revival preacher in Anaheim made me realize how sick with sin I was and how much I needed a Savior. It was something I had to spend a few nights thinking about, but the conclusion that I came to was that I really loved this Jesus fellow for dying for me and really believed that His resurrection from the dead was powerful enough to make all of my sins irrelevant if I just surrendered my life to his control. And I've never had a doubt since then."

It was Preston's turn to be silent. This was the deepest spiritual discussion the two of them had ever had, and they had been together since Annapolis, though they had only been close friends since joining *Houston* in Manila the previous October. Preston had not given Galloway enough credit before, but he was determined to do so from then on.

"That's good, Terry. That's really swell," Preston replied sincerely.

The conversation might have continued had they not needed to report to the bridge. Preston virtually crawled onto the deck of the bridge from the ladder and strained to stand up. His combined four hours of rest that afternoon had done nothing for him. He went through the standard procedure of relieving the previous watch-stander, took the man's binoculars from him, and assumed his post at the front of the bridge, looking out over the cruiser's forecastle and bow. *Perth* sailed about 900 yards ahead, silhouetted by the nearly set sun.

"See anything out there, Mr. Brown?" Captain Rooks inquired.

"No, sir. All's clear so far."

The 50-year-old captain nodded but scanned the water ahead himself as if to double-check.

"Watch that shoreline, men," he encouraged the officers and enlisted men on the bridge. "The moon's out tonight, but those mountains provide a terrific backdrop for enemy ships. With nothing in the background to silhouette them, we might never see them out there."

"Aye-aye, sir," Preston acknowledged.

Rooks gave a little nod and replied, "Carry on," before pacing to the opposite edge of the deck.

Preston and Galloway immediately began giving more attention to the shoreline, very much concerned by the captain's warning. They paid no heed to what was taking place aboard *Perth*, though they would not have been able to see or hear anything anyway.

No one on *Houston* realized that Captain Waller was just then attempting to send a signal to what he thought might be a Dutch patrol boat off the column's starboard bow. Captain Rooks sighted the unknown vessel as well.

"Mr. Brown, does that look like a patrol boat to you?" the captain asked.

Preston put his binoculars to his eyes and peered into the moonlit darkness at the shadowy object the captain was pointing out.

"I can't tell, sir. I'm sorry."

"That's all right." Rooks studied it himself for a few more seconds. Then he pulled his binoculars away from his eyes and with great conviction said, "It's moving too quickly to be a patrol boat. Mr. Hamlin," he called into the pilothouse to the OOD, "Sound general quarters!"

The general quarters alarm began to blare rudely. Its grating shrieks filled the ship, having the peculiar effect of charging each sleepy crew member with a new bolt of energy and causing him to fly to his battle station.

"Mr. Brown, Mr. Galloway, proceed to your battle stations," the captain ordered them.

The two young officers obeyed promptly, giving the shadow ship one last glance before racing off the bridge, Preston bound for his familiar tractor seat in Director Two, Galloway headed belowdecks to his station in the gunnery plotting room.

Before either could get to his destination, *Perth*'s main battery roared, and its flash illuminated the upper deck and superstructure of *Houston* for a brief moment. Preston dashed past the 5-inch guns on the starboard side as a flare from the Japanese destroyer behind him cast a red glow around him. Seconds later, the 5-inch guns spat forth star shell rounds that burst short of the enemy, again failing to create useful silhouettes. The battle for *Houston* and *Perth*'s survival was joined.

CHAPTER EIGHT

The thought racing through Preston's mind as he climbed to his battle station was that this battle was all that stood between him and his wife. If his ship and *Perth* won it, he would see her again. If they did not, he would not. It was all very simple to him at that point, and instead of distracting him, it actually focused him on his job, just as it had in the Java Sea battle the day before.

"Lord," he prayed aloud through panting breaths, "please get us through this. I'm not asking for any favors, and I'm not cutting any deals. I just want to live, and I want these guys on these two ships to live. I don't want anyone else going to hell tonight."

That was the last time Preston would think about anything not directly related to combat for more than an hour.

Commander Maher, from his station at the top of the foremast, was already ordering *Houston*'s first main battery salvo when Preston climbed into the director and took his seat. Seaman Madison shut the hatch behind him, somewhat insulating the director's crew from the clamor outside.

The first salvo went off with a deep-throated boom and a shudder. Preston put his eyes to the rangefinder binoculars and fiddled with the knobs, trying to bring the outside into focus. The Japanese ships had fired star shells of their own, which streaked and sputtered in graceful arcs traced by perforated trails of smoke that reflected the harsh light.

He swept the director around 360 degrees, sizing up the situation. As estimates of the enemy force's strength came in over the intercom, Preston could see that *Houston* and *Perth* were surrounded. He could see shadowy outlines of Japanese ships on all sides, and a remarkable number seemed to be firing at the Allied ships.

Houston and *Perth* had sailed into Banten Bay, an indentation on the Java coast guarded to the north by two islands — one quite large, the other much smaller. The two Allied cruisers had entered the bay through the middle strait and begun to thread their way north again through the western strait, hoping to make a left turn around St. Nicholas Point on the tip of Java and enter Sunda Strait. Just dawning on the Allied sailors, however, was the realization that the Japanese had chosen Banten Bay as the landing point for their western invasion force, which was separate from the one Admiral Doorman had hunted unsuccessfully the previous day.

The Japanese had decided to land on both ends of Java. This second invasion force had not been detected by the Dutch, and a report from an Australian cruiser telling of its sighting still languished on the desk of a Dutch general as *Houston* and *Perth* suddenly found themselves in its midst.

Preston recognized enough of the dark shapes to understand that they had finally found the enemy transports, though he would not realize until later that they were not the same transports that had been reported near Soerabaja.

"Fellas," he addressed his men, "you may not believe this, but we just found ourselves the Jap invasion fleet!"

The enlisted men gave each other wide-eyed looks. They understood that this news meant they could cause the enemy some serious damage, but they also realized that they were in for a tremendous fight.

The verbal reports from Director One and Spot One on the foremast confirmed this. *"One destroyer, five unknowns"... "One cruiser, five destroyers"... "Five cruisers, ten destroyers."*

"Holy cow!" Madison exclaimed anxiously. "The whole Jap navy's out there!"

The count continued to climb. *"Twenty destroyers"* was the next count.

Preston had finally processed all the information. Not only had *Houston* and *Perth* popped up unannounced in the middle of a Japanese landing force, they had every ship in the Japanese screening force, from cruisers down to torpedo boats, converging on them from all points on the compass.

The director mount would not rotate quickly enough to allow Preston to keep up with the action. Darkness no longer hindered his vision, for the star shells had turned the final minutes of February 28 into late morning. The many and varied flashes — from star shells, gun muzzles, and searchlights — played tricks on his eyes, dizzying him and impairing his sense of equilibrium. He felt the ship lurch from side to side, and he at first thought he was imagining the movement, but he was not. Captain Rooks was conning the cruiser one way and then the other trying to avoid the torpedoes zipping in from the Japanese destroyers that assailed *Houston* and *Perth* in packs of three and four.

The first batch of torpedoes missed and continued on toward the beach ... and the Japanese transports. Sharp reports reached Preston's ears from shore, and he swung the director around far enough to see transports now burning at anchor, victims of friendly fire.

The Japanese became victims of hostile fire, too, however, as both Allied cruisers split their guns between the enemy warships to the east and the enemy transports and torpedo boats to the west. There were so many targets, that the Allied gunners could not concentrate on many long enough to sink them. The fare being offered them in Banten Bay was "all you can eat," but the Japanese covering force was fast bringing the gunnery feast to an end.

Back to starboard, the Japanese destroyers continued to play their searchlights on *Houston* and *Perth*'s superstructures, bathing them in white light that made each individual crew member feel like the sole target of the Imperial Navy's wrath. *Houston*'s .50 caliber machine-gunners, stationed in the foremast, trained their weapons on the enemy searchlight platforms, and poured streams of red tracers into them, trying to snuff out each light almost as quickly as it appeared. The Japanese operators, meanwhile, responded by revealing each lamp for only a few seconds at a time before shuttering it and opening up another elsewhere. Not lost on Preston was the significance of the .50 caliber gunners — many of them Marines — having a part to play in a surface action. Typical naval battles such as the one in the Java Sea could be compared to a game of horseshoes, but this fight at the mouth of Sunda Strait was a no-holds-barred wrestling match of epic proportions. No man could be a spectator in this fight; from the foremast to the engine rooms, each crew member bore some responsibility for the lives of his shipmates.

Even Preston found himself directly engaged, finally. Commander Maher's station sat high enough for him to spot enemy torpedoes approaching from astern and call steering commands down to the helmsman so he could take appropriate action to avoid them, but it was so high that directing the ship's guns at so many close-range targets was almost impossible.

"Director Two, take control," Maher's talker's voice suddenly rang through the intercom.

Preston was ready. "Aye-aye, sir," he replied crisply and confidently and began searching for targets.

Among the smaller pops of the destroyers' five-inch guns, he heard the deeper booms of distant eight-inch guns. There were Japanese cruisers out there somewhere, but he could not see them. He scanned the surface a couple of times, but every time he thought he had made a sighting upon which he could range, *Houston's* own five-inchers discharged, their muzzle flashes blinding him.

He pulled back from the binoculars. "Director One, this is Director Two. I can't see anything either. Our five-inch flashes are glaring right in my scope."

Madison repeated the message into his telephone headset.

"Okay," Maher's talker called back. *"Turrets, this is Director One. Assume local control; fire independently."*

The two turret officers replied affirmatively, and they set about picking their own targets. They had little more luck than Preston had had, however; and Commander Maher soon took back control.

For all the havoc and destruction the Japanese had unleashed upon their own transports, they had not been very successful in touching either Allied cruiser until they finally began registering hits on *Perth* at 11:26 p.m., with one shell hit on the starboard side starting some flooding. Then they stuck a torpedo close to her forward engine room, shutting it down and cutting the ship's speed. More shells began to strike secondary gun mounts, and the main battery turrets reached the ends of their depleted stocks of shells. The surviving gunners at nearly all the mounts began firing practice rounds and star shells at the enemy because they had no live rounds left to shoot. A second torpedo strike knocked Captain Waller and the bridge watch to their knees, and he knew that *Perth* had fought her last. He ordered "abandon ship" and commanded that the ship's engines be left running so that she would steam clear of the floating survivors before sinking, thus sparing them from being sucked down when she finally plunged to the sea floor.

The Australian cruiser continued to take torpedoes as her crew jumped over the side. The ship tipped over as it sailed and sank at 12:05 a.m. while still underway.

Houston's hours were numbered as well. At approximately 12:15 a.m., Preston's battle station rocked violently as an underwater explosion reverberated throughout the ship's steel frame. Billows of steam suddenly burst into the director through the ventilator shaft. Preston knew an engine room had taken a torpedo and the high-pressure steam from the ship's propulsion system was now venting upward, just as when *Exeter* had been hit in a boiler room the previous day. The steam had, almost without a doubt, scalded the entire crew of the after engine room to death, and Preston feared the same fate for him and his team if they did not scramble outside quickly.

"Boys, let's get out of here!" he ordered them sharply.

No one argued, and soon they had all abandoned the director and made their way through the scorching cloud to the deck below. The steam turned out not to be deadly for the director crew, though it produced enough heat to keep them and five-inch gunners at a safe distance until it ceased rising from the ship's bowels.

The scene as viewed from the open deck was many times more terrifying and chaotic than when witnessed through the rangefinder in an enclosed director. Japanese ships sailed all round, most less than a mile away. They were so close that Preston could see individual men at their battle stations. Relentless, metallic crunching sounds attacked his ears, signaling repeated hits upon *Houston*. Then the ship reeled again after being hit by another torpedo, causing Preston to lose his balance.

That underwater missile had struck not far from Terry Galloway's battle station in the gunnery plotting room belowdecks and had knocked out the compartment's lights.

"Let's get over to Central Station, fellas," Galloway directed his men, who willingly followed him out of the compartment, whose starboard bulkhead formed part of the outer hull. They knew the next torpedo might burst right in their faces.

Central Station, the main battery's nerve center, lay only a few feet away across the passageway, but it was a little safer. Lt. Cdr. Sidney Smith had command there, and he and Galloway discussed their next move.

The ship continued to shudder as they felt and heard the crash of steel tearing steel. A downright unnerving, high-pitched metallic scraping against the hull caused nearly every man to jump. Galloway figured a dud torpedo had just glanced off the ship.

"Should we abandon station, sir?" Galloway asked the older officer.

Smith shrugged. "The rangekeeper's shot; there's nothing else we can do in this fight."

Galloway added, "I'm afraid that if we stay here we'll just be asking for that next Jap 'fish.' If that bulkhead gives way," he motioned across the compartment back toward the plotting room, "we're all gonna drown right here — if we don't get killed by the blast, that is."

He gazed around at the sweat-streaked faces of the men around him, red-lit in the dim luminance of the emergency battle lanterns. They all looked to be on the verge of panic, but not a one appeared ready to bolt without Smith or Galloway telling him to do so first.

Smith nodded. "Let me call the bridge." He picked up a telephone, asked for Captain Rooks, and after a pause, requested permission to abandon the station. With an "aye-aye, sir," he replaced the telephone in its cradle and faced his men. "Let's get topside." Heading for the hatch to the passageway, he waved his arm and said, "Follow me."

The men gladly did so, with Galloway bringing up the rear. They had little idea how to get out of the area, since all the watertight hatches leading upward were dogged shut so that they could not be opened except from above. Had Central Station indeed been flooded, the men inside would have been at the mercy of the crewmen on the next deck up to let them out. Otherwise, they all would have drowned banging on a locked hatch.

One vertical pathway remained available, and that was the narrow, hollow stalk of the ship's foremast. Commander Smith led the men through its hatch and up the column of unconnected rungs leading to the upper decks. One man turned off before reaching the main deck, and Galloway never found out what happened to him. Galloway himself continued after the other men in front of him, who emerged from the mast at the level of the conning tower, which sat one deck below the bridge. Galloway was still inside the mast when an unseen blast cut down the men above him. He crawled out onto the deck to see some enlisted men writhing around, clutching shrapnel wounds.

"Do you need help?" he asked them.

"No," they waved him away. "We'll be all right."

None of them knew that Captain Rooks had already given the order to abandon ship, and they had not heard the bugle call go out over the loudspeakers while they had been climbing the mast. The ship's main guns had no more ammunition, and nearly the entire crew of Turret Two had been incinerated by a flash fire ignited when sparks from an enemy shell strike lighted powder bags sitting ready for loading. Like the Turret Three fire a month before, this fire swallowed everything from the gun house down to the powder magazine, and alert crew members again avoided a greater cataclysm by flooding the magazine and starting the turret's sprinklers. Two of the ship's four propellers could no longer turn, having been immobilized by the loss of the after engine room. The ship also listed to starboard.

Galloway moved to starboard down the gently sloping passageway. As he reached the ladder that would take him back down to the main deck, he passed a Chinese mess steward kneeling next to a covered body, weeping. Galloway paused for a moment, hoping to identify the dead man.

"That's the captain," a nearby officer informed Galloway, motioning toward the body.

Galloway stared at Rooks' body in disbelief.

"Smith went to find the exec and Commander Hollowell," said the officer.

Galloway just nodded, gave another glance at the dead captain and his distraught servant, and started down the ladder into a world of worse horrors.

Bodies and parts of bodies cluttered the wooden deck, which was coated with a slick, grotesque slime that he could not identify but knew had to be blood. As he made his way aft, attempting to avoid tripping, but also attempting to avert his eyes from the carnage, he almost became part of it. The force of a blast knocked him down, and when he rolled over, he saw a hail of burning steel and debris falling directly on top of him. He started to shield his face with his hands, but out of nowhere, a Marine wearing a life jacket and a tin helmet landed on top of him. The life jacket and the helmet absorbed and deflected the shrapnel, saving both of their lives. The two lay there for about ten seconds before the Marine got up and headed aft. Before Galloway could even utter a "thank you" or ask him who he was, the Marine had disappeared. Galloway picked himself up and continued toward the quarterdeck.

Preston and his crew, meanwhile, had returned to their battle station only to leave again when "abandon ship" was sounded. Down on the deck near the aircraft hangar, the scene was terrifyingly surreal. Dead, dying, and dismembered men, some alive, lay everywhere. The star shells and searchlights lit the ship as if it were a stage, bringing large objects into clear vision but also casting shadows all about. The Japanese ships were so close now Preston felt he could probably swim to one with little effort. Their decks sparkled with the blinking flashes of small-caliber weapons, raking the superstructure and decks of Houston, mowing down huddles of American sailors waiting to jump ship. The cruiser's five-inch guns still reported with sharp cracks, now firing the white phosphorous star shells at the enemy ships because no other shells were available. Almost immediately, white flashes could be seen on the Japanese decks followed by the sound of hysterical screaming from the stricken enemy sailors. For Preston, the seemingly sanitary art of modern naval warfare, of mighty floating machines exchanging fire from a dozen miles away without any awareness of human lives being taken, had become sickeningly personal. The opposing sailors could practically see the whites of each other's eyes now and were using every designed or improvised weapon within reach to blow each other apart. *Houston*, clearly, was receiving worse punishment than she was able to return.

The once sparkling-white *Houston* that had shown the Star and Stripes throughout East Asia and taken President Franklin D. Roosevelt on many cruises was now suffering the fate that must be anticipated for all warships, just as her men were suffering the fate that all sailors must be prepared to face. Alone at sea, surrounded by a merciless enemy, on fire and flooding, *Houston* determined to live out her last moments valiantly. Before ordering "abandon ship," Captain Rooks, realizing his ship was surrounded, had turned her around toward Banten Bay and *Perth*'s grave, resolute on fighting to the death there. Sunda Strait was now a scrapped objective and its currents and submerged volcanoes bits of meaningless oceanographic trivia. Visits to Australia and California were exposed as pipe dreams. *Houston* and her men were dying, but they would not do so running. They had not run since the war had begun nearly three months earlier. Trapped in a far corner of the world, controlled by quarreling imperial allies, and cut off from any American reinforcements, *Houston* had fought the fight for Java that no one in Washington could have influenced even if they had tried.

Houston had still been underway when the initial order to abandon ship was given. Cdr. David Phillips, the executive officer now in command upon Captain Rooks' passing, reversed that order, noting that the ship was sailing out of reach of its life rafts once they were dropped into the water. Not much more time passed, however, before he decided to bow to the inevitable. The bugle call went out once again, and the *Houston* crewmen who had not already done so jumped over her sides into the balmy sea.

Preston gathered a bunch of enlisted men together to heave a raft into the water. They pushed it down the sloping port side of the hull and then slid after it. Then they swam for all they were worth, trying to get far enough away so that the ship would not drag them under when she finally went down. Bobbing in the water, Preston thought of nothing but survival. Had he been lying mortally wounded on deck, or worse, trapped in a flooding compartment with no way out because the men in the compartment above had already been killed, he would have been consumed with nostalgic thoughts of Elaine, his family, and home. But he was still alive, and was still healthy, and he knew that his next task was to get to land, which was mercifully visible just a few miles away.

When they reached a safe distance, Preston directed the men to climb into the raft. There they had premium seats from which to watch their beloved ship disappear forever. *Houston,* down by the bow, heeled over to starboard and appeared ready to capsize when she suddenly returned to an even keel. Flares zipped past the American flag still flying from the mainmast, their heat and motion creating an artificial breeze that fluttered the standard one last time. Bars of "The Star-Spangled Banner" floated through Preston's mind as the ship sank bow first, one of its guns still returning fire. A Marine gunnery sergeant manning a .50 caliber machine gun in the foremast didn't stop firing until the water reached his position, and he was never seen again. The Japanese, too, did not cease their punishment of the Galloping Ghost of the Java Coast until the Stars and Stripes had disappeared beneath the surface. Then all was quiet upon the sea.

CHAPTER NINE

Preston and the men in his raft wasted no time in trying to reach land. Two separate circumstances foiled them, however. The first was that the current was drawing them toward Sunda Strait, away from the shore. The second was that toward the shore, Japanese boats were moving about machine-gunning the survivors.

The staccato of the machine guns and the screams of the wounded further shook the sailors' already frazzled nerves.

"We can't go that way, Mr. Brown!" an unrecognizable, oil-faced gunner's mate insisted. "They're not going to pick us up; they're just going to shoot us like all the rest!"

Preston cast a wary glance over his shoulder toward the patrol boats and then turned back to his men. Scanning their black soot-and-oil-covered faces, through which their white eyes virtually shone in the darkness, he read the fear and desperation displayed there. They were all exhausted. Like him, most had only slept minimally during the past 60-some-odd hours. Some appeared alert and able-bodied, while others were clearly wounded. The wounds varied from bleeding cuts and scrapes suffered while abandoning ship to severe burns and deep shrapnel wounds. One man slumped shoulder-deep in water in one corner of the raft and struggled to keep his shattered left arm out of the saltwater. The sleeve of his light blue shirt had been ripped and the blood oozing out reflected the moonlight. These men all needed to get to land quickly, but Preston knew the Japanese would offer them no help. He decided his group would take its chances at sea.

"Don't worry," he assured the men. "We're not going ashore. Not yet at least. We'll get out into the strait, but I warn you, we're going to have to paddle or swim like madmen because once we pass St. Nicholas Point over yonder we'll be on an express train to the Indian Ocean, and once we get out there we may as well just take a dive and never come back up for air because no one will find us in the ocean anyway."

He gazed at each of the faces again. Even the most grievously wounded seemed to show a spark of determination. Preston had told them what was at stake, and they wanted to live now more than ever. If that meant fighting the Sunda Strait's deadly currents, then so be it, but they were simply not going to turn themselves over to the Japanese.

"All right," Preston continued, "rest up. We'll drift until we're in the strait and then we'll start paddling. Understood?"

"Aye-aye, sir," a middle-aged boatswain's mate first class named Caine replied stonily. "You lead, we'll follow."

Preston nodded and thanked the sailor. He would need more of that support — and more than a little of God's grace — if any of them were to survive.

Not all of *Houston*'s survivors had the luxury of a life raft. Most of those had been lost when the first "abandon ship" call went out and they had drifted astern before anyone could jump into them. Most of the cruiser's sailors wound up clinging to pieces of floating debris large enough for just one or two men each. Many wore life jackets, but some did not.

Terry Galloway and some 20 others hung onto a loose pontoon from the ship's remaining floatplane. The only other officers in the group were one of the ship's doctors, Cdr. William Epstein, and Chaplain Rentz. The doctor himself was bleeding badly from the top of his head, but seemed to be holding up as well as the rest of the men.

The pontoon drifted all night and progressively began to sink as the waves lapped into a hole on its top. Chaplain Rentz apparently recognized the danger this posed because he would occasionally attempt to swim away.

"Chaplain, get back here!" Galloway yelled at him once. "What are you doing?"

Rentz, nearing 60 and retirement, called back, "You men are young, with your lives ahead of you. I am old and have had my fun."

"Nonsense, Chaplain!" Galloway retorted, abandoning any of the meekness he would have normally used in addressing a man of God, not to mention one wearing silver oak leaves. Swimming over to him, Galloway grabbed him by the straps of his life jacket and pulled him back to the group. "None of us are going to die if you stay. We can all make it to land together," he insisted.

Of course, that claim had been most likely untrue. A few of the men were gravely wounded, and the release of some weight might just keep the pontoon afloat for a little longer, but Galloway wasn't about to let the chaplain sacrifice himself to save them.

Rentz grudgingly returned that time and several more, but only after one of the sailors swam out to retrieve him. It was a battle they could not hope to keep winning forever, however. One young seaman without a life jacket was having a particularly rough go of it. Hanging his head, he appeared to be so weak that if he dropped off the pontoon he would probably drown immediately. Rentz, typically, removed his life jacket and offered it to the sailor.

"Take this. My heart's failing me, and I can't last much longer," Galloway overheard the chaplain tell the boy, gasping for breath in such a way that the ensign knew the chaplain was telling the truth.

The sailor took the life jacket reluctantly but did not put it on. Before Galloway or any of the other men knew what had happened, Chaplain Rentz had shoved away from the pontoon and let himself slip beneath the waves. When the young sailor figured out what had just taken place, he finally put the life jacket on. It was early Sunday morning.

By sunrise Preston knew he had severely miscalculated the situation. He had known the current was strong, but he had not anticipated it being this strong. Had he and his men been floating individually on pieces of debris, they would have been scattered by now and halfway down the strait. The fact that they were all together in a raft meant that they could at least work together against the current. Some men, including Preston, had jumped over the side and tried to tow the raft toward shore by swimming, while others ripped up pieces of the wood-grate floor to use as makeshift oars. None of these efforts were good enough, however; and Preston racked his brain trying to find a way out of their dilemma. He was not about to let himself and the other nine men float effortlessly into oblivion. Preston prayed for deliverance and craned his neck in all directions looking for other survivors, islands, boats — anything.

The answer to his prayer arrived more quickly than he ever imagined an answer could. It came in the form of a motored fishing boat being piloted by a Javanese native. The men in the life raft immediately began waving and slapping the water in an attempt to get his attention. They needn't have expended the effort. The pilot had seen them long ago and had been quite determined to find them, though they would learn it was not for the reason they had hoped.

The small wooden craft puttered up to the raft, and the pilot idled the throttle and leaned over the starboard rail toward the men. He called to them in his unintelligible native tongue and pointed at them, then into his boat.

"Yes!" Preston replied. "Yes, we want to get in your boat."

The native waved Preston toward him and held his arm over the side. The American paddled over and reached up to take the fisherman's hand, but the native pulled it back quickly. Preston stared at him with a puzzled expression. The native held his hand out again, but this time his palm was upturned. He flexed and extended his fingers in a beckoning motion.

One of the sailors called to Preston, "I think he wants money, sir."

Preston was disgusted. "Money?! Who does he think we are?"

The native, though he probably could not understand English, could apparently read Preston's mannerisms and tone. He withdrew his hand again and shrugged as if to say, "If you don't pay me, I can't help you."

Preston could understand this language. He held out his arms himself and said, very slowly, "We do not have any money. Our ship is sunk. Everything we own is with the fishes."

Some of the sailors might have chuckled at his almost childish delivery if the situation had not been so serious.

The fisherman shook his head and pointed at Preston's right hand. Perhaps he understood some English because that was the hand on which Preston wore his Naval Academy class ring. The fisherman kept his finger in line with the ring until Preston looked at it. Then the native opened his palm and wiggled his fingers again.

Preston did not have much of a choice. He figured if he ever made it back to the States, Annapolis might be able to spot him a new ring, that is if he could not manage to negotiate the return of the original. He stuck both hands underwater so as to conceal the heretofore unnoticed wedding band on his left hand and pulled the Academy ring off and handed it to the native. The fisherman seemed satisfied because he smiled as he pocketed the treasure and motioned for them to quickly climb in.

"Okay, get Stansky into the boat first," Preston ordered his men to help the sailor with the shattered arm first. The gunner's mate third class had fought unconsciousness for hours, and Preston marveled that he was still alive.

It took four men pushing and the fisherman pulling to lift Stansky into the boat. Why Preston or one of the others didn't climb in first to help, he did not know. He wished someone had because he might have been able to prevent what happened next.

With Stansky secure on the fishing boat's deck, the fisherman suddenly returned to the pilothouse and opened the throttle. Before Preston or any of his men could do anything, the boat was scooting past them. The pilot, without looking back, made a sharp port turn back toward shore and motored away, leaving a thin cloud of bluish exhaust hanging above the waves.

Preston and his mates screamed and waved their arms at the native, and more than one sailor cursed him, but their entreaties accomplished nothing. The opportunistic native was gone with the Naval Academy ring that had bought him one wounded American sailor. None of the men in the water could venture a guess what might happen to their shipmate. The Javanese were known for their hostility toward white men — the Dutch in particular — and were believed to be looking forward to the Japanese invasion with great relish. Preston could only hope and pray that his ring had at least secured proper medical treatment for the enlisted man he had just met a few hours before, but he did so with a healthy dose of skepticism.

"Well, fellas," Preston turned to his enraged and dejected crew mates, "I am taking suggestions."

The humorous sarcasm was entirely forced, and the men knew it. Preston's comment failed to bring even the slightest grin to any of their faces, or to his for that matter. Silence hung depressingly heavy along with the lingering boat exhaust for many minutes. Surveying the horizon again, Preston could see their only real chance at survival was to swim and paddle madly at an angle toward the Java shore.

"There's only one thing we can do," Preston announced. "We *have* to get to the beach."

"I don't want to go there," a teenager protested. "There's too many Japs!"

"And too many stinkin' natives!" another added bitterly.

Caine, his face still red with anger, wrathfully described what he'd like to do to the fisherman if he ever saw the man again.

"Listen!" Preston brought the heated, murderous conspiracy to a close with his most emphatic command voice. "We are going to die if we do not get ashore! Forget about the Japs and forget about the natives. Unless you want to spend weeks floating in the Indian Ocean waiting to die from sunburn and thirst, then your next best option besides Java is to just drown yourselves right here."

Everyone became very quiet and still, even the boatswain's mate who was old enough to be Preston's father and who had spent the better part of the last decade in the Asiatic Fleet. One by one, they each muttered their approval, and grittily, they paddled with their arms, legs, and flimsy improvised oars toward land and life, though what type of life awaited them was a fearsome mystery.

Galloway and his group found their own piece of land on which to rest. They and their pontoon washed ashore on Topper's Island, a small chunk of earth with a lighthouse near St. Nicholas Point. Some Australian sailors had already landed there, and the *Perth* survivors helped their *Houston* brethren out of the shallow water, across the beach, and into the shelter of the trees. The Americans numbered ten, including Galloway.

"Are there any Japs here?" Galloway asked the leading Aussie.

"Not that we've seen yet," the sailor shook his head. "It won't bother me a bit if it stays that way either."

"Of course not."

"I figure we could live on our own here for some time without being discovered," the Australian declared confidently.

"Except for that lighthouse," Galloway observed.

The Aussie shrugged. "Well, we'll just have to stay clear of whoever comes out here, and hope no one saw us come ashore."

"In that case, shouldn't we get a little farther back into the bush?"

"Yeah, we should. And have some of your men drag that pontoon with them, if you please, sir."

Galloway directed two of his sailors to do just that, and he followed the Australian into the jungle that might be his home for who knew how long.

Chapter Ten

Elaine knew nothing of the battles of the Java Sea and Sunda Strait or of her husband's ordeal when she awoke in a Fremantle hotel room on Monday morning after three full days of traveling by rail. Still worried that *Houston* might have tangled with the Japanese carrier group that had bombed Darwin, she had no inkling that the ship had made its way all the way back to Java, survived a major sea battle, and then come within a few miles of surviving another and escaping to Australia. No news of the war had reached her during those days on the train, speeding across the barren, brown and orange flatness that was southwestern Australia. She was unaware of the Royal Netherlands Navy's nearly wholesale sacrifice and that it had lost over half its vessels in the East Indies and would soon lose those islands as well. She was also unaware that the legendary *Exeter* had been bombed to death the previous day along with members of the splintered and hemorrhaging U.S. Asiatic Fleet.

Wartime Australia seemed chaotic enough to her without all this discouraging news. While panic such as that present in Darwin existed nowhere else she went, the inhabitants of the continent seemed very sensitive to the hot breath of war. The fall of Singapore, she had learned, had triggered a major sea change. It had signaled the federation of former British colonies that Mother England could no longer guarantee her support for them. Australians had been at war for over two years, fighting alongside their Imperial brothers from Great Britain, New Zealand, South Africa, and India in places like Egypt and Libya, Greece and Crete, Palestine and Syria. Australian ships and sailors had distinguished themselves in the Mediterranean and the Atlantic. The war against fascism was a patriotic struggle, one for the safety of the world, though primarily the European world.

The Japanese invasion of Malaya and the East Indies had, however, created a whole new dynamic. Australians now supported the British in defense of its oriental empire, and once Singapore fell, taking nearly 15,000 Australians with it, the oriental empire seemed to have vanished. India was still firmly British, but keeping it that way would require vast expenditures, leaving little to offer Australia. "The Lucky Country" was, for all intents and purposes, on her own, and nothing illustrated this jarring fact more than British and Australian ships who had dominated Axis men-of-war in other oceans being hunted down and sunk one-by-one in the shallow littorals of the wrecked Dutch Empire. Australia would greatly miss *Perth* and Capt. "Hec" Waller in the weeks and months to come. For the time being, however, no one realized they were gone.

Elaine made this discovery when she walked up to the main gate at the Fremantle navy yard, looking for someone who might be able to tell her if her husband was still alive. The first people she met were two Aussie sailors manning the guardhouse. One of them stepped outside, rifle in hand, to greet her.

"Good morning," she greeted them cheerfully but professionally. "I'd like to speak to the ranking American naval officer here."

The sailors looked at each other skeptically and then examined her equally.

"I don't know how to help you, mum," the sailor outside replied. "There are no American ships here right now."

Somewhat surprised, Elaine responded, "Really? I thought there would be several here from Java by now."

The sailor shook his head suspiciously. "No, not yet at least. I would probably be one of the last people to know if they did show up."

Elaine paused and stared off to the side for a minute, pondering her next move. She decided to do something she never would have done under any other circumstances.

"Here," she said, reaching into her purse for a piece of paper and a pencil. She scribbled something on the paper and handed it to the sailor, knowing her mother would not have approved but not knowing what else to do at the moment. "This is my name and the telephone number and address of my hotel. Would you be so kind as to let me know when an American ship arrives here?"

The sailor looked even more uncertain now. "Sure," he replied warily.

Elaine replaced the pencil inside her purse, straightened and smiled at the sailor. "Have a good day." It was the same gracious grin that had won her so many friends in Darwin, and she figured it couldn't do any harm here.

The sailor had already turned around and started back toward the guardhouse when Elaine reconsidered. "Don't call for me unless there's an American ship in port. All I want is news so I can find out where my husband is. Understand?" She had placed a slight emphasis on the word "husband."

"No worries, mum. I'll see what I can do."

Elaine smiled again, but toned it down this time, and departed with a simple "thank you." It began to dawn on her that the completely genuine country-girl innocence that had served her so well in Darwin might be taken advantage of elsewhere, and the thought also occurred to her that her safety in Darwin might have had more to do with George's shotgun and the 30-year-old bayonet with which he claimed to have killed nine Germans than anything else.

Elaine returned to her hotel and waited, but waiting was too boring, and it also gave her too much time to worry, so she decided to take a walk around town and find a telegraph office so that she could wire home. She had intended to do so the previous evening but had been too exhausted. Neither her family in Springdale nor Preston's family in Little Rock had heard from her since Alice Springs, and she had not heard from any of them since receiving the last letter from her mother before Valentine's Day. That had been over two weeks past.

Fremantle was a very elegant, though small, port city. Infinitely more refined than Darwin, it still bore quaint charm as reflected in its century-old colonial buildings. Nevertheless, Elaine did not forget that she was in one of the few populated areas on Australia's extensive, lonely Indian Ocean coast. Along with her bigger sister city, Perth — located just a few miles up the Swan River — Fremantle was an isolated pocket of European civilization on the edge of the Australian Outback.

Elaine felt that her time there would be pleasant, but truly on her own for the first time since arriving in Darwin, she began to feel overwhelmingly lonely. It was just as well she did not know that her husband was at that moment wandering through the Javanese bush with a handful of other *Houston* survivors, hiding from Japanese troops and trying to determine which natives might be trustworthy. The hope that *Houston* might sail into port any day and discharge Preston and the rest of her crew for a happy liberty before collecting them again and carrying them off to the U.S. West Coast buoyed her sagging spirits. Then she could return to the States, and perhaps, to Arkansas. At the very least she could settle down in Honolulu or San Francisco and join their communities of Navy wives like the one she had hoped to join in Manila.

Manila had been a foolish hope, though, and she again asked herself what had possessed her to follow Preston to the Philippines in the first place when everyone knew war was so near. He had already expressed his regret upon one of his earlier visits to Darwin, but she had brushed him off. She had followed him because she loved him, and she would never regret that love. She was, however, beginning to question the wisdom of her decision, which had almost gotten her killed in Darwin and had quite possibly left poor Preston wondering if she was alive or dead. He had surely heard of the raid by now, but if he was still at sea, it was unlikely that he could have heard many details.

"Lord, if he is worried about me," she prayed, *"give him peace to know that I am safe, and please, bring us back together quickly."*

She returned to her hotel after lunch ready to take a nap. As she approached the door to her third-floor room, she spotted two men in gray suits leaning against the doorframe. They both noticed her immediately and straightened to face her.

The man on the right promptly removed the cigarette from his mouth and addressed her, "Mrs. Elaine Brown."

"Yes."

Both men withdrew badges, and the man on the right spoke again, "We're with the Fremantle Police. We'd like to ask you a few questions."

Elaine peered closely at the badges and then glanced up at them. Both fidgeted with bored annoyance.

"May I ask about what, and also what your names are?" she replied firmly. She did not want to appear scared, but the truth was that she was a little intimidated at the prospect of being questioned by foreign policemen, even if they were Aussies.

"I'm Alan Drayton," the first detective responded patiently, "and this is Bob Stone. We need to ask you some questions about your visit to the navy yard this morning."

Elaine did not even attempt to guess the specifics. That meeting had been awkward for sure, but she could not imagine why the police would be interested in it. Had they been watching her? Surely not. She was a nobody who had only been in town for one night. Did the sailors report her? Possibly, but for what?

She decided to cooperate but to also play dumb. "Okay, what do you want to know?"

Stone answered, "We want to know why you were so interested in knowing when the American ships are coming to Fremantle?"

She parried quickly. "Are they coming to Fremantle?"

Stone rolled his eyes, not happy at being countered like that.

Drayton picked up the pieces. "We all assume there will be American ships here soon enough. As to the details, we know no more than you do, unless you know more than you're telling us."

"If I knew the answers to my questions, why would I have asked those sailors in the first place?"

Drayton cringed at being foiled. Elaine certainly didn't think him to be that dense; he looked as if he were simply too tired to be playing games with her.

"Listen, lady," he continued, "if you haven't noticed, there's a war on, and those sailors you met this morning were concerned enough that you might be a spy that they told us about your visit and gave us the note you handed them."

"Well, I'm certainly not a spy. I am trying to locate my husband. He's an officer on an American cruiser, and the last time I saw him was when he left Darwin five days before the raid. I am concerned for his safety, and I was looking for another American officer who might be able to tell me if he and his ship are okay."

Stone furrowed his eyebrows. "What were you doing in Darwin?"

Elaine patiently answered his question. "I had been on a ship to Manila to see my husband when the Japanese attacked the Philippines and we got detoured to Darwin. Continuing to Manila was not an option, and I did not want to go home after having come so far, so I stayed in Darwin. If you need someone to confirm that, talk to George Fraser at George's Saltwater Café. You can also call Frank and Gladys Fraser in Alice Springs."

"So you're looking for your husband?" Drayton asked.

Elaine tried hard to conceal her growing exasperation. "Yes. Now may I go into my room?"

Stone ignored her. "Why didn't you tell the guards that when you first walked up?"

"I didn't think I needed to."

"Then why did you finally tell them that as you were leaving? That sailor thought you seemed a little nervous right then, like you were trying to cover up something."

Elaine closed her eyes and sighed. "I am not in the habit of giving my telephone number to strange men. I was desperate for news, and I thought they might be able to help me. When he turned to walk away I realized I may have given the wrong impression. They looked like upstanding boys, but you never can tell."

"No, you can't," Drayton agreed.

Stone spoke up, "*You* look Italian," pronouncing the word *eye-talian.* "Are you Italian?"

Elaine immediately saw where this new line of questioning was headed, and she did not like it. "What does that have to do with anything?" she responded indignantly.

Stone persisted. "Are you Italian?"

"My mother is."

"That's quite an admission considering that both our countries are at war with Italy. Where does she live?"

"Arkansas!"

That quieted Stone, who was clearly taken aback.

"I am not an Italian spy," she insisted. "There is a tiny little town next to my hometown that is almost entirely Italian, and I have several cousins who have already joined the armed forces ... the *American* armed forces."

The two detectives looked at each other and then back at Elaine.

Drayton spoke again, "Mrs. Brown, your story makes sense. You may be naive, but I believe you are honest. My advice to you is to not go around asking random questions about ship movements to guards, or to any military men for that matter. If an American ship shows up here in Fremantle, you'll know soon enough." As he uttered the last part of that sentence his face took on a dismayed look that said he knew what American sailors were like when they came ashore on liberty. "You can ask one of them for help, but do so carefully, understand?"

Elaine nodded. "Yes, I understand." She paused, waiting for the interrogation to continue. When it didn't, she added, "Is there anything else?"

"No," Drayton replied. "That about covers it."

"Well, gentlemen, thank you for your time." That part sounded almost sarcastic. "Have a good day." She forced a gracious smile on this occasion, and the prying detectives finally left her alone.

She entered her room and shut the door. Locking it behind her, she sighed, tried to wish herself out of this miserable situation, and realized the moral of the lesson she had just learned: life in wartime Australia was much more complicated than anything she had ever before experienced.

Chapter Eleven

While Elaine's life became vastly complicated, Preston's, oddly enough, became quite simplified. By late Tuesday afternoon, he and his men only had to worry about basic essentials such as food, water, and hiding from the Japanese and the natives. Each man had one goal in life and one goal only: stay alive. The chores of shipboard life, the strain of general quarters, and the intensity of battle had faded into the past, having given way to a literal hand-to-mouth existence as the shoeless, mostly shirtless sailors tramped their way through the jungles of Java in search of that next coconut. Those had been relatively plentiful on the beach on which they had landed two days earlier, but they were harder to find inland.

The marooned sailors marched roughly to the southeast, trying to reach the Dutch lines, wherever those happened to be. Along the way, they encountered numerous natives, but Preston forbade his men from making contact, and they never saw the unscrupulous fisherman or their missing shipmate either. In fact, they never saw any of their other shipmates or any of *Perth*'s crew. None of them realistically believed they might be the only remaining survivors for too many men had been seen in the water after the sinking. Had the Japanese machine-gunned them all? Probably not. A good many had likely swum ashore in the middle of the landing force and had been captured outright. Only those caught in Sunda Strait's current who had managed to break free of it would be wandering through the jungle.

After two days, however, the hunger and the thirst had begun to become unbearable. Several of the sailors pleaded with Preston to trust the natives, at least long enough for them to get a good meal out of the deal.

"Can't trust those good-for-nothing jerks!" Caine replied cynically. "I'll eat moss and tree roots before I let one of them feed me."

"Do as you like," Preston replied, "but I think the men are right. We need to eat. We need to find the Dutch army, and we've been out here for two days and haven't found them yet. There have to be some friendly natives."

The boatswain's mate grunted. "Aye-aye, sir, but with all due respect, I disagree."

"Your dissent is duly noted, Petty Officer Caine. We will speak to the next natives we encounter, provided the Japanese are not in view."

The men stumbled into a tiny village just minutes later. A native man saw them and walked out to greet them. He spoke no English, and none of the sailors could understand his awkward attempts at speaking Dutch. He motioned them to his hut, however, where his wife ushered them inside and offered them a meager meal of fish and rice. More substantial than the sandwiches they had consumed at their battle stations, the meal was the best they had eaten in six days.

Preston covered all of his bases, posting a lookout in each corner of the hut and having his men eat in shifts. The strategy did not prevent a jeep from roaring up the hill and into the center of the village, however. The lookouts raced back to the center of the hut.

"Mr. Brown! There's a jeep outside flying a Jap flag!" one of the lookouts informed Preston in a panic.

"Are they soldiers?"

"No, they're natives!"

Preston glanced at the boatswain's mate, who tried to avoid eye contact. Preston thought it was to avoid looking as if he was gloating.

"When you're right, you're right," Preston admitted.

Caine looked at him. "I wish I was wrong, sir."

"All right, everyone stay put, and be quiet." Preston was through taking chances with the natives. He ordered the boatswain's mate, "Restrain our hosts."

The big sailor stood and positioned himself between the native couple, his large frame looming over them and his arms poised to immediately reach out and grab them if they made any suspicious moves.

"They're headed this way!" one of the lookouts whispered urgently from near the door.

"All of you, get away from the center of the room," Preston ordered. He waved his arm around the room. "Take up positions along the walls." He intended to jump the native collaborators if they entered the hut. Some of the group could then commandeer the jeep, find the Dutch lines, and bring back help to retrieve the others.

His plan never had a chance to work, however, because more vehicles could soon be heard outside. Preston leaned in next to the lookout closest to the front door and peeked out a window. The collaborators had stopped a few yards away from the hut and were now looking toward two approaching

Japanese army trucks, each crammed with uniformed and armed soldiers.

"Fellas," Preston spoke, "this may be it. We've got two squads of Jap infantry outside now. There's no way we can fight our way out of this."

Caine spoke up, "Sir, we might be able to sneak out the back window and hide in the trees."

Preston nodded. "That's our best shot. Out the back ... now!" he whispered loudly.

He and Caine were the last ones out, and they stopped just outside the windowsill and looked back inside at their now fearful hosts.

"Sir, what are we going to do about them?" Caine asked.

Preston had no clue how to answer. He couldn't kill them for several reasons, the first being that they had no weapons, the second being that the murders would be quickly discovered and would probably bring heavy retribution if the sailors ever were caught, and third being that it simply wasn't right.

"I don't know. We just have to run."

"If you say so, sir."

As the two of them ran for the tree line, the two natives inside the hut ran for the Japanese. A brief hunt resulted in no casualties. Preston wisely ordered his men to surrender peacefully because he felt the Japanese needed no extra incentive to shoot them.

The Japanese rounded them up and marched them into the village, where the natives gathered around, staring and jeering and waving little Japanese flags. The Americans never learned who had betrayed them in the first place, though they suspected it could have been any of these hostile villagers. In fact, it was beginning to look more and more like a planned trap by the native couple. In other words, the meal had been prepared and the troops had been warned ahead of time. It was a distinct possibility that the band of survivors had been spotted earlier without their knowledge and that their betrayers had thus had time to set the trap.

Preston chafed at having been outsmarted, especially when the boatswain's mate had advised him against contacting the natives. Preston had only been looking out for his men's health, but perhaps he should have taken a harder line and made them tough it out until they found Dutch troops. He would second-guess that decision for weeks, for as it turned out, the life that lay ahead of him and his men would be much more taxing physically and mentally than a couple of more days walking in the jungle would have been.

The detectives had been right: Elaine would know as soon as an American ship entered the port of Fremantle. She discovered U.S.S. *Holland*'s arrival on Tuesday not because of crowds of American sailors but through her own observations from her hotel room window. The appearance of a gray vessel looking something like a passenger liner but flying the Stars and Stripes and bearing five-inch guns and naval life rafts prompted her to go down to the street outside the wharf and wait. After a couple of hours, a convoy of cars left the very gate she had visited the previous day, and zoomed off into the city. Guessing — and hoping — that American officers sat inside those vehicles, she followed them the best she could on foot, figuring that they were headed for one of the nearby hotels and that even if she lost sight of them temporarily, they would turn up around the next corner. Check-ins always took some time, and she had confidence that her athleticism and her flats would help her track the officers down before their rides left. If her pals Drayton and Stone happened to be trailing her — which she suspected they were because that's what G-men always did in the movies back in the States — she just dared them to keep up. She could keep a sure footing at a dead run down dirt roads, through fields, and across dry creek beds. Simply fast-walking Fremantle's sidewalks would be a cinch.

The three green sedans were easy to spot. She hurried up to the hotel — a different one than her own — and entered the lobby. Several American officers in khaki service dress uniforms were just boarding an elevator. She possessed too much dignity to race after them and make a scene, but she imagined the men would have to eat soon, so she took a seat in the lobby and waited, checking her watch frequently so that the concierge might believe she really was waiting for someone instead of just loitering.

She almost reached the point where she would have to leave and get something to eat herself when the elevator doors opened again, and five officers stepped out. As they approached, Elaine could tell most of them were senior officers, the highest-ranking one being a captain with four gold stripes on his black shoulder boards and the rest being three-stripe commanders and two-and-a-half-stripe lieutenant commanders. She boldly stood and walked toward them.

"Excuse me, Captain. May I have a word with you?"

The captain and his entourage stopped and looked her over warily as if surprised to run into an American woman there.

"Yes, you may," the captain replied. "What do you need?"

"My name is Elaine Brown, and my husband, Ensign Preston Brown, is an assistant gunnery officer on the U.S.S. *Houston*. I last saw him in Darwin the day before the air raid, and I've been trying to locate him. Can you help me?"

The captain looked suspicious just as the guards and detectives had the previous day. "Why are you in Australia?"

Elaine explained how she had become stranded in Darwin at the start of the war.

The captain didn't seem to believe her. "Why were you headed to Manila when you were? Didn't you know there could be a war?"

"We did, but didn't think it would become what it did. By the time my husband and his ship left Manila, I had already sailed, and we were in the middle of the ocean on December 7. Who knew the Japanese would attack so quickly? And who would have thought they would have captured Manila so quickly?"

The captain smirked knowingly. "None of us did."

"Looking back, it was a dumb thing to do, but Preston and I didn't think so then."

"So you fled Darwin after the raid. How long have you been here?"

"Since Sunday night. Captain, is there anything you can tell me?"

The captain glanced back-and-forth at his officers and then looked Elaine in the eye. "Mrs. Brown, I believe your story, but there's nothing I can tell you except that *Houston* was involved in a major surface battle along with other Allied ships on Friday."

Friday? If she had anticipated bad news at all, she had anticipated hearing that something had happened to *Houston* soon after the Darwin raid. Instead, everything must have been fine until just four days ago.

"Is that all?" she asked, certain there had to be more that he could tell her.

The captain sighed. "That's all I'm at liberty to say."

Elaine needed to sit down, but she did not. She was determined to stay on her feet through this. The captain's information didn't really mean anything. It had only been a few days, after all. *Houston* would need more time than that to reach Fremantle, and she doubted the ship was headed back to Darwin. Maybe *Houston*'s radio had been damaged in a fight. Her imagination formulated any number of plausible explanations for why Preston's ship was missing, but none of them could relieve the burning sensation in her stomach.

The captain read her silence correctly. "I'm sorry, Mrs. Brown. Everyone is hoping and praying that *Houston* will turn up, and she still might."

"Is that really all you know?" Elaine asked, noticing that by admitting the cruiser was missing he had just told her more than he had said he would.

"For now, yes. Since you are a civilian, I'm not sure if I will ever be able to give you more specific information, but you are entitled to know your husband's status. Tell me how I can reach you in Fremantle, and I will have one of my officers stay in touch with you."

Elaine nodded. "Okay, sir," she agreed as she began digging through her purse for that notepad and pen. She withdrew both and held them very shakily before handing them to the captain.

"How about you write, sir?" she said.

The captain nodded understandingly and copied down the name of her hotel. "I will have someone contact you as soon as more information becomes available. I will be sure to include any information you would have received in a telegram from the Navy Department if you were at home. Fair enough?" He tore off the top sheet of paper and handed the pad and the pen back to her.

Elaine nodded and retrieved the items, placing them back into her purse.

"Yes, sir, it's very fair. Thank you for your help."

"Again, I'm sorry for the anxiety you are feeling right now."

"That's all right, Captain. My husband's in God's hands."

The captain said nothing but nodded and motioned for his men to follow him out. "Have a good day, Mrs. Brown."

"You too, sir," she responded almost absently.

The captain offered a courteous nod and maneuvered around her to the door.

Elaine turned and called after him. "Captain?"

The captain now turned to look at her. "Yes?"

"What is your name?"

"I'm so sorry," he immediately apologized. "I'm Captain John Wilkes."

"It's a pleasure to meet you, Captain Wilkes."

"Likewise, I'm sure, though I wish it would have been under better circumstances."

"I'm not sure that would be possible. We're in the middle of a war, after all."

Captain Wilkes nodded understandingly. "Indeed we are. I just regret you had to get this news from me."

"Thank you again for your help, sir."

"Don't mention it, Mrs. Brown," he said, backing slowly toward the door. "Please excuse me."

Elaine watched as the captain and his officers left the lobby and climbed back into the waiting cars. After they drove off, she made her way back to her hotel room. She was no longer hungry, and all she wanted to do was try to sleep. Perhaps she would wake up and *Holland* would no longer be in the port and the whole episode would have been a bad dream.

CHAPTER TWELVE

U.S.S. *Enterprise* finally returned to Pearl Harbor from its second air raid tour on March 10. The planes of Air Group Six took off from the carrier's deck while the ship was still out at sea and flew into the airfield at Ford Island, in the middle of Pearl Harbor. They followed the same approach path that Floyd Craven and his fellow fliers had used on December 7, 1941, while dodging Japanese bullets and American anti-aircraft bursts. H.L. Hopping was one of those pilots who had made that landing but was not returning for this one. Their bodies were entombed in their shattered aircraft somewhere on the bottom of the Pacific Ocean, not far from the hulks of the minor auxiliary ships that more of Admiral Halsey's bombers had sunk. *Enterprise*'s pilots had performed well, and their strike against Marcus Island on the 3rd had been the closest yet to the Japanese home islands, but Floyd and many of his comrades felt that their accomplishments and those of aircrews from other carriers — *Yorktown* and *Lexington* — had been empty, especially when they learned the rough details of ABDA's collapse in the Netherlands East Indies, which the Dutch had surrendered just the previous day.

The situation in the Philippines remained dire as well as its American and Filipino defenders had been backed into the Bataan Peninsula, from which there was no feasible escape.

The pilots of Bombing Six received all of this information from their intelligence officer, Ens. Harry Giles, who just happened to be seated as a passenger in Floyd's SBD that day. Giles had been at Pearl Harbor on December 7 as a member of the battleship *Nevada*'s crew, and had joined Bombing Six just before its first Pacific cruise, which had been highlighted by the strike on Kwajalein.

Looking ahead at the conglomeration of combat ships and auxiliaries gathered in the harbor, as well as the upturned red hull of the battleship *Oklahoma* and the blackened superstructure of *West Virginia,* Floyd again felt all the emotions he had left there on Valentine's Day when *Enterprise* had set out for Wake. At sea, it was easy for him to concentrate on flying; but in Hawaii, it was hard for him to concentrate on anything but the memories of December 7 when the Pacific Fleet had been ambushed and several of his friends had been killed by friendly fire while trying to land at Ford Island. He dealt with these emotions by diverting himself the best he could with alcohol and women, of which he had seen neither since leaving Pearl the last time. He would fill those voids as soon as he was on liberty, but he needed to do something else before then.

"Strapped in tight back there?" he casually asked Giles.

"All set, Floyd," came the reply.

Taking no more than five seconds to plan his move, Floyd retracted his landing gear and his flaps and pushed the throttle all the way open. Nosing the SBD into a shallow dive, he headed for the waves. His headset immediately filled with nervous chatter and a few curses from his squadron. Everyone wanted to know what Craven was up to, plunging head-on toward the island, and perpendicular to the runway at that.

Harry Giles wanted to know as well. "Floyd, what are you doing?" he asked, more than a bit concerned.

"Giving myself a challenge," Floyd called back. "Haven't had one for awhile." It was a subtle reference to the routineness of the missions.

Floyd leveled off just a couple of hundred yards away from Ford Island. He zoomed mast-high over a destroyer and came over land at an altitude of no more than 70 feet. Vehicles, hangars, roads, and runways flashed by so close that Giles could see the men standing inside the control tower, gawking at the wayward plane.

Ford Island disappeared in a matter of seconds, and Floyd pressed on toward *Oklahoma* and *West Virginia.* Flying over their wrecks at better than 200 knots, Floyd didn't pull up until reaching the far eastern shore of the harbor, whereupon he climbed sharply and then eased back into level flight. He then banked to the left and headed north to begin a normal landing approach.

"What was *that?*" Giles demanded to know from the back.

Floyd didn't know what to call it. It could have been considered something of a tribute, though it was really nothing more than a bold act of rebellion. It had been as impulsive as a sudden passing maneuver on the racetrack, yet Floyd had executed it flawlessly as if he had been making his control movements in slow motion, just as it seemed he did when driving.

"*That* was the most fun I've had since my last liberty!" he replied loudly but not too happily. He had blown off some steam but not enough to put a smile on his face. In fact, it would take quite a bit to put a smile on his face these days.

Giles wasn't the last person to demand an explanation for Floyd's aerobatics. The airfield commander immediately assailed the air group commander, who then ordered the squadron commander to get to the bottom of things. The squadron commander was waiting for Floyd's plane when he taxied it to a stop on the flight line.

"Craven!" Lt. Richard Best roared. "What kind of stupid stunt was that? You didn't get killed out there by the Japs so you decided to go get yourself killed here, huh?! What in the world were you thinking?"

Giles climbed down the other side of the fuselage and stood at the end of the right wing until it was all over.

Floyd spoke his mind. "I was letting off some steam."

"Letting off steam? Are you kidding me?"

"What are you gonna do, Skipper, kick me out of the Navy?" Floyd countered defiantly.

"I dang well oughta! You nearly killed yourself and your passenger!" the squadron commander shouted, jabbing an accusatory finger at Floyd. He then thumped himself on the chest with his thumb. *"I've* got two lieutenant commanders threatening me with the same thing! And if Admiral Nimitz happened to see your little tantrum," he spread his arms like wings and wagged them, "we all might be sent on a trip to San Francisco in a life raft with nothing but a compass and a fishing pole!"

"At least it'd be more of a fight than bombing Jap bathtub toys!"

Best looked like he could have hauled off and punched Floyd. In fact, he looked so convincing that Floyd actually took a half step back toward his plane in preparation.

"Mr. Craven, you're grounded until I say otherwise, and your liberty is suspended for the duration of our stay here. If you're lucky, the higher-ups will think that's enough, and you *might* fly again. If not, you'll be about as well off as a chicken."

"Then I'll just go home. We have plenty of chickens there, and I'll at least be in better company."

Best lowered his voice a notch. "Don't push me, Floyd. I'm willing to let you off with a grounding and no liberty. You'd best keep your voice down or someone else will make this conversation their business and get you reassigned to a minesweeper. Understand? Drop it and leave. Walk away ... now."

Floyd stared hard at his commander, who he could have sworn didn't blink for 15 seconds. Floyd blinked first.

"Okay. I'll shut up," Floyd agreed. "And no hard feelings, sir. I earned it."

The squadron commander just glared at him and made no attempt to accept the apology. He had called Floyd's bluff, for the younger pilot wasn't very sorry anyway.

"Get outta here, Craven." Best then spotted Giles on the other side of the plane. "Mr. Giles!" he called out. "Make sure Mr. Craven gets to his quarters."

Giles nodded. "Aye-aye, sir." He then hurried to catch up with Floyd, who was stomping off the ramp toward the hangars.

Preston and his men had arrived in the town of Serang on Sunday, March 8. He had been locked in the jail with other *Houston* officers as well as Dutchmen, Brits, and Australians, while the enlisted men in his group had all been crammed into a movie theater and forced to sit motionless on the bare, sloping concrete floor where rows of seats had once been.

Life in the jail was not any more pleasant. The officers slept with no bedding on the concrete floors of their crowded jail cells. Sanitation facilities were completely improvised, and the food rations amounted to nothing more than spoonfuls of rice. While the enlisted men in the theater could do nothing but sit all day long, the officers were targeted for interrogation by their captors. When his turn came to answer questions on Saturday, however, Preston could not appreciate his opportunity to breathe fresh air for his anxiety about being delivered to the Japanese secret military police, the Kempeitai.

The Japanese drove him across town in an open jeep to a private house, the grounds of which crawled with soldiers coming and going in jeeps and on motorcycles. Preston's jeep stopped outside the house, and his guards prodded him out of the vehicle and into the building at bayonet point. They pushed him down a narrow hallway and into a small, dimly lit office. Bands of sunlight streamed in through the gaps in the drawn window shades, and a desk lamp provided the only artificial light. A Japanese officer sat behind a desk across from a single wooden chair, into which the guards shoved Preston after insuring that he bowed properly to the officer.

"State your name, rank, and serial number," the officer demanded in accented English.

"Brown, Preston. Ensign. One-two-four-eight-nine-four."

"What was the name of your ship?"

"U.S.S. *Houston*."

"Impossible!" the officer scoffed. "We had already sunk *Houston*."

"Where?" Preston challenged. "In the Philippines, the Flores Sea, or Darwin?"

The officer's face grew red and he narrowed his eyes at Preston. He shoved his chair away from the desk, stood, and strode around to where Preston sat. Then he hauled off with his right arm and gave Preston a fierce backhanded slap.

"You liar!" the Japanese shouted. "What ship did you come from?"

"U.S.S. *Houston*."

Another slap.

"What ship?!"

"U.S.S. *Houston*." Preston braced for another blow, but it never came.

Oddly enough, the Japanese officer seemed satisfied and retreated a few feet to ask his next question, though he did not sit back down. Preston figured he had had the same experience with every other *Houston* officer and knew they were all telling the truth.

"What is the general American attitude about the war, Ensign Brown?"

Preston shrugged. "I haven't been in the States for over five months, so I'm not terribly sure."

The officer faced Preston and planted his hands firmly on his hips, apparently suspecting more sarcasm.

"What do you *think* the American attitude is? What has your family said in their letters?"

Preston could answer that question. "Well, Pearl Harbor riled everyone up pretty well. My parents know people who used to be isolationists who went out and joined the service that very week. It seems like every able-bodied man in my entire home state who's old enough to enlist has enlisted."

"And what is your home state, Ensign Brown?"

Preston immediately recognized that the interrogator had overstepped his bounds even with that fairly benign question. "With all due respect, sir, I will not answer any questions regarding my personal life. Let's stick to the war."

"All right, let us do that." The officer's tone mocked Preston's confidence. "Do you think America can win this war?"

"Heck, yes," Preston replied with a smirk. "I know we can win this war."

"Why is that?"

Preston felt this question gave him liberty to brag. "Well, besides all of those boys I told you about who are lining up to join the armed forces back home, there's the men like my shipmates you captured. The only reason your ships sank ours is because we ran out of ammunition. We had not yet begun to fight."

"Oh, you mean like John Paul Jones," the officer responded with raised eyebrows, mocking Preston by pompously emphasizing each syllable of the Revolutionary War naval hero's name. The Japanese officer apparently knew his history as well as his English.

Preston again smirked with satisfaction. His adaptation of the famous quote, "I have not yet begun to fight" had been an intentional nod to the "Father of the U.S. Navy" entombed beneath the Naval Academy's chapel.

"Well, I commend you and your shipmates for their fighting spirit," the officer continued. "They did, after all, help sink seven of the Emperor's warships."

Preston arched his eyebrows now. He had a feeling it was a lie, but it was an impressive one nonetheless. "What do you mean, *help* sank? It was us and the one Aussie ship and nobody else."

"You had battleships, correct?"

"No."

The officer stepped closer. "Are you sure?"

"Yes! Absolutely," Preston insisted.

The officer leaned down so close to Preston's face that the American could smell stale rice and *sake* on the man's breath. Preston held fast.

"You mean to tell me that you had no battleships helping you on the night of February the 28th?"

"That's exactly what I'm saying. Every American ship your navy has encountered in the Netherlands East Indies was from the Asiatic Fleet. The Pacific Fleet, to my knowledge, hasn't come anywhere near here."

"What about aircraft carriers?"

Preston snorted. The Asiatic Fleet had never had any aircraft carriers, and the Pacific Fleet carriers had spent the past month in the open sea. "Now you're just getting ridiculous."

Another slap. Preston could feel blood flowing freely from the corner of his mouth now.

The officer grabbed Preston by his shirt and yanked him to his feet. He kicked the chair away, punched Preston in the gut, and threw him to the floor before shouting something in Japanese to the guards, who stepped forward and pulled Preston up. He regained his footing slowly, but the guards didn't care. They dragged him out of the room even as Preston began to hear hysterical male screams coming from somewhere down the hall. Preston imagined his impertinence had just earned him an early execution or perhaps a round of torture like that poor unseen fellow was just then being treated to, but the guards simply took him out the way they had brought him in, shoved him back into the jeep, and returned him to the jail. There he returned to his few square feet of concrete and curled up on the floor.

"What'd you do to earn that?" Commander Maher asked him about his wounds from across the cell.

"Got a little sarcastic, that's all, sir," Preston groaned. "I did my best John Paul Jones impression."

"Yeah, Japs don't like sarcasm."

"I know. It was actually kind of fun."

Maher chuckled. "Save some of that spunk for the long haul, will you? You're going to need it."

"Don't worry, sir. I'd have taken it easy today if I had known it would hurt this much. Besides, I've got plenty more where that came from."

"Really?"

"Yes, sir. That wasn't me talking to them today."

A strange look appeared on Maher's face. "I didn't realize spunk was a gift from God, Mr. Brown."

Preston grinned and shook his head. He painfully sat up and faced the gun boss, *Houston*'s senior surviving officer and the nominal commander of the 360 or so survivors out of the ship's original 1,168 crewmen. "No, sir, I don't believe it is. I'm trusting God to give me physical and mental strength to hold out until we're rescued. That spunk ... well ... that was my wife talking there. She'd have said the same things if she had been in that interrogation."

"Gee, do I feel sorry for you, having to live with her."

Preston grinned through gritted teeth. "Sometimes she turns it against me, but mostly, she's an angel. And if she made it out of Darwin alive, she's probably got every naval officer she can find by the collar trying to figure out what happened to us."

"Well, in that case," Maher commented, "do I feel sorry for *them*."

CHAPTER THIRTEEN

Harry Giles took it upon himself to keep Floyd Craven out of trouble during their time in Honolulu. Craven had been allowed to stay with the rest of Air Group Six's officers in the plush Royal Hawaiian hotel, but Lieutenant Best had placed him under "room arrest." The reason behind this punishment was that for the officers who stayed there, the Royal Hawaiian *was* liberty. They had no real reason to go elsewhere in search of recreation and other diversions. Various forms of it were all available at or near the hotel, and the officers would not have to compete against the crowds of enlisted men elsewhere in the city, the civilian criminals who lurked around the honky-tonks, and the Shore Patrolmen who always ran them off. Liberty at the Royal Hawaiian lacked the seediness of liberty elsewhere in the city, but Floyd's enjoyment of the charm would be limited by his inability to travel beyond the hotel's third floor.

Since most of the pilots in the group were busy enjoying liberty themselves, ensuring that Craven stayed put was easier said than done. The squadron commander had decided that requesting a Shore Patrol guard to stand outside the room would be too humiliating for the squadron, so the responsibility fell to whichever pilot happened to be walking by at the time to knock on the door and check. Giles conscientiously did this a few times a day, and even made a couple of special trips to his own room — next door to Craven's — each evening, something none of the other officers ever did.

Four nights passed without incident and only two more remained. At the start of the next week the group would be headed back to its planes for training flights. After that, another cruise seemed likely, though no word had reached the men as to where they might be headed next.

That Saturday evening, Giles excused himself early from a formal dinner in the restaurant downstairs and returned to his room to prepare for an evening swim. He had scarcely shut the door behind him when he heard Craven's door shut as well. Giles gave it no consideration.

Floyd's probably just stretching his legs, he thought.

Giles finished changing out of his dress whites and into swim trunks and a T-shirt. He grabbed his beach towel and headed for the door. Stepping back out into the hallway, he looked both directions for Craven, but did not see him. Puzzled and suspicious, Giles made a quick circuit of all of the floor's hallways but discovered that Craven was not in any of them. Giles hurried back to his room, grabbed a coat hanger, twisted it out of shape, and stepped over to Craven's door. He shoved the sharp end of the straightened coat hanger hook into the lock and rattled it around until he heard a distinctive click. Carefully opening the door, Giles peeked in and found the room to be completely empty.

Craven was gone, that was certain. Giles just had to find out where he had gone. He knew the pilot had friends on the island, but all of them were either officers or women who would most likely be found near the Royal Hawaiian during liberty periods. Surely Craven wouldn't be so foolish as to stick around the hotel after sneaking out. But if he had left the immediate area, he could have gone anywhere, and Giles did not know enough about Craven's acquaintances to be able to track him down. Giles quickly decided he had better learn.

Figuring that whatever intrusions he made into Craven's privacy were better than those their CO might make, Giles rifled through the notepad by the telephone on the nightstand, the nightstand itself, and Craven's bags, in addition to the pockets of his uniforms hanging in the closet. Not a single scrap of paper or pocketbook bearing a single telephone number could be found. Giles imagined it would only have been logical for Craven to have taken such evidence with him.

Satisfied with the completeness of his search, but frustrated by his lack of results, Giles stood in the center of the room with his hands on his hips and swept it one more time with his eyes. They stopped at the open closet. Giles walked over to it and flipped through the uniforms. Curiously, his dress whites, service khakis, and working khakis were all present. Giles had already found Craven's swimming clothes, so the possibility that he had gone for a swim had disappeared as quickly as it presented itself. Only one option remained and that was that, if Craven was like Giles, he had brought a set of civilian clothes ashore with him. In that case, not only was Craven out somewhere in Honolulu's busy nightlife scene without permission, he was out there in civilian clothes, making him that much harder to spot by someone used to seeing him only in uniform.

Giles could only shake his head. "That crazy jerk," he muttered aloud to himself.

He then tidied the room up the best he could and left.

The beer was warm, but it was better than nothing as far as Floyd was concerned. He was not about to complain, considering it might be his last drink as a naval aviator. If he were caught in the Hotel Street bar, his days as a pilot, not to mention his days as a free man, were probably over. He imagined Lieutenant Best would not hesitate to bring him up on charges. Be that as it may, he was not about to let anyone yank him around. If he was going to fight in this war, he was going to fight his way or not at all. The inclination to just do his job and let the admirals worry about the details had disappeared weeks ago.

He had one thing going for him and that was his civilian clothes. These worked to his advantage in two ways. First, they protected him from immediate identification by the Shore Patrol, who might be looking for him at that very moment. Second, they guaranteed him unlimited drinks, whereas the enlisted sailors and soldiers bumping into his elbows and crowding every square foot of the dark, dusty establishment were strictly held to a maximum of two drinks apiece.

Floyd drained his mug and pushed it across the bar. "Give me another one," he asked the bartender.

"You sure, buddy?" the man asked him uncertainly. "That'll be your third, and you've only been here about 15 minutes."

Floyd looked the bartender in the eye. "I'll take another one, please."

The bartender shook his head and said, "If you say so," before he refilled the glass and pushed it back into Floyd's waiting hands.

Floyd had the glass halfway to his mouth when somebody fell into him from behind. Floyd lurched forward and sloshed half of his beer all over the counter.

"Hey!" he protested, wheeling around on his stool to identify the culprit.

An Army private was staggering to regain his footing. Floyd gave him a push to straighten him, not so much in an attempt to be helpful but in an attempt to get the kid off of him. Floyd looked past the soldier and saw a seaman first class standing about five feet away.

"What in the world do you think you're doing?" Floyd demanded to know from the soldier.

"Sailor boy shoved me into you, mister."

The sailor stepped closer. "You were trying to come between me and my girl!" he hollered at the private.

Floyd looked around the bickering servicemen and spotted an attractive young Hawaiian woman standing near where the sailor had been and appearing to be doing her best to look invisible.

"Naw, that's what you did, mac!" the soldier argued. "She was my girl last weekend before you came into port."

"Yeah, well apparently she decided she prefers men who are actually doing something to fight this war!"

Floyd recognized the insult as a dig against the soldier's status as a coastal artilleryman, which he inferred from the young man's unit patch on his left shoulder. The coast artillerymen were, by wartime standards, full-time residents of the Hawaiian Islands, and many other servicemen considered them to be soft. The soldiers, meanwhile, resented the sailors who rotated through once every few months on liberty and stole their girls and their seats at the bars.

"Oh yeah?" The soldier spoke to the girl. "Well, I'll tell you something about these swabbies. They prefer whatever girl will actually believe their bragging!"

"How many Japs have you killed?" the sailor shot back.

Floyd, doubting neither one had ever killed any of the enemy up close, had listened to enough of the childish banter. He picked up his mug and began to relocate, offering some words of advice to the soldier as he went.

"Give it up, mac. Wait for next weekend."

The soldier grabbed him by the sleeve. "Who asked for your help, mister?"

Floyd, feeling sober enough to stay clear of a fight but buzzed enough to take great offense at being touched by an enlisted man, replied, "Get your dirty hands off of me, private!"

The soldier smirked at him and replied, "I don't take orders from civilians. Put on a uniform and do your duty, and then I'll think about it!"

Floyd snapped back. "Watch your mouth, private! You're talking to an officer."

Too drunk to take him seriously, the soldier looked over Floyd's rumpled shirt and slacks and replied with another smirk, "You're not an officer, and I'll touch you if I want." The soldier then hauled off and punched Floyd in the mouth.

Dazed momentarily, Floyd shook away the cobwebs and planted a return strike on the soldier's right cheek, knocking him backward into the bar. Floyd didn't want to make any more of a scene, so he quickly retreated. The arguing sailor gladly took his place. Floyd could hear the dispute resume with increased intensity as he pushed through the crowd toward the door. He set his mug on a table on his way out, and offered a despising glare to any soldier who looked at him too closely. He emerged from the bar and stood on the sidewalk looking both ways down the street, trying to decide where to go next. He was facing one direction when a hand grabbed him from behind. He swung his arm around instinctively and connected with his unseen assailant's face.

"Oww! Good grief, Craven, simmer down!"

Floyd had now turned far enough to see the man he had just hit. There stood a uniformed Harry Giles, hunched over clutching his jaw.

"Giles, for Pete's sake, what are you doing here?" he replied without apologizing. "Does the skipper know I'm gone?"

Giles shook his head, still holding his jaw. "Not when I left. I came to find you and to take you back before you get yourself into more trouble than you're already in." Then, noticing the racket emanating from the bar's interior, he eyed Floyd and asked, "You didn't have anything to do with that did you?"

Floyd shook his head.

Giles pointed at Floyd's face. "You liar. Your lip is bleeding."

"An Army private hit me first."

"And you hit him back, of course. Is he okay?"

"The enlisted men of the U.S. Navy are determining that as we speak."

Giles finally let go of his jaw and shook his head in disappointment. "Come on, Floyd. Let's just get out of here." He stepped to the curb and hailed a cab.

"Are you going to tell the skipper that I sneaked out?"

Giles didn't look at him. "I haven't decided yet. We don't have much of a chance of getting back unnoticed, so I suggest you be prepared to start packing your sea bag for California."

A cab pulled up to the curb and Giles opened the door. He motioned for Floyd to get inside first. "Whatever bed you've made for yourself, you're going to have to sleep in, my friend. I'm not sure anything I say is going to make a difference."

After Giles gave driving instructions to the Kanaka cabby, the two officers rode in silence for some time.

"Harry, I'm sorry about all this. I've been an idiot this week."

"Is that you talking or is it the beer?"

"Uh ... probably the beer," Floyd stammered.

"Well, it knows what it's talking about."

"You think I've been an idiot, too?"

Giles looked at him and replied without blinking, "I think you've been a first class one."

Floyd didn't respond but just looked away and stared out the window of the cab, which soon pulled into the driveway of the hotel. He and Giles got out, and Giles paid the driver. They made it back to their floor without running into anyone else from their squadron, but as they stepped off the elevator, Best was there waiting for them. He marched angrily toward them.

"Where have you two been?" he demanded to know. He pointed behind himself with his thumb. "I've been banging on your doors for five minutes."

"Drinking," Floyd replied with a slight slur. "Or at least I have been. He found me," he said, pointing to Giles.

"You brought him back here, Giles?"

"Yes, sir. I figured it would be better for me to find him and retrieve him before you discovered he had sneaked out and you called the Shore Patrol or something."

Best squinted at Giles. "You weren't planning to sneak him back in were you? You were going to tell me about this, right?"

Giles had to level with him. "I thought about keeping it to myself, but I wouldn't have been able to."

"Well, it doesn't matter now anyway." Best faced Floyd. "Craven, get in your room. I'll be in to talk to you in a minute." Then shaking his head as Floyd left, he commented to

Giles, "The kid's like a three-year-old, and I'm his babysitter. It's disgusting." He paused in thought for a moment before saying, "Thank you for your help, Giles. You're dismissed."

"Sir, a word please."

"What is it?" the skipper asked.

Giles closed the gap between him and Best so that he could be heard in a low tone of voice. "Skipper, however you decide to punish Craven, whether you put him up on charges or what, he'll be getting what he deserves. He's acted stupidly and childishly, and you're not going to hear excuses for him coming from me. I do just want to ask you if you've considered what this squadron might lose if he gets court-martialed."

The skipper replied bluntly, "It'll lose an immature, drunken moron."

Giles shook his head. "No, sir — I mean, yes, it'll lose that — but I think it'll lose a very good pilot, too."

Best squinted at him again. "You sure you weren't out drinking with him?"

"Yes, sir, I'm dead sober," Giles insisted earnestly. "Craven's a fine dive bomber pilot, and when it's time for a mission, he's as serious and focused as they come from the time he enters the ready room for our briefings to the time he leaves after our debriefings. You've seen that, haven't you, sir?"

The skipper nodded.

"I think he's frustrated, though, because for all the seriousness and effort he puts into doing his job in combat, all the news he hears from the outside makes him think that this country's not serious about fighting the Japs."

Best scowled at Giles. "That's nonsense," he scoffed. "We're giving those Japs heck every day out there."

Giles tried to keep his exasperated expression respectful. "Skipper, you know as well as I that we haven't persuaded the Japs of anything yet with those raids of ours. We've shown them that we have carriers and airplanes capable of sinking harbor craft but incapable of relieving our Marines at Wake. They hear the same stuff Craven and all of us hear. "Europe first" is what Washington is saying. Meanwhile, Java falls to the Japs and MacArthur is told to just hang on at Bataan until his men get too sick and hungry to fight. We haven't shown them anything, Skipper, and it's men like Craven who can't wait to do it."

"I thought you weren't going to make excuses for him," Best challenged.

Giles shook his head ardently. "No, sir, I'm not excusing him. I'm explaining why he's rebelling."

"He's rebelling because he's a childish brat who's a disgrace to the uniform."

"Yes, but he's also a daredevil, and daredevils are warriors. They live to prove that they can't die. But that doesn't mean anything if what they survive is simple child's play, and they feel that to die in such comparatively trivial pursuits would be disgraceful. Craven doesn't want to end up like the men we lost over Wake and over Marcus, but he also doesn't want to keep surviving so comfortably either. He either wants to go back home a hero or to burn up strapped into his SBD over an enemy flattop. Those are his ambitions for this war."

The skipper looked skeptical. "Did he tell you this, Mr. Giles?"

Giles shook his head again. "No, sir, but he didn't have to. I'm not a pilot or a race car driver, but up until a couple of months ago, I was living my life on the edge, too, except it was here in Honolulu on Saturday nights instead of in battle. I understand the mentality of men like him."

"Is that why they made you an intel officer?"

"No, they made me an intel officer because I'm good with facts, figures, photographs, and maps, and I can speak Japanese."

"Okay, so what are you driving at? What's your point?"

"I hope you'll consider giving him another chance, sir."

Best looked incredulous. "You're kidding me, right?"

"No, sir. Listen, Skipper, he's in his room right now thinking he's done flying and that he's going to spend the rest of his Navy career in the brig. If you walk in there and tell him he's got one chance left — just one — to prove he's responsible enough to fly in your squadron, it'll shock him so badly that I truly think you'll have his attention and cooperation from now on."

The skipper was not yet convinced. "And if not, if somebody gets hurt next time he decides to barnstorm an airfield or flight deck, then what?"

Giles spread his arms wide and shrugged. "It's your decision."

Best looked let down. "Thanks a lot, Giles."

He stood there silently and stared at the carpet. After about 20 seconds, he told Giles he could leave. When Giles shut the door to his room, the skipper was still rooted in deep thought. Giles made no attempt to overhear through the wall the subsequent conversation with Craven. He finally went downstairs for his swim and by the time he returned, the skipper was gone. Giles then simply went to bed.

The next morning, Giles was awakened by firm pounding on his door. He climbed out of bed, pulled his khaki trousers on over his shorts and hurried to answer it.

Before him stood Floyd Craven, who looked remarkably alert considering the amount of alcohol he had consumed the night before.

"What did you say to him?" Floyd demanded.

Giles squinted at him because of the contrast between the bright hallway and the dark hotel room. "What?"

"The skipper told me he'd put me on probation and that it was all your idea. Why in the world did you do that?"

Giles stared at his friend, trying to determine if Craven's expression betrayed anger, annoyance, or gratitude.

Trying to clear the sleep from his brain and wipe it from his eyes at the same time, Giles replied almost as drunkenly as Craven had spoken the night before, "I … uh … I thought it might be worth giving you a second chance because you're a good pilot who really wants to have a chance to fight in this war."

"The skipper said you agreed with him that I'm an immature, irresponsible moron."

Straining to remember just what he had said before, Giles responded, "Yeah … yeah, I did. Actually," he added, "he called you an immature, *drunken* moron, and I agreed. But irresponsible fits, too."

Craven gave him a confused look. "So what made you think I deserved another chance, *especially* after I sneaked out last night?"

"You didn't deserve one," came the flat reply.

"Then why did the skipper give me one?"

"I don't know. He must have thought that what I told him sounded good and decided to give you a little bit of grace."

"He wouldn't have done it, though, if you hadn't talked him into it. What gave you the idea that I might be worth a second chance?"

Giles's head was clearing now. "Not what, Floyd, who."

Craven looked more confused now than ever.

"God. The concept of grace started with Him, and Jesus Christ offers grace for all of our mistakes."

Craven froze and backed away ever so slightly. "Whoa, there, pard. Don't start sermonizing now. I was braced for a lecture all the way back from that bar last night, but it never came. Don't let me down now. I know you're into that church stuff, but I've had my fill already back home."

"I feel like I'd be letting you down more if I didn't say anything," Giles replied sincerely. "If a chaplain at Pearl Harbor hadn't led me to Christ ten weeks ago, I wouldn't have been inclined to take your case to the skipper last night."

Craven was quiet for a few seconds. "All right, that's fair enough," he finally replied. "Thank you for what you did, and I'll try not to let you and the skipper down."

"You're welcome. And see that you don't let us down because unlike Jesus' ability to forgive, I think the skipper's forgiveness has limitations."

Craven arched his left eyebrow knowingly and nodded in agreement. "I think you're probably right."

CHAPTER FOURTEEN

Elaine was not content to sit on her hands and wait for news of Preston and his ship to reach Fremantle. She literally could not afford to. Drawing on her work experience in Darwin, she found a job at a small café located near her hotel and the wharf in the historic Fremantle Markets. There had been some strategy to her job search. She hoped to place herself in the best position to interact with as many military men as possible, who were multiplying on an almost daily basis. Though her hotel room window did not provide her with a view of the actual wharf, she could see the entrance to the port, and since *Holland* had docked at the beginning of March she had noticed several surfaced submarines arrive. Increasing numbers of American, British, and Dutch sailors appeared on the city's streets and in Elaine's own café, but none of them knew anything about *Houston*. All they ever told her was that they were submariners and that they felt sorry for her because it seemed as if they had been the only ones to have gotten out of Java. These comments, needless to say, failed to encourage her.

Captain Wilkes still had not followed through on his promise to send her word of *Houston*. Surely he had received some information by now, and how could he have forgotten their meeting in the hotel lobby? At any rate, she still considered the possibility that the officer had indeed forgotten her and that she would only ever get the news she needed if she found it herself. Wary of their suspicions, Elaine gently quizzed one sailor after another, explaining her interest in the ship and keeping at least one eye out for nosy detectives.

One day she realized she might have more to worry about than the police. An American lieutenant commander wearing khaki service dress entered the café that morning and made a beeline for her. Officers frequently visited the establishment, but none had ever sought her out specifically before.

"Are you Mrs. Elaine Brown?" asked the officer, a tall, thin, studious-looking man with wire-rimmed glasses.

"Yes."

"I understand you're interested in the fate of an American cruiser named U.S.S. *Houston*."

"Yes, I am," Elaine answered cautiously, wiping her hands on her apron. "Who are you?"

"I'm Stan Townsend, intelligence officer for the Southwest Pacific Submarine Force. I have a message for you from Captain Wilkes."

Elaine froze. "Captain Wilkes?"

"Yes. He's my commanding officer."

"I've met him."

"I know. I was there when the two of you met. Here." She looked down at the officer's hands, not recalling whether she had seen him before or not. He had extended a brown envelope toward her.

She snatched it from him, tore it open, and withdrew a single handwritten sheet of Navy stationery. She turned her back to Townsend and put her hand to her mouth as she read.

Fremantle, Western Australia

16 March 1942

Dear Mrs. Brown,

I have not forgotten our meeting approximately two weeks ago. I promised you I would give you any information I obtained about Ensign Brown's ship, U.S.S. Houston. I have indeed learned that after the major fleet engagement off Java on 27 February, Houston and an Australian ship, H.M.A.S. Perth, retired to Batavia, the Dutch colonial capital. They left Batavia on the evening of the 28th and apparently engaged Japanese vessels in the vicinity of the Sunda Strait at around 11:30 P.M. It is with great regret that I admit to you that no one has heard from either ship since and they can only be presumed to have been sunk.

As depressing as this sounds, and as difficult as this is for me to write to you, your husband is not necessarily dead. If you had been at home in the States, you would have received a telegram in the next few days informing you that Ensign Brown is "missing in action." That is very accurate, for he may be a prisoner of war, or may even be hiding from the enemy. There are any number of possibilities, and I encourage you to consider all of them. Do not lose hope. The Navy is working very hard to determine exactly what happened to your husband's ship, and I will keep you informed of our progress. Until then, if you need anything, please just ask Lieutenant Commander Townsend. He will pass your messages along to me. I apologize for not being able to contact you personally, but my duties require virtually all of my attention in these grave times.

Yours truly,

John Wilkes, Captain, U.S.N.

Elaine quickly folded up the note and slipped it into her apron pocket. Wiping a couple of emerging tears from her eyes she turned around to face Townsend.

"Thank you for bringing this to me," she told him hoarsely. "Captain Wilkes says you will forward my messages to him."

Townsend nodded. "Yes, that's right."

"Then thank him for his note and for his encouragement and tell him that I have no intention of leaving Australia until my husband is found. If I ever leave Fremantle, I will tell Captain Wilkes first, so he will know where to contact me."

Townsend nodded. "Very well, Mrs. Brown. I'll pass that along. Is there anything else I can do for you?"

Elaine shook her head, fighting back tears. "No. No, there isn't."

"Okay." Townsend pulled another piece of paper from his pocket, this one just a scrap with a telephone number written on it. "Here is the telephone number where you can reach me."

Elaine took the paper from him and put it in her pocket, too. "Thank you, Mr. Townsend."

"Please call me Stan, Mrs. Brown."

Elaine cracked the slightest of grins. The man couldn't have been much older than 30, but his rank compared with Preston's intimidated her. "My husband's only an ensign, sir. He'd never address you by your first name, so I would feel awkward being on a first-name basis with you."

Townsend shrugged and grinned slightly. "As you wish. Have a good day, Mrs. Brown."

"I'll try."

Townsend nodded respectfully and walked out of the café leaving Elaine to process the "number of possibilities," as Wilkes had called them. She turned around again and leaned against the counter. It was evident that she would not be able to process them all here. She walked around the counter and entered the kitchen, where the head waiter stood waiting to collect the various dishes for an order.

"Bert," Elaine called out to him.

He looked over his shoulder at her. "Yeah?"

"I need to leave."

"You can't leave yet. It's almost lunch time."

Elaine walked over to him and stood close enough to whisper, even in the cacophonous kitchen. "Listen, Bert, I need to leave. I just got word about my husband. He's missing in action, and I really need a few hours to think this over. Do you understand?"

Bert knew all about Elaine's situation, and his previously hard expression softened at the sight of her nearly in tears. "All right. You can go. Will you be back tomorrow?"

She nodded. "Yes. That should not be a problem. I just need the rest of today off."

"Well, then hurry along. I'll see you tomorrow."

"Thank you, Bert. You're wonderful. Goodbye." Elaine hurried to untie her apron and headed for the door.

"I'm sorry about your husband, Elaine," he called after her.

She stopped at the door to the dining room and looked back at him. Searching for a suitable response, all she could muster was a half-choked "Thank you."

She then reentered the dining room and hastily proceeded to the front door. Sobbing by the time she reached the sidewalk, she could barely see through the tears by the time she reached the hotel. Avoiding as many people as possible and trying to keep from drawing attention to herself, she dashed up the stairs to her room where she fell onto her bed and finally let herself cry unashamedly.

Captain Wilkes' message had not been the worst news she could have heard, but it was bad enough. Many different thoughts and pictures flooded through her mind. She pictured Preston dead, his body trapped in the sunken ship perhaps horribly burned. She imagined him floating out at sea, awaiting rescuers who would probably never come. And she imagined him in Japanese captivity enduring who knew what kind of privations. She didn't know how they treated their prisoners, but with how badly the war was going at the time, it didn't matter if they were providing him with lodging in one of Batavia's finest hotels. They were keeping Preston away from her, and if the Japanese won the war, they might keep him forever.

Overwhelmed by the various dismal scenarios, she rolled herself off the bed and knelt alongside it. She started praying for Preston's safety, but she was so emotionally spent that she fell asleep doing so and did not awaken until dinnertime. She forced herself downstairs to eat at the hotel restaurant, and as she sat there alone, she considered what it might be like to live the rest of her life without her husband. The thought ruined her appetite, and she returned to her room and went to bed early. She slept fitfully that night, plagued by nightmares of both Preston's uncertain recent past and his and her equally uncertain future.

Though she had been raised Baptist, Elaine began attending Scots Church on the corner of South Terrace and Parry streets her first Sunday in Fremantle. She fit more naturally into the Presbyterian congregation than she would have in any of the Anglican or Roman Catholic churches in town, and besides, Scots Church was the closest church to her hotel. The small limestone and red-brick building sat next door to the

Fremantle Markets, its octagonal steeple at the top of a steep roof reaching far above all other nearby roofs.

Elaine always sat near the inside end of a pew on the third row from the back. The Sunday after she received the message from Captain Wilkes, she was surprised to look behind her and see Townsend entering through the door in his dress whites. He quickly spotted her and walked toward her.

"Do you mind if I sit here?" he inquired upon reaching her pew.

She scooted to her right a few inches to create more room. "Not at all, sir. Be my guest."

"Elaine, you are going to have to stop calling me 'sir,'" he told her in a low voice as the choir filed into the room and prepared to lead the congregation in singing.

She leaned over and whispered back. "I like formal titles, Mr. Townsend. If it's all the same to you, I prefer to address you as an officer, and I prefer to be addressed as Mrs. Brown."

Townsend's face reddened a bit. "I'm sorry if I offended you."

Elaine nodded firmly and replied, "It's all right," before standing with the congregation and facing toward the front of the sanctuary.

The first hymn sung by the choir and congregation that morning was "Eternal Father, Strong to Save," one Elaine had only heard on a few occasions but recognized nonetheless.

"This is the 'Navy Hymn,'" Townsend leaned over to inform her as they flipped through the pages of their hymnals.

Elaine, of course, knew this for that was how she recognized the song in the first place. She nodded appreciatively, kept her eyes on her hymnal, and sang along with the choir and organ.

Eternal Father, Strong to save,
Whose arm hath bound the restless wave,
Who bid'st the mighty Ocean deep
Its own appointed limits keep;
O hear us when we cry to Thee,
For those in peril on the sea.

Those last two lines brought tears to Elaine's eyes as she thought of Preston, and a catch formed in her throat that kept her from singing the second verse. The congregation and choir sang on.

O Christ! Whose voice the waters heard
And hushed their raging at Thy word,
Who walked'st on the foaming deep,
and calm amidst its rage didst sleep;
O hear us when we cry to Thee
For those in peril on the sea.

By the third verse she had recovered, thankfully without having drawn any undue attention from Townsend, and she finished the fourth verse strongly.

Most Holy Spirit! Who didst brood
Upon the chaos dark and rude,
And bid its angry tumult cease,
And give, for wild confusion, peace;
O hear us when we cry to Thee

For those in peril on the sea!

O Trinity of love and power!

Our brethren shield in danger's hour;

From rock and tempest, fire and foe,

Protect them wheresoe'er they go;

Thus evermore shall rise to Thee,

Glad hymns of praise from land and sea.

Elaine and Townsend did not attempt to speak to each other again until after the service, and they were interrupted right away by an elderly woman sitting behind them. Elaine recognized the lady as Judith Kentish, the wife of a semi-wealthy retired sea captain. They had conversed briefly several times before, and on this occasion, Mrs. Kentish reached across the pew back and put her hand on Elaine's shoulder while she was still sitting.

"Good morning, Elaine. Do you have any plans for lunch today?" the old lady asked.

Elaine turned to look at her new friend. "Well, no, I was just planning to eat at the hotel again like usual."

Mrs. Kentish patted her on the shoulder. "Come home with Gerald and me, will you, dear?" she said with sincere warmth. "Have a good home-cooked meal."

Elaine tilted her head and responded, "Are you sure, ma'am? I don't want to be a bother."

"If you were going to be a bother, I wouldn't have asked you," Mrs. Kentish assured her. "Please come."

Elaine closed her eyes and smiled softly. "That would be very nice. It's been a hard week for me."

Mrs. Kentish nodded knowingly. "I've heard, dear. I want to do everything I can to help you."

Elaine took the old lady's hand in hers, not even bothered by the efficiency of the Fremantle grapevine. "Thank you so much. I will be honored to join you and your husband for lunch."

"Good," Mrs. Kentish replied with a satisfied smile and a nod. Her eyes then traveled over to Townsend. "And who is this?"

Caught off guard, Elaine took a couple of seconds to process the inquiry before remembering that Townsend was still sitting right next to her.

"Oh, I'm sorry," she apologized. "This is Lieutenant Commander Stan Townsend. He's a staff officer with the new American submarine command here, and he's the one who told me about my husband's ship."

Mrs. Kentish cordially greeted Townsend and shook his hand before introducing him to her husband, who had until then been distracted by another conversation.

"Would you care to join us for lunch as well, Commander?" Mrs. Kentish asked Townsend.

The officer seemed only too willing to agree. "If it would be no imposition, then I would be glad to."

An even greater grin spread across the white-haired lady's face. "Wonderful! You may ride with us in our car if you are ready."

Elaine and Townsend both agreed, and the four parishioners left Scots Church together for the Kentish home.

Over lunch, the conversation first centered on Townsend. The Kentishes asked some general questions about his personal history, including his family, where he had been born and raised, and what the highlights of his naval career had been thus far. Elaine learned that he was 32 and a native of rural New York, having been born and raised near Buffalo.

He was the oldest of four children, having two brothers and a sister all between the ages of 20 and 30. He had graduated from Annapolis in 1931 and had spent much time at sea before being assigned to intelligence. He and Mr. Kentish shared some fond and some frightening memories of the Indian Ocean before Mrs. Kentish steered the conversation toward Elaine.

"Have you heard from your family back home yet, Elaine?" she asked.

"Only by telegram. I don't expect to receive any letters for a couple of more weeks. The war has slowed down the mail delivery something awful."

"What are your plans now that you know for certain that your husband's missing?"

"I plan to stay here," Elaine replied frankly. "I want to stay as close to Press as possible and do whatever I can to help the war effort."

Mrs. Kentish looked concerned. "But don't you want to be with your family?"

"If I go back to the States, I'll be with my family, sure, but I'll feel even more helpless there than I do here. The day I married Press, I loosened some of my ties to Arkansas and to my family, and I decided to follow him wherever God led him. I was willing to go to Manila and to Darwin and now here, and I feel no need to go back home now."

"You're a plucky sheila, I'll give you that," Mr. Kentish commented.

Elaine smiled. "People have been telling me that all my life, except for the sheila part, of course."

The Kentishes and Townsend chuckled.

"A lot of folks back home don't like me the way I am. They say I'm too independent. Those same people will probably be appalled when they find out that I'm staying alone in Australia; they'll be afraid that something terrible will happen to me."

"I don't blame them," Mrs. Kentish replied.

"No, I don't suppose I do either, except that they don't understand that I'm staying here only out of loyalty to Press and because I believe this is where God wants me to be. My independence is what allows me to do this, while my love for my husband and for God is what motivates me to do it."

Mr. Kentish declared his hearty support. "Here-here! You sound a lot like our own Jill. She's all the way out in Sydney living alone with three kids while she waits for her husband to come home from Egypt."

"He's in the AIF, you see," Mrs. Kentish explained, referring to the Australian Imperial Force, the country's overseas army.

"The Ninth Division," Mr. Kentish added. "Fine outfit he's a part of. Has given Rommel and the 'jerries' quite a difficult time."

Mrs. Kentish grinned proudly, but could sense that her husband was about to launch off into a divergent monologue, so she brought the discussion back to center.

"Does your family support you?"

Elaine nodded. "As a matter of fact, they do. They wish I would come home, of course, but they've not pleaded with me to come back."

"Well, we support you fully as well, Elaine. If there's ever anything you need, just ask."

Elaine thanked her and they finished their meal. Mrs. Kentish then showed Elaine and Townsend to the nautically decorated parlor before departing to clear the table with her husband's help. She insisted that Elaine sit with Townsend until they returned.

"Quite an admirable thing you're doing, Elaine," Townsend complimented her.

Elaine smiled modestly. "Thank you, sir. I'm not doing it to be admired, though."

"Oh, I know. You made your motivations very clear."

"Did I?"

Townsend gave her a puzzled look. "What do you mean? Of course you did."

"Then you understand the significance of the fact that I'm a married woman?"

"Yes. What ever made you think I didn't?"

"Your repeated attempts at informality with me and your sitting with me in church," she replied bluntly.

"Elaine … er … Mrs. Brown, you let me sit with you."

"What was I supposed to do, say 'no'?"

"I think you're a little too sensitive about this. I'm only trying to be friendly. And I *am* a Christian. This morning wasn't for show."

"Well, I apologize if I've misjudged you, but I've always assumed Yankees were a bit more … eh … shall we say, 'reserved' than you are."

Townsend laughed slightly. "That's the most Southern thing I've heard you say yet."

"You can take the woman out of the South but you can't take the South out of the woman, as they say," she responded good-naturedly.

"Apparently." Townsend bowed his head slightly and looked at her over the top of his glasses. "Listen, Mrs. Brown, *I* apologize for giving you the wrong impression. Yes, you have misjudged me, but I cannot blame you for doing so. I am only trying to carry out Captain Wilkes' instructions in the most complete way possible. My little sister is your age, and I know I would want somebody like me looking after her if she were in your shoes. Understand?"

Elaine nodded. "Yes, I do understand, but I have the Kentishes to look after me when I can't look after myself. I appreciate your and Captain Wilkes' willingness to provide me with information about my husband, but I really do not need any other assistance from the Navy as a whole or from you personally."

"Suit yourself, Mrs. Brown."

"And I don't think we should continue to be seen sitting together in church or eating together," she added.

"A sound conclusion," he agreed.

"Good. Thank you." His responses to her suggestions had been so matter-of-fact that Elaine immediately wondered if she had only been imagining interest coming from him and she worried she might have offended him with her rebukes. She didn't have time to consider that, though, because Mr. and Mrs. Kentish returned from the kitchen just then and sat down in two matching armchairs facing perpendicular to Elaine and Townsend's seats.

"Elaine," Mrs. Kentish said, "Gerald and I have something we want to ask you."

"Yes?"

"Would you consider moving in with us while you are in Fremantle?

The question took Elaine completely aback. "Oh, my."

"We understand it won't quite match your independent spirit, but it will save you much money and will be safer. No matter how self-sufficient you are, a hotel will be no place for a woman to be living by herself when this town becomes flooded with sailors, and more are arriving every day."

Mr. Kentish piped up, "Consider it a Christian service from us. Don't think that we're trying to manage your life. We're only wanting to make it easier for you to stay in Australia and to give you some support that your family can't give you right now."

Elaine smiled to herself and pondered the offer.

"I'd take them up on it if I were you," Townsend advised her.

It did sound very tempting. Elaine enjoyed being independent enough to follow Preston around the world, but she was so lonely without him. Every minute she spent in her hotel room, she was torn between thoughts of his potential death and thoughts of their happy reunion — either on Earth or in Heaven — and the only way she could resolve these clashes was through prayer and Bible study. She had cried or prayed herself to sleep every night for nearly a week and had woken up from nightmares more than once. She was beginning to feel the emotional strain physically, and she knew the wise thing to do would be to move in with the Kentishes. She was, after all, just 20. She was not too young to be married and living overseas, but she was also not too old to accept outside help. And so she decided to give up a bit of her independence in the interest of maintaining her sanity, for she knew that her wait for Preston might be a very long one.

"Okay," she announced simply. "Your offer is extremely generous, and I think I would be stupid to turn it down. I'll move in as soon as you'll let me."

The Kentishes both beamed, and Mrs. Kentish stood and walked over to where Elaine was sitting and gave the younger woman a great hug.

"We're so glad." She released her grip and held Elaine at arm's length. Looking deep into Elaine's eyes, Mrs. Kentish said, "You have an Australian family now."

CHAPTER FIFTEEN

Terry Galloway had faithfully tallied the days that his band of *Houston* and *Perth* survivors had lived on Topper's Island without being captured by the Japanese. On the morning of March 24, he used a sharp piece of bark to scratch the 24th notch into a tree near the patch of ground where he slept. The men had scraped out an existence on this deserted island while all that any of them needed to do to see civilization was to walk to the beach and observe Japanese soldiers and sailors and Javanese civilians offloading the transports in Banten Bay. Galloway wasn't sure the Japanese even cared they were there. It seemed so surreal to be un-captured while living within a few thousand yards of their sunken ships and the enemy.

That last fact particularly bothered Galloway. Not a night passed without him reliving the sheer terror of the battle in his mind. He would stare out into the bay toward *Houston*'s grave and try to imagine what she looked like on the sea floor, with her hull plating buckled and punctured, her decks splintered, her interior wrecked, and her dead sailors resting in peace, never to be retrieved and returned home to their loved ones for proper burials. Anyone who had ever sailed the high seas had to be conscious of the likelihood that his body would be unrecoverable upon his death, but Galloway had not allowed that to stop him from joining the Navy. Now, though he was not reconsidering his fateful choice, he was thinking of all those men's families who would never be able to hold a true funeral for their loved ones and would have to live with the knowledge that their bodies were slowly disintegrating in a deep, dark saltwater bath. Galloway tried to keep such morbid thoughts to a minimum, but the memories were just too fresh. He did not feel as if *Houston*'s sinking was in the past; he felt as if he were still living it.

He and his fellow castaways took their first step toward closure that day when the local native police chief finally visited the island and presented a note to Doctor Epstein and the ranking Australian petty officer. They then gathered their men and made an address.

"Men," the Aussie announced, "the police chief has come here to demand our surrender. He promises that we will be well-treated."

"Take that with a grain of salt, gentlemen," Epstein interjected.

The Australian petty officer continued, "This may be our best chance at survival, for we cannot keep on living like this forever. We have already been machine-gunned once a couple of weeks ago by those destroyers. If we do not surrender, we will either die here of eventual starvation or be killed when the Japs finally decide to flush us out. I strongly suggest that we go to Java with the police chief."

The men murmured amongst themselves briefly before resigning them to the fact that their leaders were probably right. They gathered up their few belongings and climbed into the small boats that the police chief and his native companions had brought with them. The first phase of their survival was over, but Galloway felt little relief in leaving the small island. The outcome of his captivity was now more uncertain than ever for he was about to be turned over to the Japanese. All bets were now officially off.

Preston did not know whether to be relieved or depressed by the appearance at the Serang jail of Galloway, Epstein, and four other *Houston* survivors accompanied by a small group of Australians. On the one hand, he was glad to know they were alive (and particularly glad to see Galloway). On the other hand, since they were more than two weeks late in arriving, he wondered how long they had been in Japanese custody and how close they might have been to escaping. He would have to ask Galloway all of those questions once he got settled in his cell. Until then, Preston and the officers already present could complete their list of survivors. With Epstein's arrival, both of the ship's doctors were now accounted for. Lt. Clement Burroughs was also imprisoned at Serang, along with Commander Maher and 12 other officers. Captain Rooks, Commander Phillips, and Commander Holloway were among those believed to have died in the battle.

Preston did not recognize any of the three enlisted sailors and one Marine private just brought to Serang, which meant that he was likely the only survivor of Director Two. He imagined that Madison and the others had been cut down when the Japanese machine-gunned the quarterdeck and the aircraft hangars, just yards from where he had been standing. Likewise, there had been no trace of Stansky, the injured man from the raft who had been "rescued" by the Javanese fisherman.

The living members of the *Houston* family were finally all in one place after being scattered for three-and-a-half weeks. The men lying at the bottom of Banten Bay would never be forgotten, but Preston knew he and his fellow survivors would have to start living as if they and their ship had never existed if they were to make it through their captivity. Whether rescue came within days, months, or years, only hopeful speculation about the future would sustain them mentally. Nostalgic recollections of their ship's glory days would only strengthen their sense of loss. Their sailing days were over, and as the days in the Serang jail added up, Preston began to develop a new identity that superseded that of "naval officer." That new identity was "prisoner of war."

Phillip Brown rested his elbows on the sturdy oak desk in his downtown Little Rock law office and scanned the telegram from the Navy Department for what must have been the thousandth time in five days. The telegram informed him and his wife, Olivia, that their son Preston was "missing in action" after his ship, U.S.S. *Houston*, had apparently been sunk by enemy fire in the waters around Java. It also conveyed Secretary of the Navy Frank Knox's greatest sympathies for the Brown family's anxiety.

Phillip did not consider the telegram to be hollow, just frustratingly incomplete. It was the only information he had about his son besides a brief telegram from Elaine in Australia, and both had told him virtually nothing. Phillip wished he was back in the Navy himself. He still held a commission as a reserve officer, but he had not been called up yet, and he wondered if it was time for him to take the initiative.

If he returned to the Navy, not only might he be able to get his hands on inside information behind the fate of *Houston*, but he would also be able to actively avenge his son's death or fight in his stead, depending on whether Preston had been killed or had been captured. Phillip was 50, not too old to return to sea. As a lieutenant commander who had served as an engineering officer and exec aboard destroyers in the '10s, '20s, and early '30s — with seven active-duty years that spanned the First World War — he would probably be given a minor sea command or perhaps another assignment as an exec. It would be well worth his effort if he could convince Olivia to let him go.

Phillip leaned back in his chair and gazed around his plush office. He had maintained his late father's practice quite efficiently over the past seven years and had even built it far beyond the first Preston Brown's ambitions. Phillip took pride in his success, but with every second that passed with the telegram burning his hands, its luster diminished. He had never put his career ahead of his family, and he had no reason to start doing so now.

He reached forward and picked up the phone. One of his old shipmates was now a captain in the Navy's Bureau of Personnel in Washington, D.C. Phillip knew his pal could pull the necessary strings to get him back into uniform. Olivia would just have to understand. This war had become deeply personal since it had swallowed their only son into oblivion, and Phillip felt that naval service was his only choice.

He spoke into the receiver and gave his secretary instructions on how to connect him with his friend in the capital. Then he waited to hear a voice on the other end.

A couple of hundred miles to the northwest, in the Ozark foothills, four high school buddies met for the last time at the drug store in Springdale, Arkansas, before going off to war. Elaine's brother Danny, dressed in the white cap and blue "crackerjack" uniform of a seaman second class, opened the door for his friends, Marine Corps Privates Matt and Mike Mayfield, and for his younger brother, Nick. The Mayfield twins entered the empty shop proudly wearing their green service dress uniforms, while Nick followed in street clothes, only able to wish for the day when he could enlist and join them.

Danny let the door shut behind him and called out for the soda jerk. "Andy? You in here?"

An even younger high school boy emerged from the back room, wiping his hands on his apron. "Yeah, Danny!" he called. "What can I get for you fellas?"

"Just the usual," Danny replied.

Andy scrambled to fix four chocolate sodas, filling one glass at a time while holding the other three. Mike reached across the counter and took two of the glasses. "Let me help you," he said before passing the tall glasses down the counter to his brother and to Danny, who passed his to Nick.

"How long are you in town?" Andy asked them.

"Just a few more days," Danny replied. "Is Mr. Richardson here?"

"Sure is," the soda jerk replied, handing the last two glasses to Mike and to Danny. "Let me go get him." Andy disappeared into the back room and returned a few seconds later with the gray-haired, bespectacled druggist.

"Well, boys!" he greeted them jovially. "You're looking good in those uniforms. How long are you here for?"

"Just until Friday," Matt responded. "We're making our last rounds."

"Figure it might be some time before we get back," Mike added.

Mr. Richardson leaned over the counter across from the boys, and Andy took up a position on the other side of the soda fountain.

"Where are you headed?" the druggist inquired.

"Matt and I are headed back to Camp Pendleton," Mike told the man. "We've been assigned to the First Marine Division."

Mr. Richardson nodded, appearing to be impressed. He turned to Danny. "And you, Danny?"

"Somewhere on the East Coast," he replied. "I don't know what ship I'll be assigned to, but I reckon I'll be sent to sea pretty soon. I'm going to be a signalman, and that's mostly a shipboard job."

Mr. Richardson's eyes proceeded on to Nick. "And what about you, son? When do you get to join up?"

"As soon as I turn 18," the freckle-faced, brown-haired kid replied. "That's just about a year away. I'm almost 17 now."

Danny sipped his soda. "He'd leave at 17 if Mom and Dad would let him."

"I hear a lot of boys are doing that," Mr. Richardson commented.

Danny shook his head while still sipping through his straw. "Mom's too smart, though, and even Dad wouldn't let Nick get away with that. They're nervous enough about letting us go fight, but with Elaine being down in Australia and her husband missing, they're especially worried."

"I'll bet. What is the last you heard from your sister?"

"She's living in a city called Fremantle with a couple of old folks from her church and is working in a restaurant."

Mr. Richardson looked amused. "Old folks, huh? Am I one of those 'old folks'?"

Danny just ducked his head and grinned sheepishly while the other boys chuckled.

The friendly druggist returned to the original subject. "And what about Elaine's husband?"

Danny shrugged. "No one knows anything. It's been two weeks since we first heard that Preston's ship had been sunk, and we haven't heard anything new since then. Elaine's still asking every sailor she can find, and nobody knows. He's either a prisoner or he's dead, and neither one sounds very good right now."

The druggist shook his head sadly. "No, son, they certainly don't. This whole war is going very badly for us, and it's up to fellas like you to turn it around." He stopped and looked each boy in the eye. "We're counting on you boys. We're counting on you to get those Japs back for Pearl Harbor and to stop Hitler and Tojo from taking over the world. My generation did it once in the last war; now it's your turn. When you're out there on the front, don't forget us back here in Springdale. We'll be praying for you every day."

"Thank you, Mr. Richardson," Danny replied softly.

Changing the subject after a brief but heavy silence, Mr. Richardson asked, "Is there anything else I can get you boys?"

Matt spoke up, "Our mom wanted us to pick up some aspirin."

"Okay. Andy, get that for them, will you?"

Andy hurried into action. "Sure thing, Mr. Richardson."

"Now," the druggist said again, looking at the four nearly empty soda glasses, "how about another round on the house, huh? Andy!" he said, turning to find his employee, who had not quite reached the aspirin. "Get them each another soda and then fix one for yourself and for me. Oh, wait … never mind. You finish getting that aspirin, and I'll get the sodas."

"Yes, sir!" the soda jerk, who was already halfway back to the fountain, replied obediently without a hint of exasperation.

Mr. Richardson handed out each glass as he filled it, and Andy soon brought the sack of aspirin to the Mayfields. The boy started to ring up the purchase on the cash register, but Mr. Richardson waved him off.

"The aspirin's on the house today, too," he said.

As soon as the sodas were all distributed, Mr. Richardson raised his glass and addressed his customers. "Men," — being called men by Mr. Richardson was quite an honor — "I salute you as you prepare to serve your country. Here's wishing you victory against the enemy, a safe return home, and many more visits to my humble establishment."

The boys raised their glasses in acknowledgment and then each drank his soda down to the very bottom of the glass.

"We'll definitely be seeing you again soon," Danny replied confidently.

With a few parting words of thanks the boys left the drug store. Mr. Richardson and Andy walked them to the door, and then watched them stride down the sidewalk on Emma Avenue and disappear around a corner. With the exception of Nick, Mr. Richardson and Andy were uncertain if they would ever see any of the boys alive again.

Chapter Sixteen

Preston heard them when they were still about a mile away from the Serang jail. He immediately got Galloway's attention and the two young officers hurried to the outer window of their cell. Through the bars, they watched a column of Japanese army trucks file into the center of town and roll to a stop between the jail and the theater. A few soldiers climbed out and greeted the jail's native guards, while Japanese guards at the theater came forward to meet the new arrivals.

"I don't like the looks of this, Preston," Galloway commented. "I don't think they're just coming for officers this time."

Preston nodded and grunted in agreement. It had been less than a week since the last time trucks had visited them and had taken away all of *Houston*'s officers, save Preston, Galloway, Lt. Harold Hamlin, Ens. Charles Smith, Drs. Epstein and Burroughs, and the very ill Lt. Russell Ross. Commander Maher and the others were rumored to be on their way to Japan, and those they left behind hoped those rumors were true. If not, the other officers were probably already dead. They certainly were not on their way home.

The Javanese guards re-entered the jail yelling and waving their arms for everyone to stand and file outside when their cell doors were unlocked. Preston, Galloway, and their companions obediently did so. Outside, a Japanese officer ordered them to stand against the jail wall.

"Officer? Any officer?" the Japanese inquired, apparently not realizing that all of the men present were officers.

Preston and Galloway both started to raise their hands when Hamlin, the turret officer from Turret One, spoke up and stepped forward. "Yes, I'm an officer," he answered.

The Japanese strolled over to the American lieutenant and asked him a few questions about himself before inquiring as to which ship he had served upon.

"U.S.S. *Houston*," Hamlin replied.

The Japanese officer's face lit up. Ever since the Kempeitai interrogations, the Japanese had seemed proud to have finally sunk the "Galloping Ghost," even though they had initially tried to deny that they had failed on so many previous occasions.

"You realize you sank a hospital ship in Banten Bay that night, don't you?" the officer prodded.

Hamlin shook his head. None of them could know what they had or had not sunk in their last battle, and Preston seriously doubted that the Japanese officer was telling the truth about the hospital ship anyway.

Nonetheless, the officer commented on the subject in his fragmented English. "No good. No good," he said. After a pause, he looked hard at Hamlin. "Who is the better man, Tojo or Roosevelt?"

Hamlin needed no time to respond to such an easy question. "Roosevelt."

The officer turned around and shouted an order to his troops. The soldiers scattered, and Preston's heart rate quickened not slightly when he saw the machine-gunners standing in the beds of the trucks swing their weapons toward the American officers.

"Holy mackerel," Galloway muttered under his breath.

Preston, meanwhile, preferred not to breathe.

The Japanese officer approached Hamlin again. "Who is the better man, Tojo or Roosevelt?"

Every prisoner in the formation knew what the response would be because each one of them would have given it if asked. The President was not only their commander-in-chief, but had spent many cruises aboard *Houston* before the war. None of the prisoners had been aboard to witness those happy times, but stories of those voyages had been so ingrained in the ship's lore that each officer felt as if he had sailed with the President.

"Roosevelt," Hamlin again replied.

The gunners then focused their sights exclusively on Hamlin. The Japanese officer repeated the exact question again, and this time Hamlin responded truthfully but diplomatically. "Roosevelt is my leader," he said.

The officer stared at him long and hard once more, his mouth curved downward into a contemplative, squinting frown. Without taking his eyes off the brave American officer, he shouted another command to his troops, and the machine-gunners began dismantling their weapons.

Hamlin returned to the line and received a few whispered compliments from his shipmates before the soldiers began hustling them into the backs of the trucks.

"I sure thought we were dead men back there," Galloway commented to Preston once they were riding through Serang's mud streets.

"I thought so, too," Preston replied, "but I'm almost ashamed to admit that I was a little relieved when they all took aim at Lieutenant Hamlin."

Galloway chuckled. "That guy's got guts."

"Yeah, but guts alone don't keep you alive," Preston pointed out. "He'd have gotten himself shot if he hadn't used his brain to get that Jap to shut up."

"I guess. Where do you think they're taking us anyway?"

Preston shrugged and shook his head. "I don't have a clue. We may be thankful that we don't know."

A guard sitting near the cab several feet away shot him a cross stare, and Preston quit talking.

The men rode in silence, and the town scenery gave way to that of the Java jungle as the trucks rattled and bounced their way east. They would occasionally pass through a village decorated ubiquitously with homemade Japanese flags. Young Muslim boys dressed in baggy garments and wearing skullcaps raced up to the side of the road to wave at the Japanese soldiers and gawk at the raggedly clothed and unshaven white men. The thought that these kids actually saw the Japanese as liberators turned Preston's stomach. However poorly the Dutch colonial authorities might have treated the natives, Dutch sailors would never have machine-gunned enemy survivors in the water, and though his experience with the Japanese as captors had only lasted about a month thus far, he had a fairly solid impression that life under Japanese control would not be easy for the survivors of *Houston* and *Perth* or for the Javanese natives, no matter their affection for the Nipponese flag.

After about 90 minutes the scenery changed again and Preston realized that the convoy was about to enter the capital city of Batavia, though the port area which he had visited six weeks before was nowhere in sight. The trucks wound through town and approached a fenced-in compound with a gate. Soldiers standing by pulled the gate open ahead of the convoy. As the trucks rolled through, Preston checked out his surroundings. They were in the middle of what appeared to be a military compound. On either side of the paved road stood single-story concrete barracks with red-tile roofs and porches running their lengths.

Preston's truck lurched to a halt and the guards prodded him and the rest of the prisoners out onto the street. The Japanese sent the Americans, Australians, Brits, and Dutchmen each different ways, and separated the officers from the enlisted men. Preston looked over his shoulder toward the road as his group was led off toward their quarters and saw that the truck convoy was still filing in through the gate. Practically every Allied prisoner in Serang had been transported to the new facility, which the men soon learned was called "Bicycle Camp." The guards herded the American officers into one building and then left them on their own.

"Home sweet home, fellas," Hamlin announced as they all examined the bare concrete interior. Walls sectioned the building off into cubicles, and bamboo platforms attached to the walls provided the only apparent locations for sleeping. Preston was the one who discovered that the bathroom had running water and drains, a welcome upgrade from the Serang jail, where the only running water had been a stream that ran through the cells from the outside.

"This place doesn't look half bad compared to the dump we just left," Galloway commented as he stretched out on one of the bamboo beds. "And I think I could get used to sleeping on this, too."

"Yeah, right," Preston responded skeptically. He was plenty glad to still be alive after the execution scare earlier in the day, but he wasn't sure he could ever get used to captivity. He had been in it for a month-and-a-half already and still itched to get out. The Allied troops rumored to be coming to rescue them for the past several weeks could not arrive quickly enough.

That night, Preston could not sleep for the hardness of the bamboo, the buzzing of the mosquitoes, and the turbulence of his own thoughts. He stared at the ceiling, eyes wide open, wondering about all the things he was missing by being cooped up in this prisoner pen.

Someone stifled a sneeze nearby, and Preston rolled his head to see that it was Galloway, who was lying at a right angle to him, his head almost touching Preston's where the two sleeping platforms met.

"I guess you're awake," Preston commented.

"Yeah, but I didn't realize you were, too," came a whispered reply.

"What's your problem?"

"This confounded bed!"

"It's harder to get used to than you thought, isn't it?"

"Yeah, sure is."

"Is that all that's keeping you awake?"

"No, but if you'd like I'll make you a list in the morning."

Preston grinned up at the ceiling. "That's okay. I can see that your optimism has faded a bit."

"I'm always trying to keep a good attitude about things, but once the sun goes down and everyone else goes to sleep, and I'm alone with my thoughts, it gets too hard and I quit trying. You know what I mean?"

"I know exactly what you mean. That's just how I feel."

"What are you thinking about?" Galloway asked.

"My folks and my sister and where Lainy is and what she's doing — if she's still alive and how much I wish we were all back home together," Preston replied.

"I figured." Galloway craned his neck in an attempt to make eye contact in the dark and quickly added, "Feel free to talk about them as much as you want, though. It'll help me keep my mind off my family."

"You don't talk about your family very much."

"Not much to talk about. My dad's an accountant for a shipping company in Long Beach, and my mom stays at home. My older brother and his wife are living somewhere in Arizona ... I think he's running a service station on Route 66, though he may have enlisted by now. He was something of a black sheep, even more so once I got appointed to Annapolis. He married a gal my folks didn't like and then moved away to take a job our dad would have sneezed at. I haven't heard from him in ages, but I don't think Bud wants to talk to us anyway. I think he was glad to put us and California out of his mind."

"You have a sister, too, don't you?"

"Yeah, Debbie. She's older, too. She's not doing too badly for herself. She got a degree from USC and is trying to break into acting for one of the smaller studios in Hollywood. She hasn't married yet, though, and that has my folks a little uptight. They think she's too independent."

"They're not believers are they?"

"No, none of them are. Like I told you before, I got saved during a revival. No one in my family wanted to hear anything of it when I started talking about my new life. I think my academy appointment was the only thing that kept me in their good graces."

"Hmm. I'll be sure to pray for them. Anything else you want to tell your best friend?" Preston asked sarcastically, hinting at how privately annoyed he was that his shipboard cabinmate had kept so much to himself for so long.

"Not at the moment. Sorry you're just finding this stuff out now."

"Don't worry about it. You can tell me anything anytime, though, you know?"

"Yeah, I know."

"The two of us are going to have to stick closer together now more than ever if we want to come out of this alive. Despite what you said about your family, we both have a lot of people who are going to miss us if we don't come home."

"Yeah."

The conversation had sapped the last of Preston's energy. "Good night, Terry," he said through a great yawn.

"Good night, Preston ... and I'll be praying for your family, too."

"Thanks."

That word was the last Preston uttered before falling asleep.

Chapter Seventeen

U.S.S. *Enterprise* and its escorting cruisers and destroyers that comprised Task Force 16 cut through choppy seas at the International Date Line northeast of Hawaii shortly after sunrise. Men standing along the starboard railing of the gallery deck just outside the noisy aircraft hangars and beneath the flight deck could see the gray shapes of another task force approaching on a converging course.

"There's *Hornet*," Harry Giles informed Floyd Craven as they stood side-by-side.

They could see another flattop, with lines very similar to those of *Enterprise*, growing gradually larger on the haze-gray horizon. This was the rendezvous the men of Task Force 16 had been anticipating since leaving Pearl Harbor five days earlier. *Hornet*'s Task Force 18 was to join them in a secret mission about which no one seemed to know anything except that it was taking them northwest.

"What are those on her flight deck, Harry?" Floyd asked, peering into the distance, trying to discern the unfamiliar shapes gathered atop *Hornet*.

Giles leaned into the railing as well, and stared across the expanse of rolling saltwater. "You're the pilot; you tell me."

"You're the intel officer," Floyd retorted, "you tell me."

"I don't know what they are," Giles replied as the ship dipped to starboard and a puff of spray blew across him and Floyd. "I get my information on a need-to-know basis. When I need to know something, Admiral Halsey's staff or Commander McClusky tells me. Until then, I know as little as you do, but you know more about aircraft recognition." Giles nodded his head toward the other carrier. "What do you think they are?"

Floyd took another gander. "They almost look like Mitchells. But that's ridiculous. You can't launch Army medium bombers from a carrier!"

Giles straightened and rubbed his eyes. "Maybe we're delivering them to the Aleutians."

Floyd found that suggestion plausible. "Could be. Or we might be taking them to the Ruskies in Kamchatka," he mused.

"Perhaps."

Floyd looked at Giles with amusement. "You really don't know, do you?"

Giles shook his head.

"Well, as long as you find out what you need to tell us before we take off on a mission, I guess I'm happy."

Enterprise's loudspeakers suddenly buzzed to life, and the metallically modulated voice of Capt. George Murray boomed through them and into every compartment, from the firerooms to the bakery to the ready rooms.

"This is your captain speaking," Murray greeted the crew formally and without any sort of emotion. *"Admiral Halsey wishes me to inform you that within a few minutes, our task force*

will be joining with Hornet *and Task Force 18 and proceeding on a new course that will take us within a few hundred miles of Tokyo. Upon our arrival at our destination,* Hornet *will launch its new complement of B-25 Mitchell bombers, which, manned by Army crews, will take off to bomb Tokyo."*

Floyd shot Giles a disbelieving glance. "Is he kidding?"

Giles could only shake his head as they both looked back out to Hornet and the cluster of twin-engine bombers huddled on her flight deck.

"Lieutenant Colonel Doolittle and his men have practiced ashore for several weeks a special take-off technique which will allow them to get airborne from an aircraft carrier's deck at a minimum airspeed. Our responsibility in this secret mission will be to set up a combat air patrol to protect Hornet *from enemy attack, since her own aircraft will be prevented from launching until the B-25s have taken off. Pilots, your squadron commanders will have relevant instructions for you when it becomes available. Crewmen, you will receive additional briefings from your department officers when the time comes. That is all."*

The announcement ended, leaving the 2,500 men of *Enterprise* to process what their skipper had just told them.

Floyd could not quite bring himself to believe that they were about to launch an attack on Tokyo.

"Can this be true, Harry?" he asked Giles. "After all the raids we've flown the past few months, are we really going to bomb Japan? That's almost too good to be true."

"You heard the captain. He wouldn't lie to us."

An actual happy smile crept onto Floyd's face for the first time in weeks. "I'll bet Admiral Halsey's going nuts up there right now," he said, pointing to the overhead and the bridge several decks above it. "I wouldn't be surprised if he went over to *Hornet* and flew right-seat in one of those Mitchells!"

Giles laughed at the joke.

Floyd's enthusiasm was growing by the second. "I'm tempted to swim over there right now myself! Holy cow, why can't they send us in to do the job?"

"Because you'd all get murdered over Tokyo, that's why, and then the Japs'd fly out here and sink our carriers because we had to get so darn close to launch. Whoever thought of using long-range Army planes was pretty smart."

"Smart? He's a danged genius! As long as those Army fliers don't hog all the credit, I'm willing to give them the chance to be the heroes."

"I'm sure Admiral Halsey will be relieved to know that the mission meets with Ensign Floyd Craven's approval," Giles poked at his friend sarcastically.

Floyd brushed off the jibe. "Now, Harry, just keep your fingers crossed so something doesn't come along and foul this all up."

The mission did indeed come close to being fouled up. Five days later, in the wee hours of April 18, radar spotted two Japanese patrol vessels just ten miles away. Admiral Halsey switched to a northerly course to avoid them, and planes from *Enterprise*'s air group, including Floyd's from Bombing Six, took off on combat air patrol. About three hours later, while flying some 40 miles west of the task force and on the wing of Lt. Osborne Wiseman's aircraft, Floyd's gunner gazed down from his perch and spotted two tiny boats on the sea.

"Mr. Craven, I have two Jap pickets, sailing east directly below us and slightly to our five o'clock!" the teenager called to him through the intercom.

Floyd instinctively tried to look over his right shoulder, but his view was naturally blocked by the back of his seat as well as the SBD's wing.

"Good eyes, Schumaker!" Floyd placed his oxygen mask to his mouth so he could speak through the microphone inside and transmit over the plane-to-plane frequency. "Mr. Wiseman, my gunner reports two Jap patrol boats below us and sailing east to my five o'clock. Do you see them?"

There was a pause as Wiseman banked his plane to the left and descended toward the ocean surface. Floyd followed.

"That's affirmative, Mr. Craven," Wiseman called back. *"I see them."*

Floyd now had his plane lined up on the small vessels as well.

"Should we attack?" he asked Wiseman.

"Negative," came the reply. *"Let's fly back to the ship. I'll have my radioman drop a message on the flight deck."*

"They have probably sighted us already, sir. Are you sure you don't want to attack?"

"Yes, Mr. Craven, I'm sure. Let's get back to the ship on the double and let Admiral Halsey know what's up."

"Okay, I'm following you."

The two SBDs climbed again and raced back to *Enterprise*. Wiseman flew low over the flight deck, and his crewman dropped a weighted paper containing the message too sensitive to be transmitted by voice or morse code.

The picket sighting forced Halsey and Doolittle to adjust their plans. Instead of a late afternoon launch for a night attack, they were now forced into an early morning launch for a daylight raid, and the task force was more than 150 miles short of the planned takeoff point. This meant the bombers would barely have enough fuel to reach their landing fields in China. Carrier takeoffs in the Mitchells were at least theoretically possible, but landings had not even been theorized. The Army crews had long known they would have to set down in China, but now they would have to do it flying on fumes.

Floyd circled the task force in his dive bomber as the B-25s warmed up on *Hornet*'s flight deck. Every few seconds, he would sneak a downward peek, checking to see if any of the twin-engine planes had made it into the air yet. For once in his naval career, he wished to be aboard ship instead of in the air. He knew Giles was watching the drama unfold from a front-row seat on one of *Enterprise*'s bridge levels, and Floyd was jealous.

Giles leaned on the railing outside the primary fly station, high above *Enterprise*'s deck, eyes transfixed on *Hornet* as the pair of carriers swung into the wind so that *Hornet* could launch her Mitchells and *Enterprise* could recover her patrols. In the distance, light cruiser *Nashville* charged off after a Japanese patrol boat that had been sighted too close to the task force. The escort's prow threw up an elegant arc of white spray as the ship, rocking back-and-forth on the heavy seas, raced to confront the snooper.

The carriers were pitching almost as much as the cruisers. The weather had turned overcast and blustery, and Giles had to grip the railing and spread his feet apart to keep his balance. As the bows of both flattops plunged into the wave troughs, the front edges of their flight decks met the ocean surface, dousing the decks with green water and spray. The ships then climbed out of the troughs at such an angle that their keels nearly emerged from the sea. Such conditions were hazardous for normal carrier air operations, let alone the launch of twin-engine bombers, a feat that had never before been attempted in the history of aviation.

Colonel Doolittle's B-25 was the first to take off. To Giles it appeared to be barely moving at all, certainly not quickly enough to become airborne. Indeed, the bombers were only able to muster some 60 knots worth of speed on their own power as they rumbled down the short flight deck, but to that meager momentum was added a headwind of about 50 knots from *Hornet*'s own speed and the weather. The Mitchell rolled off the edge of the deck and seemed to just hang there, straining for every inch of altitude. Giles and the other spectators held their breath, waiting pensively to see if the bomber — stripped of all unnecessary weight, including machine guns — would remain aloft or drift into the drink. Somehow, it steadily gained altitude, and Giles exhaled in relief. But that relief was only partial. There still remained 15 Mitchells to go.

One after another, Giles watched them go as he held the steel railing in a white-knuckled grip. *Nashville*'s 6-inch guns boomed in the distance, hurling shells at the patrol boat and reminding all hands how close they were to Japan, and how vulnerable they would be if they were attacked. Dive bombers near the cruiser apparently spotted the target, and Giles glanced up to see them make their runs like tiny pelicans that had spied out some fish. Meanwhile, the Mitchells continued their heroic struggle to achieve flight. More than one skimmed the rolling waves for several hundred yards before finally climbing. At least one dropped off the flight deck so suddenly that its crash appeared imminent, only for its pilots to pull it out of the stall at the last possible second. They would need much more of that skill to get them to Japan and on to China.

The last B-25 launched at 8:24 a.m., one hour after Doolittle's. Admiral Halsey ordered an easterly course, and the task force steamed homeward. Doolittle's raiders would catch the Japanese completely unprepared, and though each aircraft bore only 2,000 pounds worth of bombs, which caused little material damage, they greatly damaged Japanese egos.

The Mitchells continued on to China, not one of them having been shot down over Japan. Most crews bailed out over China and were rescued by friendly civilians. Others crash-landed. Eight crew members were captured by the Japanese, and three were later executed. One crew landed its bomber intact in the Soviet Union but was subsequently interned by the suspicious Russians.

The raid sent a wave of uncertainty rippling through the Japanese high command. Once complacent in their apparent invincibility, the Japanese military leaders now began to become concerned about further long-range strikes. The Japanese patrol boats had, indeed, sighted Halsey's task force, and had informed Tokyo. The Japanese authorities had determined that the carriers were no threat at that distance, however, and had refrained from attacking them. When the Mitchells arrived over Japan at midday, the Japanese believed they had originated from land, not from the carriers. Shaken by the sudden appearance of land-based American bombers over the Empire, the Japanese began taking steps to secure the home islands against future attacks from American airbases. Among the American territories targeted for invasion, partially as a result of the raid, was a three-island coral atoll 1,200 miles northeast of Hawaii called Midway.

CHAPTER EIGHTEEN

Life at Bicycle Camp soon settled into monotony. The Japanese put their prisoners to work at the Batavia dockyards during daylight hours, but the time the prisoners spent within the prison compound itself was characterized by alternating boredom and terror, relieved only by a few hours of sleep each night. Diseases, particularly malaria and dysentery, had already become major problems, claiming the lives of Lt. Russell Ross — ill since Serang — and an Australian soldier. The men had died largely due to the late arrival of medicine that Harold Hamlin and a British colonel had begged the Japanese to order. The Japanese had at last relented, but not in time to save Ross and the Australian. This left Hamlin as the senior American officer in Bicycle Camp.

These tragedies aside, deaths were not common; physical abuse was. The Japanese guards demanded the utmost respect from all prisoners, regardless of rank, and even the most minor violations — which might not have been true violations at all — earned them brutal beatings. The prisoners had at first been demoralized by this treatment, but once they observed the guards meting out abuse on each other according to rank they began to accept the violence as a way of life.

Preston emerged from the officers' barracks one Tuesday morning in mid-May and stretched his upper body as he descended the steps from the porch. Galloway hustled to catch up to him and they were halfway across the yard when they heard a familiar cry from a comrade.

"Kiotsuke!" an unseen American officer called everyone in that section of the compound to attention in Japanese.

Preston and Galloway both stopped dead in their tracks and stiffened with their arms at their sides, their heels touching, and the fronts of their feet spread slightly apart. Out of the corner of his eye, Preston saw a lone Japanese private strolling past the gate into the American compound. Glancing quickly around the yard without moving his head, Preston counted at least 30 other Americans standing rigid at random intervals. They would have to remain there until the Japanese left. The guard appeared to be minding his own business that morning and not looking for trouble. As long as none of the Americans decided to give him any, they would all be able to enjoy their breakfast — such as it was — pain free.

Preston never intended to cause trouble. It was not his fault that since he was a little kid, he had had a peculiar tendency to sneeze early in the morning. It started with a light, tickling, burning sensation in his nose. He started to inhale through his mouth and reflexively reached up with his right hand to stifle the sneeze. In this he was successful; in staying invisible, he was not.

The guard froze, wheeled to his left, and glared straight at Preston, who was just lowering his arm. The guard raced toward him and didn't even stop before swinging the butt end of his rifle up and into Preston's left shoulder. The blow knocked Preston off-balance, and he stumbled off to his right, only to be met by the other end of the rifle across the right side of his face. That blow hurt worse than the first, but since it came from the skinnier part of the rifle, it did not stagger him as badly. With Preston still rocking on his heels, the Japanese guard rammed the rifle butt into Preston's solar plexus region, knocking the wind out of him and ensuring that he dropped backward to the ground.

His shoulder and jaw throbbing and his very empty stomach feeling as sick as possible, Preston groaned and tried to roll over onto his hands and knees. He had about two seconds to catch his breath before one of the guard's feet booted him directly in the behind, causing him to pitch forward face-first into the dirt. The guard circled around to Preston's right side and kicked him twice in the ribs, forcing from Preston's lungs whatever breath he had left. Then the guard piledrove the rifle butt into the small of Preston's back. Preston flattened himself against the dirt, too exhausted to try to stand again. The guard took care of this for him. Grabbing the back of Preston's shirt collar, the guard dragged him to his feet and, adjusting his limbs as if he were a clay figurine, forced him to stand at attention. He gave Preston a quick slap and a backhand across the face and then grabbed his jaw to set his head looking forward.

"Kiotsuke!" the guard screamed. Then, apparently satisfied, he shouldered his rifle and sauntered away.

Every muscle and joint in Preston's legs strained to resist the urge to collapse until the Japanese was out of sight. Then he crumpled to the ground. Galloway, who had stood at attention no more than four feet away through the entire beating, caught him before he hit the dirt.

Galloway summoned a couple of enlisted men to help him. "Quick, fellas, help me get him to the hospital!"

Preston didn't say a word on the way to the hospital, but he felt every step and every misplaced arm or hand of the men who were helping him walk. When they arrived, they set Preston down on a bamboo bed so that Dr. Epstein could examine him. Then one of the pharmacist's mates helped tend to his bleeding wounds — notably around his mouth — and his ribs, of which the doctor said two were broken. Galloway sat nearby and watched.

"He sure got you good, didn't he?" Galloway commented.

"Yup," Preston replied through gritted teeth. "I'll tell you what, that's the last time I'm taking that kind of abuse from a *private*."

Galloway patted him on an unbruised section of his back. "Easy. You wanna get out of here alive, don't you?"

Preston just groaned gutturally. "Of course I do. That's why I'm so frustrated. If I didn't have a reason to live, I wouldn't hesitate to go out and fight one of those Japs to the death. I might get killed in the process, but at least I'd have a chance at taking one with me."

"Yeah, and you'd be sending him straight to hell," Galloway commented.

Preston glared at Galloway. "How many hundreds of Jap sailors did we do that to while we were on the ship?"

"There's a difference between killing someone in battle and killing someone out of pure hatred. Killing Japs is not your responsibility anymore. Staying alive is."

Preston gave up the argument, but only grudgingly. He was in too much pain to argue.

"I have to say I agree with Terry," the pharmacist's mate interjected. "If we lay low and just stay out of the way, we might just live long enough to get rescued."

Preston closed his eyes and shook his head. Concentrating his foggy mind on speaking the right words, he asked threateningly, "What did you call Ensign Galloway, sailor?"

The pharmacist's mate looked up at Preston. His face had turned white in an instant. "I called him by his first name, sir, but he hasn't seemed to mind before."

Preston shot a glare at Galloway. "Is that true?"

Galloway shrugged. "We're all in this together."

Preston looked back at the pharmacist's mate and said in an annoyed tone, "Listen, the Navy regulations didn't sink with our ship. They apply here just as they did before we became prisoners of war. I don't care what Ensign Galloway says, I'm telling you to maintain proper courtesies when addressing officers. Is that understood?"

The pharmacist's mate nodded. "Yes, sir. I apologize."

"Apology accepted," Preston replied with a sigh, leaning back against the wall and wincing in pain.

The pharmacist's mate rose to his feet. "You can lie down now, sir. I don't think Doc Epstein will want you to leave for the rest of the morning. He might let you out later."

"Thanks."

Galloway stood as well. "I'm going to leave now. Take it easy, okay?"

"Sure thing," Preston mumbled as his friend disappeared around the corner.

Hamlin soon appeared in his place. "How are you feeling, Mr. Brown?" he asked. "The boys say that little yellow rascal really worked you over."

"He did, sir," Preston replied. "Sorry I can't get up," he said, referring to his inability to stand at attention in the presence of a superior officer.

"Don't worry about it. You've earned the right to lie down."

Preston snickered at that. That did remind him of the incident just a few moments before. "Sir, there is something I need to report to you."

Hamlin furrowed his eyebrows in concern. "What is it?"

"Have you noticed many of the enlisted men addressing officers by their first names?"

Hamlin appeared to think about that for a second before he replied, "No, but I've heard some nicknames get used."

"Well, I just heard it happen, sir. That pharmacist's mate over there addressed Galloway as 'Terry.'" Preston rolled his head to discreetly identify the offender. "Galloway explained it by saying, 'We're all in this together,' and in a sense I think he's right. We're all in the same boat — or rather, out of the same boat — but that doesn't mean that you and Galloway and I ceased to be officers and they all ceased to be enlisted men. Don't you think we have to maintain order, sir?

"If we don't maintain our way of life, then we lose all control over the situation and will have ultimately handed it over to the Japs. We can't let the chain of command break down. We have to insure that this unit stays together and stays disciplined. It's the only way any of us will make it out alive."

Hamlin nodded understandingly. "I think you're exactly right, Mr. Brown, and I intend to have a meeting this evening with the officers and the chiefs. I'm concerned about these incidents and some of the cartoons floating around."

Preston gave a closed-mouth smile of recognition. "You mean the satirical ones that Marine has been drawing of us?"

Hamlin nodded. "Those are the ones. Things will get out of hand if I let them. The men are also stealing things from the docks. That has to stop, too. If the doctors let you out today, I want you to be at that meeting."

"I'll be there, sir."

"Good. Now, I need to go. I'll see you again soon."

"All right, sir," Preston said as Hamlin turned and left his bedside. Preston just lay on the bamboo bed and stared at the ceiling, counting the sore spots on his body as he did so. That day was one of the longest of his life.

Elaine prepared herself for bad news when she saw Townsend enter the Fremantle Markets café. She wiped her hands on her apron even though her hands were not dirty — it had become a nervous habit.

"Good afternoon, Mrs. Brown," Townsend greeted her pleasantly, wearing his working khakis and depositing his cap upside down on the counter between them.

"Good afternoon, sir," she replied, a bit more relaxed now. If he had come with bad news, he would not have been smiling. "Are you here to give me news or to order something?"

"I came for some tea, actually. There's no news yet on your husband."

"I suppose no news is good news, then."

"Probably. If we hear anything about the fellows on that ship at this point, it won't likely be news that they've been recovered."

"Hmm," Elaine responded, allowing herself to slip momentarily into a state of deep reflection, the kind that usually resulted in sleepless nights. She consciously put an end to her daydreaming. "I'll get you that tea," she responded.

Townsend held up a hand and called her back as she headed away from the counter. He lowered his voice and asked, "You think you could slip some ice into mine? I haven't had a good glass of iced tea since the last time I was in Manila. These Aussies don't know what they're missing."

A smile broke on Elaine's face. She had violated the Australian custom of drinking only hot tea a couple of times herself. "All right, I'll do that."

"At no extra charge?"

She shook her head and continued to grin. "No extra charge."

Elaine fixed the cup of iced tea in an inconspicuous ceramic cup and brought it to Townsend. He drank it deeply, draining the small cup in a couple of gulps and betraying to anyone paying attention that the beverage was not actually hot. He smacked his lips lightly in satisfaction when he finished drinking.

"I do have news about the war," he announced. "Did you hear about the major events this weekend?"

"The good ones or the bad ones?" Elaine replied, confident that she had already read in the newspapers what Townsend was about to tell her.

"Both, actually. The Coral Sea and Corregidor?"

Elaine nodded. "I read about both. I feel horrible about all those boys on Corregidor who had to surrender. They must have had a terrible time of it. And the ones on Bataan..." her voice trailed off. Imagining the fate of the U.S. and Filipino survivors of the Philippines only compounded her own personal pain. On the one hand, she knew Preston — if he was alive — was not alone in his suffering. On the other hand, her concern for him was joined by her concern for the thousands of faceless soldiers who were now also Japanese prisoners. And she could not avoid considering what might have happened to her if she had ever arrived in Manila. She would likely have been taken prisoner as well.

"We caught a huge break in the Coral Sea, though, you have to admit," Townsend commented. "The Japs were on their way to take Port Moresby and to bomb Queensland. If our carriers hadn't stopped them, they'd be close to securing all of Papua and might be able to invade this country."

Elaine nodded in agreement. "We lost a carrier, though, didn't we?"

"Yes, but in some ways we broke even with the Japs. One of our big carriers, a destroyer, and an oiler in exchange for one of their small carriers and heavy damage to two of their big ones. At any rate, we turned them back — that's what matters."

"I suppose," she sighed. "It's good to have a victory for once."

"That's for sure."

There was a brief pause before Elaine asked, "Any word on which carrier it was that got sunk?"

"Ours or theirs?"

"Ours."

"It was *Lexington*," Townsend replied.

Elaine furrowed her eyebrows. "I haven't heard of that one. One of the boys from my town is a dive bomber pilot, and I'm wondering if he was on that ship."

"Do you know the name of his squadron?"

She shook her head. "No, I don't. I haven't seen him in months anyway. He's not at all a friend of mine, but he's still from Springdale, and he's still an American." She thought about this for a second and chuckled to herself.

"What?" Townsend asked.

"Oh ... nothing. I'm just thinking how ironic it is that during wartime all your enemies at home become your heroes because they are less of a threat to you than the enemy you're at war against."

"Is this pilot that bad a fella?"

She chuckled slightly again. "That's almost exactly what my husband asked me one time." Her gaze fell to the countertop and she absently wiped up some water with a rag that had been lying nearby. "I grew up with him, and from about the time he turned 15 to the time he dropped out of college, he turned into one of the most vile men I've ever known." She looked up at Townsend and smiled. "And now he's fighting a war against the country that may have killed my husband. I suppose I should be indebted to him."

"War kind of makes you rethink your priorities, doesn't it?" Townsend commented.

"Yes, it does. As much as I despise Floyd, I pray that he will change some day. Christ can change anyone, but ..." her voice trailed off again.

A quizzical smile played on Townsend's lips. "But what?"

"But I don't want to see Floyd again until he *is* changed," she remarked with raised eyebrows before taking Townsend's empty tea cup away for washing. When she returned, he was preparing to leave.

"I need to get back to the headquarters, Mrs. Brown," he informed her.

"Well, then have a good day, sir."

"I will do my best. Pray for us, too, if you don't mind."

"I already do, Mr. Townsend — all the time," she replied with the greatest sincerity. "Come visit again."

Townsend promised that he would, picked up his cap, and walked out of the café and back into his world of helping fight the war, leaving Elaine to go about her odd business of brewing tea in the shadow of it.

CHAPTER NINETEEN

Drs. Epstein and Burroughs released Preston from the hospital in the middle of the afternoon and gave him strict orders not to perform any strenuous labor. They need not have worried. Preston's body throbbed all over, and even breathing hurt. He had no intention of performing any strenuous labor.

He left the hospital and hobbled back toward his barracks. Most of the enlisted men and a few of the officers were working down at the docks or at the Dunlop tire factory by now, and the prison had something of a ghostly feel to it. Outside the barbed wire, however, life went on. Vehicles drove past and bicycles appeared frequently with most of the drivers and riders not even venturing a glance inside the camp. One bicyclist stopped, however, and called out to Preston as he climbed the steps to enter the barracks.

"Hey, American!" an accented woman's voice shouted at him.

He turned to see a young, blonde Dutchwoman standing just on the other side of the fence and straddling her bicycle.

"Come here!" she motioned to him urgently.

Preston feared something was wrong, but when he approached the woman, he could see that she was smiling.

"I have something for you," she informed him, reaching into her satchel. She pulled out a chocolate bar and poked it through the fence.

Preston's sore face broke into a grin and he reached to take it. He hadn't seen chocolate since the night his ship had been sunk, and the two candy bars Galloway had bought for him in Batavia now lay somewhere at the bottom of Banten Bay. He also hadn't eaten anything all day due to his hospitalization. Dr. Epstein had been afraid of feeding him until it was clear that he had no internal injuries.

"God bless you," he told the woman gratefully. Taking the bar from her, he said, "Thank you very much."

"Anything for you brave men," she replied. "I know you would rather be fighting and not be locked up in there. I would rather not be out here knowing that my sailor husband is probably dead. But we cannot give up. We must fight the war in our own little ways."

Preston looked at her curiously. "What ship was your husband on?"

"The destroyer *Kortenaer*," she replied.

His expression darkened. "Oh, I'm sorry," he told her, intentionally neglecting to mention that he had seen her husband's ship sink. Perhaps he had been one of the stalwart survivors who had given *Houston* a thumbs-up as their ship sank beneath them. Perhaps he had also been one of the oil-soaked men who had been dragged aboard *Encounter* a few hours later. Or perhaps he really was dead, entombed with his shipmates in their shattered steel coffin at the bottom of the Java Sea.

"It will be all right," she replied. "God is with us."

Preston smiled at her faithful confidence. "Yes, He is." He waved the candy at her. "Thank you again for this chocolate."

"Share it with your friends," she encouraged him.

"Oh, I will," he assured her.

"Is there anything else that you need?"

Preston pondered the question carefully. He wasn't sure that he wanted to put this woman at any greater risk, but he was also inclined to take advantage of her generosity.

"Could you find me an English-language Bible?" he finally asked.

The woman's eyes lit up and she didn't even hesitate to respond. "Yes, I can. I know just where to find one."

Just then a Japanese guard emerged from the gate about 15 yards away. He saw the meeting taking place and charged at the woman, screaming hysterically. With well-trained reflexes, the Dutch woman rose back to her seat, placed her feet on the pedals and started away from the fence.

"I will see you again," she called over her shoulder to Preston as she fled.

"Okay," he replied, slipping the chocolate into his shirt pocket and turning his back to the guard while the Japanese was still chasing the woman. Preston hurried to get up on the barracks porch, and then turned to watch the woman make good her escape. By the time the guard turned around, Preston was hidden inside and on his way to his bunk to enjoy his portion of the sweet gift.

Lieutenant Hamlin held his meeting that night in the officers' barracks. All of the surviving chief petty officers were present as well. Hamlin addressed the specific discipline problems that had arisen in the ranks and recited the appropriate chapters and verses from *Navy Regulations* in order to justify his concern that *Houston*'s crew remain a well-coordinated team functioning with a distinct chain of command. Most of the officers and chief petty officers voiced their support for their *de facto* skipper's initiatives. Hamlin led his officers in dividing the enlisted personnel into divisions similar to those they had been members of aboard ship. Each officer, except the doctors, was placed in command of a division — even Preston, who lounged uncomfortably in the corner listening — and each chief was assigned to assist an officer.

"I intend to hold 'captain's mast,'" Hamlin informed them all. "Violations of the regulations will be punished with extra work duties. Commander Epstein, you will be in charge of our medical department. The men will stand watch on rotating schedules and will keep their barracks clean at all times. Everything, as much as is practical, will be just as it was aboard ship.

"Mr. Brown: the two yeomen, Reas and Harrell, are in your division. Assign them to that office the Japs set up for us and have them put together personnel records. Have them give a copy to the Japs and keep a secret copy for ourselves."

Preston nodded weakly. "Aye-aye, sir."

"Mr. Rogers," Hamlin turned to his new "exec," Lt. (j.g.) Leon Rogers, "start working on compiling written reports of our battles in the Java Sea and in Banten Bay. We will need those someday."

Hamlin's crisp delivery of clear objectives inspired Preston to approach his captivity with new energy. He had a sense of purpose and mission now, and Hamlin's presentation had a galvanizing effect on him similar to that of the Dutchwoman's simple but heroic act of generosity earlier in the day. Preston hoped Hamlin never got himself "bashed" by the guards, because if anything happened to that young lieutenant, it would fall to someone like Preston to pick up the slack, something Preston was not sure he was capable of doing in his present physical state.

Two mornings later, Preston could still feel the bashing, and he could tell that the guard's last strikes would be the last to heal. The kicks in the side had caused the broken ribs, and the rifle butt to the lower back had caused bruising so severe that Dr. Epstein feared one or both of Preston's kidneys had been damaged. The doctor decided to keep the junior officer under close observation. Preston didn't much care what was specifically wrong with him, he just knew that he had never hurt so much in his life and that sleeping on the bumpy bamboo did not help things any.

Standing at attention through the morning *tenko* (roll call) was all he could manage. Later that morning, he and Galloway sat on the edge of the barracks porch discussing the organization of their respective divisions when a commotion outside the fence distracted them. Around the end of the Dutch prisoners' mess hall on the opposite side of the camp appeared a column of green-clad men carrying duffle bags over their shoulders.

"Who in the world is that?" Galloway questioned rhetorically.

Preston laid a hand on his friend's shoulder and used it to pull himself up straighter. He then leaned forward to stare at the approaching formation.

The men were soldiers, of that there was no doubt, and it did not take long for Preston to recognize the olive-green uniforms as being U.S. Army service dress.

"Those are our soldiers, Terry," he said in disbelief. "Those are our soldiers!"

"You gotta be kidding me!" Galloway exclaimed in return. "I thought all that talk of rescue was just a bunch of talk, but look at that, will you?"

Preston already was looking, of course, and soon they both saw something that burst their briefly inflated spirits.

A Japanese soldier appeared walking alongside, holding his rifle down at his waist, its bayoneted tip pointing at the American soldiers. Then another Japanese appeared, and another.

Galloway sighed out of frustration. "Oh, good grief."

"I knew it was too good to be true," Preston muttered.

Slumping dejectedly, the two Navy men watched as their Army countrymen filed in through the gate and lined up on the road dividing Bicycle Camp in half. The Japanese guards unlocked the interior gate to the American section and showed the soldiers to their new home. The men loitered inside the yard, waiting for someone to tell them what to do, while the *Houston* sailors gathered around to examine the new arrivals. The soldiers were doing their fair amount of examining as well. In contrast to the soldiers, the sailors were dressed raggedly in what they had worn to Batavia from Serang, which in many cases was what they had worn from Sunda Strait. After a few minutes, the two groups began to intermingle, and conversations arose.

Preston let himself slide off the porch onto his feet, and he groaned with the effort. "Let's go meet these fellas," he told Galloway.

"Right behind you."

The two men approached a second lieutenant who was standing with his hands on his hips, taking in his new surroundings with a skeptical gaze.

"Welcome to Bicycle Camp," Preston greeted him with an extended hand. "I'm Ensign Preston Brown. This is Ensign Terry Galloway."

"Second Lieutenant Jake Dunn," the young Army officer replied with a drawl. "Pleased to meet you, present circumstances not withstanding."

Preston gave a cynical snort. "We thought for a few seconds there that you were the American troops that we heard had landed on Java weeks ago."

Dunn shook his head sympathetically. "No, sorry. We're the only American soldiers on Java, and until we marched into here, we thought we were the only Americans, period."

"What unit are you with?" Preston inquired.

"Second Battalion, 131st Field Artillery Regiment, 36th Infantry Division, Texas National Guard," Dunn replied. "And before you get your hopes up again, the rest of the 36th Infantry Division and the Texas National Guard ain't nowhere near Java. We were the only ones, sent to the Philippines to help General MacArthur, and then sidetracked here while we were still on the transport ships. We stopped in Brisbane on our way over, and then fought beside the Aussies and the Dutch until March when those Dutch cowards rolled over belly-up, stuck their paws in the air, and told us to do the same. Not sure I'll ever be able to look a Dutch officer in the eye again as long as I live. What ship did you fellas come off of?"

"U.S.S. *Houston*," Galloway replied, "speaking of Texas," he added with a wry grin.

Dunn wasn't amused. "Dang. You're the ones we were told might have been able to pick us up at Tjilatjap. We thought about trying to march there instead of surrendering like the Dutch told us to, but decided it was too much of a risk. I reckon we turned out to be right."

"I reckon you did," Preston commented glumly. "You thought we were about to rescue you, and we thought you were about to rescue us. And now we're inmates together."

"Cryin' shame," Dunn responded without emotion. "I reckon we'd just better make the best of what's been dealt to us, though."

While Preston wondered how many more times Dunn could use the word "reckon" in a single conversation, Dunn looked Preston and Galloway over and then pointed to the duffle bag at his feet. "What do you fellas need? I've got plenty of extra clothes and gear and stuff in here, and I'm willing to share. Come on, you name it, I've probably got it."

Preston stroked his chin thoughtfully and remembered how unshaven he was. "You have an extra razor?"

"Think so," Dunn replied as he crouched down to start digging through his duffle.

"How about a blanket or two?" Galloway asked. Pointing his elbow at Preston he said, "This guy got beat up really badly by a Jap guard the other morning, and he's been sleeping on bare bamboo ever since then."

"I've got one extra blanket," Dunn answered without looking up, "but I'm sure we'll be able to find another from someone else." He looked up at them. "How about some fresh shirts? That is, if you don't mind wearing Army duds."

Preston and Galloway exchanged pleased glances. "Khaki's khaki, isn't it?" Preston responded.

Dunn reached up and stuffed a poorly folded shirt into each of their hands and a razor into Preston's. "Here."

"You have everything, don't you?" Preston commented with a chuckle.

"Hey, you ain't seen nothin' yet. They're just now bringing in the field kitchen."

The men directed their eyes to the gate where the last of the battalion was filing in, carrying with them loads of equipment that normally would have been transported by truck.

"Oh my word," Galloway marveled.

"Yeah, and we brought cash, too. I've seen a lot of locals around here. We can probably buy supplies from them."

"Probably," Preston responded. "A Dutchwoman sneaked some chocolate through the fence to me two days ago, and I see other Dutch women and kids slipping stuff to the guys every now and then. They're very brave and seem to be pretty resourceful, too."

Galloway opined, "All we'll have to do is just sit here and wait to get rescued. As long as we stay clear of the guards, all should be well."

"I'm not quite as optimistic," Dunn told them as he stood again, "but you can think what you want to. I suppose morale would be pretty low around here if no one had any hope."

Preston and Galloway nodded thoughtfully in response and, unbeknownst to Dunn, reconsidered their prior optimism.

"So the Japs just decided to dump us in here," the Texan observed. "Where's our suite?" he added sarcastically.

"I don't know where Lieutenant Hamlin will want to put you all," Preston told him, "but let's go find out."

Preston and Galloway took the lead carrying their new clothes, and the two of them, with Dunn lugging his duffle bag along with him, pressed through the crowd in search of the Navy lieutenant who was, no doubt, considering his organizational response to the unexpected influx of additional prisoners. For Preston, the arrival of Texas National Guardsmen was a welcome development as it already appeared that the artillerymen would provide a morale boost to the Navy company. Still though, the discovery of their capture only reinforced the magnitude of the Allied defeat on Java and reduced his hope that rescue might come soon. Far from being harbingers of deliverance, the soldiers represented the uncertainty and open-endedness of the war, which they would be fighting together for a daunting, indefinite period of time.

CHAPTER TWENTY

Spirits were high among the crowd loiter-ing about the Woolloomooloo Pier on Sydney Harbour the night of Sunday, May 31. Brilliant floodlights illuminated nearby Garden Island Naval Station and the various and sundry Allied vessels moored around it and anchored further out into the harbor. Dozens of Australian sailors on liberty milled around, enjoying the pleasant if overcast evening and the fresh air, which was a precious commodity aboard ship. Even more than that, though, many of them enjoyed the company of pretty local girls, who were even harder to find outside of port than fresh air.

Ordinary Seaman Tony Fraser, the waiter who helped Elaine leave Darwin, was one of these sailors. On liberty from the heavy cruiser *Canberra* — a gorgeous, white, three-stack vessel anchored off Farm Cove less than a mile away — he was savoring his last couple of hours with charming, blonde Isabel Finley. Isabel was only 17, but that had not stopped the just-19 Tony from asking the younger sister of his best mate's girlfriend for a date at the beginning of May while *Canberra* was in Sydney for an overhaul. They had quickly become inseparable.

His only cruise thus far had been a brief voyage to Melbourne escorting a supply convoy. He had returned as in love with the sea and his ship as he had been with Isabel when he had left. *Canberra* returned to Sydney and remained there, much to Tony's dismay. Isabel, meanwhile, probably realizing that the extended layover could not last for long and that Tony would soon be sent to the real war, clung to him whenever they were together. Her attention eased his frustration and gave him something to enjoy about being on land with nowhere to go and no Japanese to fight. They sat together on the pier, facing Garden Island, with their arms around each other, discussing Isabel's family.

Her father was a shoe salesman, and her mother was a homemaker, but the mundane details ended there. One uncle had been killed when the Japanese captured the island of Rabaul, east of New Guinea, and another was missing ever since *Perth* had been sunk. The shoe-salesman father burned with anger over these tragedies. Isabel's only brother had enlisted in the militia and was on his way north to the Papua territory on New Guinea, which worried her to no end because the Japanese had made no secret of their desire to invade it. After all, the Coral Sea operation had been intended to take its capital, Port Moresby.

The terrible uncertainty that surrounded both of their futures weighed heavily on Tony's and Isabel's hearts even as they soaked in their pleasant surroundings to the sound of cheerful chatter from the other sailors and girls. Isabel wrapped her arms around Tony's right arm and lay her head on his shoulder.

"What time do you have to get back to your ship?" she asked him.

"Midnight," he replied quietly.

"What time is it now?"

Tony lifted his left arm and searched for the luminescent hands in the dim glow provided by the lights on the pier. "About 10:30," he answered her.

Her only response was a sad sigh. Tony leaned over and kissed the top of her head. "Don't be sad. I'll have liberty again in a couple of nights."

"I get so lonely, though, when you're not around. I don't know what I'll do when you go to sea."

Tony was trying to compose some tender, romantic words of comfort when a muffled explosion broke his concentration. The chatter on the pier ceased immediately as all heads turned to the east toward the harbor mouth. Then everyone began talking again at once. *What was that? Was that an underwater explosion? Someone hit a mine! There ain't no mines out there! Submarine! It's a Jap submarine!*

Tony rose to his feet, attempting the impossible feat of seeing through Potts Point, which sat opposite Garden Island to the south and blocked his view. Isabel rose as well and regained her grip on his arm.

"What *was* that?" she demanded to know in a soft but worried voice. "Can you see anything?"

Tony shook his head, keeping his eyes directed to the east. "Come with me," he insisted.

He pulled her down the pier, past the gawking, murmuring crowd, and into the street.

"Where are we going?" Isabel wanted to know, stumbling along, trying to keep up in the pair of high heels she had just bought that afternoon as part of her attempt to look older on the waterfront.

"We'll be able to see the harbor better from Potts Point," he explained. "I'm no expert, but that sounded like an underwater explosion to me. I think the blokes on patrol out there just bagged a Jap sub."

Fear now edged Isabel's voice, replacing the earlier tone of concerned curiosity. "You really think it was a Jap?"

"Oh, it could have only been one of their midget submarines, baby. Ones like they sneaked into Pearl Harbor. They're nothing to be scared about."

Tony would have been better off if he had not invoked Pearl Harbor. Isabel stopped in her tracks and yanked him to an abrupt halt. "Nothing to be scared about?" she fairly well shrieked. "What if the Japanese are about to bomb Sydney?"

"Listen," Tony told her firmly, "it's the middle of the night. If they're going to bomb us, it won't be until after dawn, and I'll have plenty of time to get you home. Let's just walk up here and take a look to see what we can see, okay?"

Reassured, though only slightly, Isabel nodded. "Okay."

Tony led her to a spot near the water where they could see the entire harbor on that side of Garden Island. Before them lay several small Australian ships and, a little further out, the American heavy cruiser *Chicago*. *Canberra* was now out of sight behind them. Moored next to Garden Island were a Dutch submarine and a small Australian barracks ship, *Kuttabul*.

An orange flash from *Chicago* split the darkness as a sharp crack of gunfire reverberated across the waterfront. Isabel jumped and wrapped her arms around Tony. Together they watched as a geyser of water immediately rose in the harbor.

"The Yanks've spotted that sub," Tony told her.

A few more shots were followed by silence. Tony and Isabel sat for a seemingly interminable ten minutes or so before more explosions rocked the harbor, having originated toward its mouth to the east.

"There must be more than one of them," Tony muttered. He heard Isabel let out a slight whimper and looked down to see that she was crying silently. At a loss for words — he wasn't that scared, but he didn't know how to ease her fears — he just squeezed her a little tighter and continued to scan the harbor.

The sound of more naval gunfire came from around Garden Island, and all the ships in the harbor suddenly went dark. Then Tony and Isabel sat and waited and waited and waited. Midnight approached with no more excitement, and Tony knew it was time to head back to his ship.

"I'd better get you home, Issy," he told her. "I only have 20 minutes left."

"Okay," she replied softly. They stood and turned their backs on the harbor, though they repeatedly looked over their shoulders for several blocks.

Tony left Isabel on her parents' doorstep, just as he always did (high heels or not, she was not old enough to walk the streets alone at night) and returned to Farm Cove just in time, only to discover that the launch waiting to take him and his shipmates back aboard was not going to make a trip until the alert ended. So Tony sat with his shipmates and waited. The floodlights at Garden Island had been doused and all was dark and silent. None of the sailors as much as smoked a cigarette, whose orange pinprick of light might enable a sub skipper to get his bearings in the treacherous harbor.

At 12:30, an explosion louder than any of the others shook the harbor. Looking back to the east, Tony could just see the tip of a geyser hanging over Garden Island. Another explosion followed closely, and Tony saw another geyser. The rest of the sailors were now looking that way, and word soon reached them that a ship had been hit. Tony and his shipmates dashed to Garden Island and when they reached the east side, they saw *Kuttabul* settling rapidly with sailors scrambling to jump overboard and swim to shore. Others jumped off the island's seawall and swam to the old converted harbor ferry to help rescue men. By the time Tony got close enough, there was nothing left to be done. *Kuttabul* had sunk down to the main deck, and water washed through its railing. The survivors lay atop the seawall, soaked to the skin, coughing up water and checking themselves for injuries.

A naval dock worker hurried past, and Tony called out to him. "What happened?"

"Torpedo exploded against the seawall, right next to the boat. The old girl couldn't stand the blast. It blew her bottom out. Pitch in and lend a hand, mate!"

The dock worker left Tony staring at the scene of the tragedy, his mind vividly reliving the air raid in Darwin. He had joined the Navy to catch up with the war, but it seemed as if the war had caught up with him. Australia had been attacked twice, and he had not yet had the opportunity to fight back. Tony set his jaw and jogged toward the seawall.

CHAPTER TWENTY-ONE

After returning from the Tokyo Raid, *Enterprise, Hornet,* and the rest of Halsey's Task Force 16 set to sea again in an attempt to join up with Rear Adm. Frank Jack Fletcher's *Yorktown* carrier group and Rear Adm. Aubrey W. Fitch's *Lexington* carrier group, which were sailing in the waters northeast of Australia attempting to halt a Japanese thrust through the Solomon Islands toward Papua, New Guinea, and Queensland. They arrived one week too late to participate in the Battle of the Coral Sea, in which *Lexington* had been sunk and *Yorktown* had been crippled by bombs. The Japanese retired after the battle and gave up their attempt to invade Papua. *Enterprise,* despite its late arrival, maintained station east of the Solomons for several days.

Adm. Chester W. Nimitz, commander of the U.S. Pacific Fleet, then ordered Halsey's force back to Pearl Harbor, where it arrived on May 26, 1942. Two days later, it was back out at sea but under a new commander. Halsey had been hospitalized with a skin infection and had been replaced by Rear Adm. Raymond A. Spruance. It was he who led *Enterprise* and *Hornet* with their sailors and airmen out of Pearl Harbor on the 28th on an unknown mission that might have a decisive influence on the course of the war in the Pacific. Two days later Fletcher, flying his flag in *Yorktown* — to which three months of repairs had incredibly been made in three days — left Pearl Harbor for a rendezvous with Spruance, which was accomplished on June 2.

Floyd Craven was aboard *Enterprise* as well. Having been restricted from all liberty during the ship's two brief stints in Oahu — that was Lieutenant Best's continued punishment for sneaking out the last time — he was relieved to go back to sea. Perhaps if they stayed out long enough, some statute of limitations might form in Best's mind and Floyd might get his next possible liberty. On the other hand, with such short spaces between cruises, if Floyd didn't hurry and "serve enough time," Best might have him locked up during liberty until 1943.

Truthfully, though, liberty was the last thing on Floyd's mind as he sat in his cabin, walked the decks, and flew patrol missions. Many of *Enterprise*'s fliers were green, just out of flight school, and feeling as if they owned the world. Floyd had been one of them once, but his memories of that time had long since faded into a distant recollection. Slowly but surely, his freewheeling, irresponsible character had given way to a morose, wary spirit hardened by the reality of war. The transformation had begun during the Pearl Harbor attack and had not reversed since. Even his March rebellion had been born out of frustration and grief over too much loss with such little gain. But his vices had ceased to become methods of recreation and had instead become defense mechanisms against depression. He took no part in the rowdy crowing over Honolulu liberty activities, not only because he had not had anything to crow about for months, but because he was more aware than his junior comrades that death lay over the horizon.

They had all heard the announcements from Admiral Spruance that *Enterprise, Hornet,* and *Yorktown*, with their attendant cruisers and destroyers, had been dispatched to intercept a Japanese invasion force bound for Midway, a coral atoll northwest of Hawaii that served as an American airbase. Its loss would be more devastating than that of Wake, and Admiral Nimitz's intelligence staff had determined that the Japanese force including four or five flattops sought not only to capture Midway but to destroy the United States Pacific Fleet in the process. This would all supposedly take place while a second Japanese force bore down on Alaska's Aleutian Islands in hopes of convincing Nimitz to split his forces and, therefore, make victory at Midway even more certain.

How Naval Intelligence had figured any of this out was beyond Floyd's comprehension. Recently promoted Lt. (j.g.) Harry Giles didn't even know. Somehow, Nimitz had gained access to the entire Japanese battle plan and had sent out his three remaining carriers (*Saratoga* was undergoing repairs in San Diego) to stop the Imperial Navy. Spruance and Fletcher's rendezvous station had been christened "Point Luck," and lay some 325 miles northeast of Midway. From there the carriers circled and launched round-the-clock patrols that were supplemented by PBY Catalinas flying from Midway. The element of surprise would be essential to the success of this mission. Outnumbered in every category of ship, from carriers to submarines, Spruance and Fletcher needed every advantage they could get.

Two Japanese fleets — one being the actual invasion force and the other being the carrier force — loomed somewhere in the waters west of Midway, presumably unaware that the Americans were waiting for them. If they just happened to trip across the American fleet, however, the American carriers would be easy pickings for the Japanese battleships. All of the American battleships not sunk at Pearl Harbor now cruised off California, and they were too slow to keep up with the carriers, so Nimitz had kept them at home. This battle, like the Coral Sea, would have to be an aviator's battle. If it devolved into a surface clash, the destruction of the Pacific Fleet was a mathematical certainty.

This grim outlook charged Floyd with low-key excitement. Here was the challenge for which he had been waiting for months. The Doolittle Raid had been a moral victory, but it had not dealt a decisive blow to the Japanese home islands, and what blows had been dealt had been thrown by the Army flyboys at that. All the naval aviators could claim to have accomplished was the sinking of several small patrol boats, which to Floyd seemed to be nothing out of the ordinary. This Midway operation, though, this was the real McCoy. There were Japanese carriers out there, and Floyd was itching to get them. Yes, with the prospect of an epic battle came the enlarged specter of death, but Floyd was more occupied with making certain the Grim Reaper spent most of his time in the Japanese field than with worrying that the ghostly agriculturalist's scythe might be hooking itself over his own shoulder. That was why SBDs had rear gunners.

Air Group Six's pilots ate breakfast around 1:30 a.m. on June 4. Reports of contact with the Japanese had been streaming in from Midway's Catalina flying boats for nearly 24 hours, and they and some Army B-17s had bombed the invasion force several times, claiming extraordinary success against heavy gunnery ships and transports. None of Spruance's or Fletcher's fliers or the Midway searchers spotted the Japanese carriers, however. Air Group Six manned its planes twice overnight — and after breakfast — only to be recalled to the ready rooms. Much grumbling ensued and rumors spread that the original orders had been given by Spruance's chief of staff, the testy Capt. Miles Browning, but had been rescinded by Spruance himself. That Browning had been Halsey's chief of staff and that Spruance, unlike Halsey, was not an aviator had led many of the men to doubt

Spruance's judgment versus Browning's. It was not so much Spruance's judgment that mattered; it was more Fletcher's since he held tactical command over both carrier task forces. When the PBYs finally sighted the Japanese flattops around 6 a.m., it was he who ordered Spruance to send *Enterprise* and *Hornet* to the southwest in pursuit while *Yorktown* tarried in order to recover her search planes.

At 6:07, a blaring alarm sounded on *Enterprise,* and the unseen voice declared, *"Now general quarters. Man your battle stations."* With a few parting intelligence reminders from Giles and encouragement from Best, Bombing Six's pilots clambered out of the ready room for the third time and boarded their aircraft. Floyd walked across the bustling flight deck at a sharp, business-like pace while the greenhorns around him dashed off to battle with the exuberance of a high school football team, despite the fact that they were launching at the outer edge of their fuel radius with slim chances of survival.

Their launch was a complete roll of the dice by Spruance. Those crews that the Japanese did not shoot down in the attack would barely have enough gasoline to make it back to their carriers. Floyd and all the pilots and crewmen in the group knew the odds but they took off anyway. They had no other choice, for this was why they had become naval aviators.

The morning of the Fourth of June was a gorgeous one. Clear skies ensured visibility of 35 to 40 miles over a calm, flawless blue sea, and temperatures hung near 70 degrees Fahrenheit with a light breeze out of the east. Despite the beautiful scenery, Floyd was not encouraged. *Enterprise* and *Hornet* had to reverse course to steer into the wind and launch the planes, and what's more, the ships had to speed up to do so, which meant the range between them and the Japanese carriers only increased while the air groups went airborne. Meanwhile, Floyd's fuel tank lightened considerably as his plane and those that took off ahead of his orbited for an hour waiting for the rest of Bombing Six, Lt. Earl Gallaher's Scouting Six, and their fighter escorts to form up. The air group commander, Lt. Cdr. Clarence Wade McClusky, then led the two dive-bomber squadrons off on their own. They would need to climb to 20,000 feet, and the slower TBD Devastators of Lt. Cdr. Eugene Lindsey's Torpedo Six could catch up by the time the SBDs reached that altitude.

Floyd donned his oxygen mask as the formation passed 14,000 feet. An hour later, they overflew the predicted course of the Japanese fleet. Floyd looked out the left side of the canopy and spied Midway in the distance, marked on the horizon by a pillar of smoke that extended far above the bomber formation's altitude.

"Take a look out to port, Schumaker," he instructed his gunner. "Looks like the Japs beat us to Midway, or at least their planes did."

The teenaged gunner replied with a low whistle. "Holy mackerel. Midway's 175 miles from here," he announced.

"Yeah, and that smoke probably reaches up to five miles," Floyd replied, marveling that he could see Midway from a distance roughly equal to that between Springdale and Little Rock, which would require several hours of driving over winding mountain roads to cover.

The insertion of aircraft into naval warfare had expanded battlefields exponentially. The Coral Sea had been the first battle in which opposing ships had never sighted each other, and now not quite a month later, Midway could become the second. Even an aviator like Floyd struggled to comprehend the radical shift, and he could only imagine the upheaval taking place within the minds of surface officers who were attempting to define the roles of their gunnery ships in this new type of sea war. Their jobs could very well be limited to shooting down enemy airplanes, a job which Floyd hoped they performed well on this day so that *Enterprise* would still be there when he returned.

He turned his attention back to the airspace in front of him and looked up to his right just in time to see an Army B-17 streak across and above his flight path, likely on its way back to Midway from a patrol. Floyd's eyes followed the bomber as it lay four white contrails in the open sky behind it. Then the contrails flashed above him, and the B-17 disappeared from sight.

Floyd glanced down at the map clipped to his kneeboard. They had reached the point where they were supposed to bank to the northwest, but McClusky, far ahead, and Best, just ahead and to the right, kept on flying for better than a quarter hour. Then McClusky finally edged his SBD into a right turn, and the rest of the dive bombers followed.

"Sir, where are we going?" Schumaker, who had been quiet up until that point, inquired from the rear seat. "Shouldn't we have made that turn a long time ago?"

Floyd sighed. "I don't know where we are going anymore, and yes, we should have made that turn a long time ago. I'm sure Commander McClusky knows what he's doing, though. If the Japs are out here, he'll find 'em."

"I hope he finds them before they find us. I haven't seen hide nor hair of our fighters since we left *Enterprise*. Where are those morons anyway?"

"Your guess is as good as mine, Schumaker. Maybe they made the turn behind us. Who knows?"

Events began to climax rapidly at that point. McClusky had turned because he had just spotted the stark, white wake of a lone Japanese destroyer making a speedy beeline to the northeast. He had directed the group to follow him as he followed the ship, supposing that it was headed back to the Japanese carrier fleet.

After the turn, Floyd suddenly began to feel light-headed. He closed his eyes and looked down toward his lap. The plane had not encountered any turbulence and the turn had been a gentle bank, but he was inexplicably dizzy nonetheless.

"Sir, I'm having trouble breathing," Schumaker called forward to him.

"Are you feeling woozy?" Floyd asked back.

"Gosh, yes, sir. I haven't felt this bad since the morning after my last night out in Honolulu."

"I thought you Cajun boys could handle hangovers better than that," Floyd quipped wearily.

Schumaker was in no joking mood. "I think it's our oxygen, sir. I think our tanks are running out," he panted. "Do something, please."

"Now just stay calm, you hear? Use the Morse key to tell the skipper and have him take us down to 15,000."

"Okay."

Floyd was already nosing his plane that direction when he heard Schumaker begin tapping out the message. Best obligingly dropped in altitude and soon the entire squadron was flying below and slightly ahead of McClusky.

Then they saw the enemy carriers. There were three of them, set out in a triangular formation. Two carriers were sailing side-by-side ahead, and the third followed behind and between the other two. Their escort ships were sprinkled about, sailing uncoordinated in all directions, leaving twisting, white wakes in their paths. Floyd viewed this scene with no context whatsoever. He had no inkling that all three American torpedo squadrons had just assailed the Japanese carrier force, and that all three had been nearly wiped out.

Lt. Cdr. John C. Waldron's Torpedo Eight from *Hornet* had been the first to strike, about an hour earlier around 9:30.

The Japanese combat air patrol and anti-aircraft batteries had shredded the low, slow formation. All 15 of Torpedo Eight's planes splashed, and only a handful managed to release their payloads. A single pilot, Ens. George Gay of Houston, Texas, escaped and spent the rest of the battle floating in the middle of the Japanese fleet. As for Bombing Eight and Fighting Eight, they missed the battle altogether. They made a left turn where Waldron had made a right, and most crashed from lack of fuel while attempting to return to *Hornet*.

No sooner had the last of Waldron's gallant fliers sunk beneath the waves into eternity, than Gene Lindsey's *Enterprise* squadron hovered in. The Japanese commander, Vice Adm. Chuichi Nagumo, now realized that an earlier reconnaissance report of a single American carrier near Midway had been an underestimate. This many torpedo bombers could not have originated from only one ship, which meant that he just might have stumbled into an American trap.

The Navy torpedo bombers had not been the first to visit Nagumo's fleet that morning. Army B-17s and B-26s and Navy and Marine Corps torpedo bombers flying from Midway had attacked earlier and been driven off without scoring any hits. This strike had prompted Nagumo to take the advice of the pilot who had led the bombing of Midway and prepare for a second attack that would subdue the atoll's defenses completely. While the returning planes of the Midway strike were still inbound, however, a pilot of the floatplane from the cruiser *Tone* informed Nagumo that he had sighted an American naval formation. Some minutes later, he updated his report by saying that he saw a carrier as well.

Nagumo had then switched plans. He decided to stop arming his aircraft for a second Midway attack and begin preparing them to attack the American carrier. Now, as his anti-aircraft guns began barking away at Lindsey's squadron, he knew there was at least one more American carrier somewhere in the vicinity.

Nagumo still had no immediate need to be concerned, however. Lindsey's pilots, every bit as brave as Waldron's but their aircraft every bit as lumbering and vulnerable, succumbed one after another to bursts of flak and streams of machine-gun bullets. Banking over like crippled ducks, they smoked and flamed their ways into the sea in clouds of fire and saltwater spray. Five aircraft dropped their torpedoes and made good their escapes. Lindsey's plane was not among them, and neither was that of Floyd's fellow Arkansan, Paul J. Riley of Hot Springs.

If Lindsey's attack had unsettled Nagumo, the attack of *Yorktown*'s Torpedo Three led by Lt. Cdr. Lance E. Massey did nothing to ease his anxiety. At least three American carriers sailed unseen in the distance, and no matter how unsuccessful their attacks had been thus far, they still posed a mortal threat to him as long as they remained hidden behind the horizon. Massey led his TBDs in according to the manner of Waldron and Lindsey and met the same horrible fate. Two TBDs and only three crew members survived after dropping their torpedoes.

For all this sacrifice, the Americans had nothing to show for it. Seventy airmen, including the three squadron commanders, were dead, and not a single torpedo had found its mark. Unbeknownst to Nagumo, however, McClusky's SBDs were even then approaching unnoticed more than three miles above, readying to pounce and avenge their slain comrades more than eightyfold.

Floyd heard Best call to McClusky over the radio: *"I'm attacking according to doctrine; my lead planes will strike the far target, my trailing ones will attack the near one."* Apparently, the third carrier to the east was none of their concern.

Floyd understood these orders and fell into column behind Best and his other wingman. There was a flash of blue metal from above, and before Floyd knew what was happening, he saw McClusky's and Gallaher's bombers plunge directly in front of Best's aircraft, dragging the rest of Scouting Six behind them. Best protested angrily over the mike, but the air group commander was already well into his dive on the nearest carrier.

"Victor Baker Six, reform," Best called to his squadron.

Still in the proper position, Floyd quickly checked around him and saw that everyone behind him had headed off after McClusky.

"I think they all followed Scouting Six, Mr. Best," Floyd explained. "I'm still back here, though."

"Good!" Best replied, still clearly annoyed at the foul-up. *"Listen, we're going to take that far carrier, okay?"*

"Wilco."

The dive flaps on the two leading planes opened, cuing Floyd to pull the lever in his cockpit. In the same manner as always, the aircraft decelerated almost to the point where Floyd felt it was just creeping along, hanging onto the air.

"Ready, Schumaker?" he asked his gunner.

"I was born ready, Mr. Craven, and I don't see any Jap fighters yet."

"They'll be around soon enough, I'm sure. Just keep your eyes peeled. When they come, they'll probably come out of the sun."

As a trained gunner, Schumaker already knew that and had already shifted in his seat to face the eastern sky.

"Hang on!" Floyd called out as he nosed the plane over into its dive.

Best's and the other aircraft had already disappeared out of sight, and Floyd picked them up again as he reached his dive angle of 70 degrees. The squadron leader and wingman were far below him, just specks really. Below them lay a Japanese carrier, its deck painted bright yellow and the biggest, reddest rising sun any dive bomber could have ever hoped to have as a target painted on the bow end of the oblong flight deck.

Floyd hung in his seat harness, suspended in a state of near-zero-gravity and patiently lined the flattop up in his scope. What a beautiful, magnificent target! This was no minesweeper or flying boat. This was a real-life, honest-to-goodness Jap carrier crammed with machinery, humanity, ammunition, and fuel. Here was a ship that had launched its planes against Pearl Harbor and against Darwin, killing thousands in the process. Now Dick Best, Floyd Craven, and the other pilot in column were seconds away from knocking this mighty vessel out of the war.

Floyd wondered when the Zero fighters would come streaking in. Surely they wouldn't concede such a precious ship without a fight. The anti-aircraft gunners on the carrier and in the screen certainly were not going to. As Floyd's ears popped with the rapidly increasing pressure, anti-aircraft shells popped around his plane, jostling it slightly but never threatening it. He could see the yellow flashes of the guns and could tell that the Japanese sailors were throwing everything they had at the dive bombers. Again, he had no knowledge of the three torpedo attacks they had shattered in the previous hour — the last one just minutes before — nor of the terrific panic the Japanese experienced when on the heels of those heroic, suicidal strikes another one came from straight above. And the Zeros were all still skimming the surface, like birds of prey circling the crumpled metal carcasses of the dead TBDs. They would be of no assistance until the American dive bombers reached the ends of their runs, at which point all the anti-aircraft gunners might be dead.

Feeling a rush of adrenaline he had never before experienced while flying or racing, Floyd bore down on the target as it churned on through the ocean, leaving a foaming wake in its path. He began to see the distinctive shapes of individual aircraft waiting to take off among the white huddle of planes gathered like a flock of geese on the fantail. He could see the deck crewmen racing about, dashing for cover, looking for some place of shelter aboard ship that might not be struck by one of the Americans' thousand-pound bombs.

Best let his bomb go, and then his wingman followed suit. They both pulled sharply out of their dives and out of Floyd's sight while he waited to see their results before releasing his own bomb. Best's thousand-pounder burst with a terrific flash in front of the carrier's bridge, igniting a tremendous fireball and punching a gaping, ragged hole in the flight deck. The second bomb struck at the head of the aircraft formation, exploding brilliantly in the same manner as the first had.

Floyd glanced at the altimeter in front of him. The needle spun down past 2,500 feet toward 2,000. He waited until that point and then let her rip. The SBD lightened, and fighting G-forces and his body's urge to black out, Floyd pulled his plane into a sharp climb, retracted the dive flaps, and craned his neck over his shoulder for a look.

The ball of fire appeared over the carrier's fantail in an instant, completely obliterating the formation of parked planes. The bomb's explosives, the fuel in tanks of the aircraft, their armaments, and goodness knew what belowdecks all seemed to go up at once in the most massive blast Floyd had ever seen. Large wood splinters, chunks of airplanes and deck equipment, and men and parts of men all streaked out into space, some trailing smoke and flame behind them and then splashing down into the sea like oversized pieces of hail plunging into a hot spring. A cloud of fire roared hungrily across the deck and over the water, overtaking everything in its way before it metamorphosed into a roiling mass of scorching black smoke that passed astern as the tormented ship raced at full steam to escape its smothering embrace.

Schumaker reacted ecstatically, lapsing into unintelligible Cajun. *"Key awau! Gardez dont ça!"* he shrieked. "You pasted her good, Mr. Craven!"

The sight was the most thrilling and horrible thing Floyd had ever seen. He only viewed it for a few seconds, but those few seconds would remain embossed on his mind for the rest of his life.

"I can see that!" he responded with perhaps a little more exuberance than he felt. In fact, he was in something of a state of shock. He had many times imagined what a hit on a capital ship would look like, and those images paled in comparison with the real thing. He would be a hero when the folks back home heard about this. How would he ever describe it to them? How *could* he? And would they believe him?

Allowing one more second's glimpse of his terrible handiwork, Floyd looked ahead again, brought the plane back into level flight, and focused on the daunting task of making it back to *Enterprise* before getting swatted from the sky by the screening ships' anti-aircraft fire or the Zeros that now zipped in from all quarters to claim the SBDs as they had the TBDs.

"The other two flattops are burning, too!" Schumaker exclaimed from the rear seat.

Floyd swiveled his neck around to see. "Both of them?" he asked incredulously as he saw, true to Schumaker's word, columns of smoke emanating from the other two carriers. "Who got the third one?"

"It wasn't Scouting Six, I can tell you that," came the reply. "I saw another column diving out to the east while we were on the way down. It must have been a squadron from *Hornet* or *Yorktown*.

Floyd shook his head. It was all too incredible. They had sailed thousands of miles from Oahu under radio silence to stop a Japanese fleet from invading Midway, and it now seemed as if everything had gone just as planned. The wrong turns and the likelihood that every SBD would run out of fuel before reaching the rendezvous point with *Enterprise* notwithstanding, they had accomplished all they had set out to accomplish in dizzying fashion by giving the Japanese a staggering wallop. Floyd and Schumaker could not celebrate just yet, however. They still had to make it out through the cruiser-destroyer screen and the combat air patrol. They might die yet, but at least they would die victoriously.

CHAPTER TWENTY-TWO

Sitting inside the air plotting room aboard *Enterprise* hundreds of miles away from the Japanese fleet, Harry Giles could not observe the action that began to unfold around 9:30 with the torpedo attacks and culminated around 10:30 with the dive-bombing strike. He could hear only garbled chatter that provided no news as to whether or not the Japanese carriers had been sighted yet. Not until 9:52 did Fighting Six's commander, Lt. James Gray, report that he had sighted the Japanese carrier force. There were no transmissions from Gene Lindsey, whose squadron Gray was supposed to be escorting, or from any of the other American squadrons. The distance was simply too great.

Unseen up on the flag bridge, Capt. Miles Browning belted out, *"Attack! I say again, ATTACK!"* to McClusky, whose voice was heard for the first time giving a cool, sarcastic, profane reply to Browning to the effect that he would attack as soon as he found the carriers.

For some reason, Giles clearly heard the dive-bombing attack over the radio, though it was difficult to decipher the frantic, high-pitched broadcasts from the young pilots. From one joyful shriek to another, Giles pieced together that McClusky's dive bombers were having a banner day. Incredulous curses and boisterous exclamations poured from the loudspeaker. Giles, the other officers in the plot, and the telephone-headset-wearing enlisted men seated at the radar scopes and standing with grease pencils in hand in front of the plexiglass charts exchanged nervous, uncertain glances. Could they be sure that the gleeful shouts were not actually tortured screams of dying pilots? Could they have really fallen upon the Jap carriers and been as successful as they sounded? It seemed too good to be true, and nobody in the plot wanted to be the first to celebrate.

Giles would have to see for himself when the aircraft returned. He made certain to be standing by the railing on the island overlooking the flight deck when the first flights came back in. The TBDs appeared first, but whereas 14 had taken off that morning, only three returned. Gray's Wildcat fighters winged in missing just one of their number. Then the SBDs began to appear, Gallaher's and Best's fliers mixed together in a random assortment. Many had already splashed down from lack of fuel, partly because Spruance's staff had miscalculated Point Option — where the planes were supposed to meet the carriers — by failing to factor in their carriers' frequent course reversals to the east for launching and recovering search aircraft.

The SBDs each bore a stenciled tail number identifying their squadrons, so Giles was able to differentiate between Bombing Six's and Scouting Six's aircraft once they landed. One after another floated in over the fantail and bounced onto the wooden deck. Their tailhooks snagged the arresting cables stretched from port to starboard, and the planes jerked to a halt, after which their crew members pulled themselves up out of their low seats and descended to the deck while plane handlers wheeled the bombers out of the landing path. Giles counted up to ten aircraft and began considering the odds that his friend Floyd had survived. Thirty-seven SBDs from the two squadrons had taken off. How many of them could have made it through safely considering the attrition suffered by Lindsey's squadron? And even then, word was trickling in from *Hornet* and *Yorktown* of the tremendous slaughter of their torpedo planes and crews.

An 11th and a 12th plane landed. Giles leaned against the railing and strained his eyes to make out the tail numbers and shook his head sadly when he saw that they belonged to Scouting Six. Looking skyward again he saw a pair of SBDs approaching from the wrong side, against established landing doctrine. The first plane touched down, and Giles immediately recognized Dick Best. The squadron commander's plane was towed clear and the second plane thumped the deck. Giles' spirits rose. Again, he needed not wait for the pilot to emerge for he recognized Floyd immediately.

In all, 19 SBDs returned, just over half the number McClusky had led away that morning. Up to 36 pilots and gunners might be dead, though many were certainly floating on rafts waiting to be rescued by a destroyer or a Catalina. Some might be unfortunate enough to be picked up by the Japanese, while others might never be found at all. Giles raced down to the ready room to begin his debriefings of the pilots.

The General Quarters alarm sounded suddenly as Floyd trotted off the deck and into the island. He backtracked and stepped outside the hatch again to see what was going on. Anti-aircraft gunners were scurrying to their battle stations, and word quickly spread that *Yorktown*, barely visible to the northwest, had fallen under attack. Floyd stood by the threshold of the hatch as the aircraft handlers rushed to push the last planes over to the elevators, which then whisked them below to the hangar deck. Moments later, the elevators rose with Wildcats on them, fueled and armed for combat. Their crews hurriedly manned the aircraft and took off to protect *Yorktown*. They had not even finished taking off when Floyd noticed a column of smoke appear above the other carrier, making it appear that the ship had been hit. He ducked back inside, where his assumption was verified by the ready room teletype machine, which spat out the news that *Yorktown* had taken three bombs.

With Floyd's arrival, the gathering of Bombing Six survivors was complete, and Giles began asking for their testimonies of the attack one at a time. The depositions ranged from ecstatically hyperbolic to somber. Floyd maintained a cool exterior, casually puffing on a cigarette as he described his aircraft's victorious dive and escape from the Japanese combat air patrol. It was all he could do to remain professional. He was physically and mentally sapped, and he had to lean against the bulkhead and hold onto something to keep the tremors in his hands and legs concealed. Driving a race car was nothing like piloting a dive bomber over an aircraft carrier, and after this experience, he figured he might never race again. It simply would not be thrilling enough anymore.

The debriefing ended shortly, and Floyd quickly sought out Best.

"Mr. Best," he addressed his skipper, "I want to thank you for not grounding me back in March. I wouldn't trade that mission we just had for anything in the world."

Laugh lines appeared on Best's face, but the lieutenant didn't crack a smile. "Good," he replied a bit hoarsely, "because we're heading out again after that fourth Jap flattop that just hit *Yorktown*. Commander McClusky's wounded, so Gallaher's taking the lead. You need to follow me down to Air Operations right now."

Floyd, as worn out as he was, could not help but grin at being given a chance to bomb another enemy carrier. "Aye-aye, sir," he responded with a twinkle in his eye and then placed the cigarette back in his mouth.

Giles walked up and patted his friend on the shoulder. "What was it like, Floyd?"

Floyd mashed the cigarette into a nearby ashtray and began his response as they ducked through the interior hatch to go to the plotting room. "Unlike anything I ever imagined. The dive was just like any other — stomach-churning, heart-racing, all that. But watching that Jap blow up ... that was just incredible. I think the other fellas described it better than I could. I've never killed that many people at once before either."

"And now you're gonna go do it again."

Floyd chuckled bitterly. "Yup. Better them than us."

Giles nodded agreeably. "That's why we're fighting this war."

In the air plotting room, the pilots from Scouting Six, Bombing Six, and the refugee SBD squadrons from *Yorktown* composed a plan to attack the fourth Japanese carrier, which was believed to be sailing north of the three that had been hit earlier in the morning. They took off without fighter escort shortly after 3:30 p.m. and reached the enemy flattop at 5. This ship was ready and waiting for them, twisting madly at full speed beneath the 24 plunging SBDs and throwing up a storm of flak at 20,000 feet. The six Zeros flying combat air patrol were dealt with easily, though one downed Best's right-side wingman. As Floyd's bomber dove lower, the anti-aircraft fire grew more intense. The muzzle flashes ringed the carrier's deck like candles, and he wondered if the sailors below were even using small arms to shoot at him and his comrades. All of the screening vessels, including a battleship, contributed to the fusillade, which decreased in some intensity once the carrier began taking hits that were just as devastating as those suffered earlier by her sister ships. The increased opposition compared with that of the morning attack spooked Floyd a bit and he accidentally released his bomb early. Pulling out of the dive, he zipped through the enemy formation without looking back, listening with dismay to Schumaker's report of their miss.

Floyd followed Best west out of the combat zone. They then flew south until they could see the funeral pyres of the other three flattops before banking back to the east and returning to *Enterprise* alive, elated, and absolutely exhausted. Floyd's hunger for a real battle had been satiated in most dramatic fashion. Fully satisfied with his accomplishments, he slept well the night of the fourth and awoke on Friday the fifth ready to fly more missions. Spruance, having retreated during Thursday night to avoid a disastrous nighttime clash with the Japanese battle fleet, held back until Friday evening. Floyd and his comrades flew unfruitful search missions that night to the end of their planes' fuel capacities and were only saved from ditching when Spruance made the bold decision to illuminate his carriers with searchlights, thereby exposing them to submarine attack but also allowing his fliers to make safe landings. Saturday, *Enterprise* and *Hornet* launched again, and the SBDs bagged a Japanese cruiser. By the close of that day, even Floyd needed a break from action, something he had never believed he would need, and he longed for liberty in Honolulu more than ever.

The Battle of Midway turned out to be a remarkable reversal of fortune for both the United States and Japan. The Midway invasion thrust had been crushed, and along with it, the greater portion of Japan's naval air arm. The Aleutian diversion had succeeded in occupying the isolated Alaskan islands of Attu and Kiska, but that minor Japanese accomplishment had no bearing on the bigger strategic situation. Midway had been a Japanese disaster, plain and simple. Four carriers — *Akagi, Kaga, Soryu,* and *Hiryu* — all veterans of Pearl Harbor, had been sunk. American dive bombers sank a heavy cruiser two days later as the Japanese force withdrew. Admiral Nimitz's intelligence windfall had proven to be worth every week the Navy codebreakers on Oahu had spent deciphering the Japanese naval codes. Admiral Spruance, meanwhile, had solidified his standing as a top-rate task force commander. Greater assignments lay in store for him in the future.

Not all the news was good, however. *Yorktown,* after taking aerial bomb and torpedo hits on June 4, was torpedoed again by a Japanese submarine on June 6. The destroyer *Hammann,* idling alongside *Yorktown,* lending assistance, took a torpedo as well and sank with heavy loss of life. *Yorktown* finally sank the next morning, and despite the smashing defeat of Japan's carrier forces, the United States Navy's carrier arm was temporarily left with only *Enterprise* and *Hornet* in operational condition. *Saratoga* soon returned to duty, and *Wasp* transferred to the Pacific from the Atlantic Fleet. All four of these carriers would have major roles to play in the remaining months of 1942 as the fighting again shifted southward, toward Australia. Within two months of the victory at Midway, the name of another theretofore obscure Pacific island — Guadalcanal — was admitted to the glossary of war, and by the time the struggle there ended, its entry would be one of the longest.

CHAPTER TWENTY-THREE

Danny Wright stood on the starboard bridge wing of the U.S.S. *Quincy* and scanned the jungle. The lush vegetation yards away seemed so close that Danny could reach out and grab a fistful of leaves. The Panama Canal truly was a world wonder, he thought. No wider than a large creek at some points or a moderate-sized lake at others, it ushered the largest ships in the world from the Atlantic Ocean to the Pacific Ocean in a few hours. Just a few decades before, *Quincy* and her companions — the aircraft carrier *Wasp*, just back from the Mediterranean, new battleship *North Carolina*, light cruiser *San Juan*, and seven destroyers — would have been doomed to a monthlong crawl around the southern tip of South America in order to reach San Diego. Now, she could sail from New York to San Diego in just two weeks. Having departed New York on June 5, *Quincy* should have been able to make California on June 19. After that, no one aboard had a credible opinion as to where the *New Orleans*-class heavy cruiser was headed next, though all hands reckoned they would soon be sent to tangle with the Imperial Japanese Navy.

Prior to Danny's arrival two months before — while *Quincy* lay in the New York Navy Yard for a well-earned overhaul — the warship had conquered the heavy seas of the North Atlantic winter in the hostile waters around Newfoundland, Iceland, and Greenland. The veterans among her crew had passed along many hair-raising tales of those long trips escorting supply convoys between Canada and Great Britain, but from the sound of it, the weather had been a more threatening enemy than the vaunted German U-boats.

Danny dared not discount the U-boats, however. He knew full well that since Germany had declared war on the United States on December 8, 1941, the German submarines had been picking off American and British cargo ships and tankers like lame deer in waters within sight of American beaches. From Galveston, Texas, to Jacksonville, Florida, and from Jacksonville to New York City itself, the enemy dominated the littorals, all while Danny and his fellow sailors whiled away their time in the city. Many nights, while standing along the shorelines of Manhattan, Brooklyn, or even Coney Island while visiting its theme park, Danny and his friends had been able to watch torpedo attacks in the distance. The unarmed merchant ships would be invisible until a German torpedo struck, sending a flare of orange flame skyward and announcing to all the helpless people ashore that another American vessel had fallen prey to the wolf packs. Daylight often revealed wreckage, oily water, and scattered bodies washing up on the shores of Long Island.

The war had not yet risen to Danny's expectations. In fact, he had not really known what to expect. He had certainly never imagined German submarines operating so close to America's coast, using the lights of her own bustling cities to silhouette their creeping, hapless targets.

Danny was learning about the world and about war slowly and uneasily. Growing up, he had rarely ever left Arkansas, even though both Missouri and Oklahoma lay less than 50 miles away. As an average student at Springdale

High School, he had been fairly unambitious and largely unconcerned with the quandaries of human existence, save for the need to learn algebra. His imagined future had taken him no further east than the edge of Washington County, no further south than the Arkansas River, and no further west than the Oklahoma line. Little Rock may as well have been in another state. If he suddenly became possessed to become a real journeyman, he might find his way up north to Kansas City someday, but not if his mother could help it. Swinging towns did not suit Antonia Wright's style.

New York was quite the swinging town, however, possessing a whole host of temptations and vices that never had been tolerated in Springdale, and never would be in the Wright household. Danny's strict, Italian Catholic-raised mother and austere but loving father had trained him too well for him to disappoint them on his first excursion away from home. Of course, there were a few men at home who had been enticed away from moral living by booze and women, but they were generally outcasts. A few were younger men like the smooth-talking, fast-driving Floyd Craven, who had chased Elaine for years and almost gotten himself shot by Douglas Wright more than once.

As humiliating as life with a big sister could be, Danny could not help but smile every time he thought of Elaine. She had declined Floyd's advances with politeness and grace, and then spent hours in her room crying because she was so embarrassed to be given so much attention by such a, to use her word, "creep." But he had eventually given up on her for easier girls, and though he and Elaine had run into each other at the university in Fayetteville from time to time, he had soon joined the Navy and, last Danny had heard, learned to be a pilot. Ironically enough, Elaine had gone on to marry another naval officer, and the Christian Preston Brown was everything Floyd Craven was not. And now, in a multiplication of that irony, all four of them were caught up in the middle of this war. Preston was either dead or in a Japanese prison camp, Elaine was waiting for him in western Australia, Floyd was flying with the fleet somewhere in the Pacific bombing enemy ships no doubt, and Danny himself was now on his way to the war zone.

A crazy thing this war, Danny thought to himself, watching a flock of tropical birds flit from one tree to another. What other type of insanity would bring enemy submarines to the mouth of New York Harbor, take an Arkansas boy to Panama, make his older sister a widow-in-waiting in Australia, and turn Springdale's black sheep into a war hero? So much upheaval had taken place in his life and in the world already, and the promise of more filled him with a sense of foreboding. He had a compelling feeling that when — if — he returned to Arkansas, nothing would be as he had remembered.

The perky jingle of a bicycle bell caught Preston's attention from the inside of his barracks one afternoon. As usual, Bicycle Camp was nearly deserted, with the enlisted men being out and about Batavia in the *kumis*, or labor parties, that the Japanese had organized. He strolled casually to the doorway and saw the young Dutch navy wife standing over her bicycle by the fence across the yard. She saw him and waved discreetly. Preston stepped cautiously onto the porch and looked both directions before approaching the fence.

Still casting wary glances over both shoulders, Preston walked up to her with a smile on his face. "Boy, am I glad to see you," he greeted her.

"Good afternoon," the woman replied with a grin. "I brought the Bible you asked for." With that she withdrew a brown paper bundle from the basket mounted on her handlebars. "Unfortunately," she commented as she held it with two hands, "it's bigger than a chocolate bar, and I don't think it will fit through the fence."

"Just toss it over," Preston instructed her coolly. "The Lord won't mind."

The young woman giggled slightly. "No, I suppose He won't." She then proceeded to scoot a couple of feet away from the fence and heave the bundle overhand over the top of the high fence. The spontaneous ease with which she accomplished the task surprised Preston, and reminded him of Elaine's resourcefulness as he hauled in the load. His wife, it seemed, could do anything at any time and in any place, regardless of whether she actually knew how to or not.

"Nice throw," he complimented the woman as he unwrapped the package and observed a mildly-worn, black-leather Bible. A loose sheet of paper protruded from its center.

"Thank you. I marked a passage for you with that piece of paper," she informed him. "I hope it will encourage you. The Lord has used it to encourage me and give me hope for my husband."

"How is your husband?" Preston inquired. "Have you heard anything about him?"

The Dutchwoman's blue eyes glistened. "Yes, he's alive, but he's a prisoner as well. I don't know where he is. He was last seen in Soerabaja."

"I will pray for both of you," Preston told her.

"Thank you. And I am praying for you. Do you have a wife?"

"Yes. She was in Australia the last I saw her."

"Does she know what happened to you?"

"Possibly."

"Then I will pray for her as well. I will pray that God will give her peace."

"Thank you," Preston replied softly. "Tell me, what's your name?"

"Rika Postuma."

"And your husband's?"

"Sebastiaan."

"If I ever hear anything about him, I will let you know," Preston told her. "And if I ever see him, I will let him know you're okay and tell him how you've helped me."

Rika beamed. "That would be wonderful. What is your name?"

"Preston Brown. My wife's name is Elaine." Preston checked their surroundings once again. "Listen, you'd better get out of here before a guard comes along like last time."

"Okay," Rika responded and climbed back onto her bike.

"Thank you again for the Bible," Preston called after her as she began to pedal away.

"You're very welcome," came the reply.

Preston didn't waste any time returning to the barracks. He hurried to his bunk and opened the Bible to the page Rika had marked. It was in the book of Jeremiah, and he saw a passage underlined in blue pencil, chapter 29, verses 11 through 14.

For I know the thoughts that I think toward you, saith the LORD, thoughts of peace, and not of evil, to give you an expected end. Then shall ye call upon me, and ye shall go and pray unto me, and I will hearken unto you. And ye shall seek me, and find me, when ye shall search for me with all your heart. And I will be found of you, saith the LORD: and I will turn away your captivity, and I will gather you from all the nations, and from all the places whither I have driven you, saith the LORD; and I will bring you again into the place whence I caused you to be carried away captive.

Though God had spoken those words to the Hebrews in Babylonian captivity thousands of years earlier, Preston felt as if they had been spoken directly to him. Of course, he knew that being a believer in Christ did not guarantee him a comfortable life and freedom from crises, but there it was in black and white, a promise from the Lord that Preston would see the end of this trial. No timeframe was given, and the struggle was likely to be long, but Preston knew he would endure as long as he kept his eyes on God in this place that, without people like Rika, would seem God-forsaken. No specific part of the passage assured him that Elaine was alive, but a growing sense of peace it had created told him that the Lord had provided for her well-being, too. Besides, reflecting again upon his wife's resourcefulness, he could not believe that she would have been killed at Darwin. She was just too smart for that.

No, Preston was certain that God had not brought him and Elaine together for a few months of war-interrupted marriage only for one or both of them to die. There was a divine plan behind this painful separation, and though Preston could not imagine what it could be, he had faith that it would end in a reunion with his beloved bride.

Surreptitious fence-side meetings with civilians were far from the only means the men of Bicycle Camp had of staying in contact with the outside world. Paid small stipends by the Japanese for their labor and actual salaries out of the 131st Field Artillery's payroll, the men had enough money to buy moderate amounts of food from local markets. The true morale booster, though, was the presence of two clandestine radios, one managed by the sailors and the other by the soldiers. The radios kept them tuned in to the true events of the world, which contrasted so dramatically with the propaganda shouted at them during every *tenko.* Through the month of May at least, the Japanese had not needed to exaggerate. The American prisoners learned from KGEI in San Francisco and the BBC that Corregidor had fallen and that *Lexington* had been sunk, but also heard about Doolittle's raid on Japan and the failure of the Japanese invasion force to reach Port Moresby and threaten Australia.

In June, though, they also heard about the Battle of Midway, and though accurate reports of the struggle would not emerge for many months — the crews of the Army B-17s claimed credit for sinking most of the Japanese carriers — the prisoners knew that the Japanese had finally been handed a clear-cut defeat. The guards at Bicycle Camp knew it as well, for the prisoners soon discerned a souring in their moods. They dared not reveal that discernment to their captors, though, nor allow their own moods to improve too much lest the existence of the radios and the typed news bulletins produced from their broadcasts become suspected by the Japanese.

No quantity of good news could halt the daily bashings or the long days of back-breaking work in the *kumis.* Only freedom could do that and return them to the business of fighting the war. U.S. military regulations required them to keep fighting, however, even behind the wire, by mandating that they attempt to escape at every opportunity. Such efforts were more easily written into regulations than performed in real life, though, and became the subject of many lively debates among the *Houston* officers.

Preston sided with those who believed in escaping, no matter what the risks, because he was one of many who had

had enough of the Japanese brutality. Unlike some of the enlisted men who had already escaped from abusive stepfathers and the like back in the States, Preston had been raised to take no maltreatment from anyone. His father was a lawyer, and Phillip Brown had instilled a demanding sense of justice in his only son. Preston had no interest in sitting back and waiting for the war to come back to them. He wanted to take it to the enemy, so to speak, but wiser colleagues knew they could not act rashly. The Japanese had presented Harold Hamlin with a pledge for all of his men to sign, promising that they would not try to escape. The *Houston* officers discussed what to do with it while sitting in their barracks one night. Hamlin, as always, presided as acting captain, with Leon Rogers sitting to his right as exec.

Hamlin sat before the officer corps, holding a copy of the pledge in his hands. "Everyone, this could be the most significant decision we make while we are here at Bicycle Camp. The Japs want us to promise not to escape and to obey all of their orders, while we are obligated to a man to recognize our own military regulations that require us to make escape attempts. The Geneva Convention recognizes our right to escape, but the Japs, as we all know, never ratified the Geneva Convention and do not care about our rights."

"We can't sign that piece of trash, sir," Preston interjected eagerly. "We can't sell our country out like that."

Another junior officer protested from the corner. "We're not selling anyone out. That document and our signatures on it won't mean a blessed thing because we all will have signed it under duress. Your old man's a lawyer, you should know that."

"But we can't simply give up on escaping!"

"Brown! Do you even have an idea of how to escape from this place? *If* getting outside the fence was possible, where would we go? We're so close to the city we'd be seen, and the jungle is full of hostile natives. That's how most of us got caught in the first place, yourself included."

"He's right, Mr. Brown," Hamlin responded calmly, subtly attempting to reduce the tension in the room. "I hear the Army boys talking about this all the time. They somehow believe they can escape from here and make it through the jungle to the sea and then find a boat to sail to Australia or some place. That's simply not feasible. We know what it's like out there, we know what the sea's like. It can't be done."

"With all due respect, sir, we shouldn't give up so easily," Preston replied.

"I appreciate your sentiment, Mr. Brown," Hamlin said firmly, "I really do. We cannot sign any pledge to the Japanese that will violate our own regulations, but we also cannot realistically entertain thoughts of escape."

Terry Galloway now joined the discussion on Hamlin's side. "The Japs have threatened to kill ten of us for every one who tries to escape, Preston, and I don't think they're kidding around."

"You don't kid around by dragging an Aussie through camp behind a truck until he's dead," another officer added.

"Anyone who tries to escape from here will be risking suicide for himself and murder for everyone he leaves behind," Galloway continued. "We can't take that sort of risk."

The other officers murmured their agreement, leaving Preston to hang his head in contemplation. He said nothing more.

Hamlin spoke next. "I can try to modify the language of the pledge so it will only require us to obey orders that do not conflict with U.S. military regulations, but I don't know if the Japs will spring for it."

"It'd be worth a shot," Rogers commented, and several others offered their support for the idea.

"Okay, I will try that," Hamlin replied. "But in the meantime, we will not sign any document promising our obedience to the Japanese and promising not to escape. That does not mean I think escape is a good idea; it's just that we cannot violate our own regulations. That is my decision."

That sentence told the junior officers that Hamlin had made up his mind and would not be dissuaded. He was the captain now, and his word was final. Preston was the only one who really harbored any lingering disagreement anyway, and that was only because he still did not recognize the Japanese as holding legitimate authority over him no matter what their abilities to kill him amounted to. His bashing a month earlier had only strengthened his resolve.

Galloway had sensed Preston's potentially destructive stubbornness before, and had especially sensed it during that night's meeting. He pulled Preston aside after it broke up and tried to warn him of the potential consequences his attitude might bear for all of them.

"Hey, pal, may I have a word with you?"

Preston nodded slightly and simply said, "Sure."

"I can tell you're getting more and more frustrated with being stuck here, and I just want to ask you to be careful. I know you're not a rebel; you're a very straight, proper officer, just like the rest of us, but the Japs hold all the cards here, and you have to accept that."

Preston glared at him uncertainly, not sure if Galloway was being disloyal to their friendship or was really trying to help him.

"I take orders from God and American officers," Preston replied.

"That's not true. You obey the Japs every day."

"That's with little things, though. I do it to keep from getting bashed again, and I'm not selling out my country when I come to attention."

"You're not selling out your country by tolerating life here either, though," Galloway insisted under his breath. "If you let yourself get so fed up with things that you do something crazy and get yourself and a bunch of us killed, then you will have sold *us* out. We have to survive this place so we can fight again! We have to survive if we want to see our families again."

"Lainy would never back down, and neither would either of my folks, or her folks for that matter."

"None of them have ever been in this big of a jam before. I'm sure they care more about your coming home than your sacrificing yourself in some empty act of symbolism. The whole island of Java's our prison; there's no escaping — not yet at least."

Preston looked at Galloway glumly, knowing that his long-time roommate was right, but not sure that he wanted to admit it.

"Thanks, Terry. I appreciate your concern." He walked away determined to restrain his growing frustration for a little while longer, but left Galloway unconvinced that the warning had accomplished anything.

A few days later, the Japanese surprised the prisoners not by modifying the language of the pledge but by offering to let the men — any of them — write messages to their families back home and broadcast them over Batavia radio. This gesture seemed suspicious to many of the men, including Preston, because the Japanese penchant for propaganda was so well-known. The prisoners were, after all, subjected to heavy doses of it on a daily basis, as were the inhabitants of

Java, who had been promised for months that the occupying forces were liberating the East Indies from European colonialism and placing them into the so-called "Greater East Asia Co-Prosperity Sphere."

The radio messages became the subject of another officers' huddle, but this time, *Houston*'s surviving leaders decided to go along with the Japanese by following the logic that letting their families know that they were alive was worth giving the Japanese an opportunity to use the information for propaganda. Preston and Galloway both began composing their addresses, hoping and praying that they might be given a chance to have a one-way conversation with their loved ones. As it turned out, the Japanese selected an Australian civilian broadcaster in Bicycle Camp to be the official on-air reader, but no matter who read the messages, news of *Houston*'s survivors would get out.

Chapter Twenty-Four

Elaine had not seen Stan Townsend in two-and-a-half weeks when he suddenly appeared on the Kentishes' stoop on a sunny Sunday afternoon. It was the first time he had come to the house since he and Elaine had dined with the Kentishes after church and the elderly couple had invited her to live with them. That had been in March, almost three whole months before. That Townsend had come so far out of his way on this day worried her.

"Hello, Elaine," he greeted her pleasantly, almost happily. "May I come in?"

Elaine grinned back politely. "Sure, but only if you'll tell me what you're doing here so I don't die from the suspense. You never come here to talk to me."

"I know," he replied, stepping inside and wiping his feet on the mat. "Don't worry, I have positive news."

Judith Kentish's voice fluttered in from the other room. "Who is it, Elaine?"

"Lieutenant Commander Townsend," Elaine called back.

"Well, bring him in!"

Having already done so, Elaine disregarded her hostess's admonition. She gave Townsend an uncertain glance. "Positive? You mean, 'good'?"

"Well, sort of," he answered. "I don't know where your husband is, if that's what you mean by 'good.' The *positive* news that I have is that the past two nights Batavia radio on Java has broadcast messages from Australian prisoners to their families at home."

"Tell me more," Elaine prodded as Mrs. Kentish strolled in, followed by the ever-casual but ever-curious Mr. Kentish.

Townsend looked up and saw the couple. "Hello, Mr. and Mrs. Kentish. How are you today?"

"Just fine, Commander," Mrs. Kentish replied sweetly. "How are you?"

"Quite well, thank you."

Elaine had little patience for small talk at this point. "Would you please tell me what Australian prisoners on Batavia radio have to do with Preston, Commander?" she asked impatiently, surprising herself with her tone of voice — the kind she had last used with her husband — and the fact that she had stumbled over the word "commander," almost addressing him as Stan instead. That violation of her own strict rule would have been a mortifying Freudian slip.

Townsend seemed not to have noticed. "If you'll calm down, I'll tell you," he told her with a grin playing on his lips.

Mrs. Kentish stepped forward and motioned toward the sofa in the parlor. "Please, come sit down and tell us all."

"All right." Townsend took a seat and waited for his hosts to do the same before telling his story. "The radio station in Batavia has announced that it will broadcast more messages, so I'm thinking Preston, if he's even there, might be one who gets selected."

Elaine scooted to the edge of her chair. "Will he be speaking himself?" she wanted to know.

"No," Townsend replied. "The actual broadcaster is an Australian civilian named Rohan Rivett."

"I've heard of him," Gerald Kentish interjected. "He reported from Singapore before its capture."

Townsend nodded. "That's right. Rivett was captured and has now, apparently, wound up in Java." Turning back to Elaine, he told her, "I have to warn you, Mrs. Brown. The odds against your husband's message being selected are overwhelming, but there is a chance it will be. If you do hear it, do not expect too much detail. The Japanese are censoring these messages quite a bit, so they will likely paint things more positively than they really are. I did notice, however, that the second Australian officer managed to slip a hint."

"Really?" Elaine asked.

"Yes, he referred to the conditions at this prison they call 'Bicycle Camp' as being 'comparable to those of Dudley Flats.'"

Mr. Kentish let out a guffaw, and Mrs. Kentish remarked, "Oh, my!"

"I think the Japs thought it was a compliment," Townsend replied.

Elaine did not understand what could be so funny. "What? What did I miss?"

Mr. Kentish stifled his grin and explained, "Dudley Flats is Melbourne's slum district. Anyone who's ever been there would know that."

"And the Jap censors had obviously never been to Melbourne," Townsend added with a wry grin.

The meaning of the Australian officer's ornery pronouncement caused its humor to be lost on Elaine. "So they're pretty bad off, huh?"

Townsend's smile disappeared and he replied, "The Japs are not known for treating their prisoners well. In fact, they can be downright brutal. They never ratified the Geneva Convention, so they recognize no international laws governing treatment of prisoners. It's likely that if your husband is in their custody he is having a very unpleasant time."

Elaine rested her elbows on her knees and dropped her face into her hands. Why did things have to work this way? Every time she received even the slightest bit of encouraging news, more negative news canceled it out. She lifted her head after a few seconds of silence in the room and asked, "How can I hear the broadcasts?"

"Well, tonight's will begin in a little over an hour, so I figured I might tune the Kentishes' radio for you, if they won't mind."

Mr. Kentish shook his head.

"Just over an hour?" Mrs. Kentish questioned.

"That's right."

"Why, that's right between tea and supper."

"I suppose so."

"And you knew that, I assume."

Townsend squinted at her as if he didn't know where she was taking this line of thought. "Yes," he replied.

"Then I imagine you'll have to join us for both tonight. You wouldn't have planned it that way, would you?"

An impish grin now spread across his face. "I might have, ma'am. After all, it's been weeks since I've tasted home cooking."

Mrs. Kentish's face broke into a huge smile. "I understand, and you are more than welcome to stay. Gerald, you help the commander tune the radio, and Elaine, you help me set the table. I'll get the food ready."

Elaine did not protest Townsend's intrusion and suspected it was motivated by nothing more than an honest desire to get a good meal or two. She helped Mrs. Kentish prepare the meal, and then after they ate it, they reconvened in the parlor to listen to the radio broadcast."

"Good evening, ladies and gentlemen," a crisp Australian voice called out through the ether, *"I'm Rohan Rivett reporting from Batavia. I have been given another letter to read from an Allied prisoner held by the Japanese at Bicycle Camp."*

Elaine leaned over to Townsend and whispered, "Why do they call it 'Bicycle Camp'?" He explained the origin of the facility's name as he had learned it from Dutch naval officers.

Rivett had spoken through their exchange. *"Tonight's letter was written by an American naval officer ..."*

"Did you hear that? An American!" Mrs. Kentish said excitedly.

Elaine's attention now came back to the broadcast, and her eyes fixed on the large wooden set as if by staring at it she could see the name of the prisoner before Mr. Rivett could read it.

"Ensign Terry Galloway of Long Beach, California, writes, 'Dear Mom, Dad, Bud, Deb, and all the Americans who are listening .... "

Elaine felt disappointment and elation all at once, disappointment that Preston's letter was not being read right then, and elation that Terry's was.

"That's Preston's roommate!" she piped up.

"Really?!" the excitable Mrs. Kentish exalted while Elaine redoubled her concentration on the radio.

Terry Galloway, through the voice of Rohan Rivett, continued, *"By now you have probably heard that my ship, U.S.S.* Houston *was sunk. It was a terrific fight, and I prom*ise you, we *gave the Japanese more than they bargained for. After the sinking, some Aussies and I swam to a small island where we lived for several weeks before deciding to turn ourselves in to the Japanese. Being completely surrounded and without supplies, we had no other choice. Captivity has been trying for all of us, but we are okay and have high spirits ... ."* The authenticity of that statement was doubtful to all. *"I was especially pleased to find my friend Preston Brown alive and well when I was reunited with the rest of my ship's survivors at Serang."*

"Oh, God *bless* him!" Elaine shouted, using her arms against the armrests of her chair to propel herself to her feet. "He must have mentioned Press just for me!" She clasped her hands in front of her chest and looked toward the ceiling. "Thank you, Lord!" she prayed aloud. She then stood rooted to the floor for the next ten minutes as Rivett read the remainder of Terry's letter, resting her chin on her clasped hands, listening for any further clues about her husband's condition. None came, and she was not surprised. The Japanese would not allow details of their brutality to be broadcast. She was thankful for the little bit that she had heard, though.

The broadcast ended, and Mr. Kentish turned off the set. Townsend stayed a while longer, ate supper with them, and then begged his leave. Elaine walked him to the door, thanking him profusely for his timely tip about the radio messages.

"I haven't felt this encouraged since the last time I saw Press," she told him. "I know he's in a terrible place right now, but I also know that he's alive, and that means there's a chance I might see him again."

"I'm glad I could help, Mrs. Brown," Townsend replied. "You have a good evening, okay?"

"I will, sir. You can bet I will."

Elaine's prayers that night were a bit more hopeful and much less tortured. Pondering the streams of moonlight filtering into her room through the slits between the curtains, she lay in her cozy bed wondering if Preston could see them, too. For the first time in four months, she felt united with her husband despite the impossible distance that still separated them.

Preston lay awake that night on his bamboo bed, whispering to Galloway in the moonlight with the Bible lying by his side. "I sure hope Lainy heard it," he commented. "I can't imagine how she would have known to listen to Batavia radio, but our names are out there now. Someone had to hear it, and someone will tell her. Someone will tell my folks." He tilted his head backward to see Galloway. "Thank you so much for doing that for me."

"Hey, pal, don't mention it. You woulda done the same for me, right?"

"Of course."

"I'm sure it was no accident that my message was the first American one to get read, so we can just assume God had something to do with it, and that your wife and your folks will get the news soon."

"That's right." Preston rolled over to face the concrete wall. "Thanks again."

"Good night, Preston," Galloway replied, hinting strongly that it was time to go to sleep.

Preston said no more and did fall asleep, into a deep, satisfying sleep.

CHAPTER TWENTY-FIVE

After the Battle of Midway, ***Enterprise*** returned to Oahu on June 13, and Floyd Craven, Harry Giles, and the other members of Bombing Squadron Six spent the period of onshore duty at the naval air station at Kaneohe, on the eastern side of the island. Liberty was usually spent in the town, which was decidedly quieter than Honolulu but not without its own humming social life. Just the same, on a pleasant early July evening, Floyd and Giles rented a car and drove over to Honolulu. Giles wanted to see some old friends from Pearl Harbor, and Floyd had gone along for the ride, hoping to find a way into the lavish Royal Hawaiian, which had become the assigned liberty domain of submariners.

Giles had arranged to meet his friends at a high-class restaurant near Waikiki, and when the two officers arrived, Floyd was surprised to discover who the friends were. Standing on the sidewalk in the place of the two fellow junior officers from old *Nevada* that Floyd had imagined stood a middle-aged couple, the man a short but well-built Navy commander in dress whites, and the woman a petite redhead.

"Those are your friends, huh?" Floyd asked. "I didn't know you made friends with commanders and their wives."

Giles evidently missed the sarcasm in Floyd's comment. "Yeah, these folks are real special to me. They're my second family in a way."

Floyd didn't say another word until they were out of the car and the introductions had started. Standing now less than five feet from the commander, Floyd could see the gold crosses on his shoulder boards indicating that he was a chaplain. Floyd's neck immediately began to sweat beneath his choker collar.

After the initial greetings, Giles said, "Chaplain and Mrs. Bates, I want you to meet my buddy Floyd Craven, one of the SBD pilots in our squadron and a brand-new lieutenant (junior grade)."

Floyd mildly appreciated Giles's pretense of bragging on his promotion of the previous day. The fact was the promotion was overdue, having been withheld for a month due to his bad behavior earlier in the spring.

Giles continued the introductions, "Floyd, this is Chaplain Henry Bates and his wife Mabel."

Floyd quickly set aside his discomfort and shook the couple's hands in the warmest Arkansas style he could remember and said, "It's a pleasure to meet you both," with the mild swagger he had learned as a naval aviator. He had a feeling he might need to charm his way through this evening.

"I made the reservations for the three of us," Chaplain Bates told Giles, "but I'm sure they won't mind if I add Lieutenant Craven. I know the maitre d' well, and I don't think he'll object."

"Excellent, sir. Floyd, would you like to join us?"

Floyd looked for an excuse but knew he had none. If he didn't stay at the restaurant he would probably wind up drunk in a bar with Giles having to bail him out of trouble again, so he agreed to stay.

The four diners stepped into the plush restaurant and stood in line to speak to the maitre d'. Chaplain and Mrs. Bates took that opportunity to go wash up before eating, and left the two junior officers waiting silently in line.

"Harry Giles, is that you?" a sweet, young female voice chimed at them from a point near the pay telephone mounted on the wall about seven feet to their right.

Floyd's head snapped over to see a pretty young woman with auburn hair and wearing an attractive evening dress walking toward them. Giles saw her, too, and Floyd noticed that he had the look of a cornered animal in his eyes.

"Debbie," he said almost breathlessly.

"You're darn right it's Debbie," the woman said with a wry grin on her face as she approached. "I thought I'd never see you again after your last letter."

"I didn't think I'd ever see you again either," Giles replied unenthusiastically.

"You know you broke my heart, right?"

"I'm sorry, Debbie. I just did what I had to do," Giles said apologetically, with the first trace of emotion Floyd had yet detected.

"Yeah, well, I couldn't argue with you, not across the ocean I couldn't."

"I thought you'd be mad at me."

"I was, for about three months. But there's other fish in the sea, and I'm not one to hold a grudge. If you want to make up, we could. I mean, since we've run into each other like this." She practically sang that last sentence and left the last phrase dangling in midair.

Giles shook his head emphatically. "No, Debbie, we can't. My decision still stands, and besides, I'm having dinner with a chaplain friend of mine and his wife. Floyd was going to join us."

The young woman raised her eyebrows. "Floyd? You mean this fellow to whom you failed to introduce me?"

Giles closed his eyes in embarrassment and quickly corrected his error. "I'm sorry, Debbie. This is Floyd Craven, a pilot friend of mine."

"Dive bomber. VB-Six." Floyd interjected a bit cockily.

"Yes, that's right. Floyd, this is Debbie Galloway. She's an old girlfriend of mine from my days being stationed in California."

"So I've gathered," Floyd responded. Turning to Debbie, he charmingly said, "I'm pleased to meet you, Miss Galloway. What brings you out to Hawaii?

"Oh, I'm acting in a movie that's being filmed in part on the island. I was one of the lucky ones to get sent out here."

"Are you here with company this evening?"

"No, actually, I just found out my date won't be able to join me. He was half an hour late, so I decided to call him. He said he got held up in a production meeting. He's the assistant director."

Floyd saw an irresistible opening here. "Oh, well, I'd certainly be eager to stand in for him so that your evening's not ruined. It would also save Harry's chaplain friend 40 bucks."

"Hey, that'd be terrific!" Debbie exclaimed. "Harry, you won't mind that, will you?"

Giles shrugged. He had heard of Floyd's legendary ability to find dates with pretty women, and he had just witnessed with his own eyes and ears the fastest rebound of all time. Had Debbie been Giles's sister, he would have definitely objected, but he knew Debbie too well to think that he could protect her because, for one thing, she was a woman who did not want protection.

"No, I don't mind." He turned to Floyd. "I'll come find you when I'm done eating, okay?"

"Okay. Take your time, though," Floyd replied, his eyes fixed on Debbie. "Where's your table?"

Debbie flashed him a grin and said, "Follow me."

Giles took a deep breath as he watched them leave knowing that neither one was what the other needed.

Floyd gazed at Debbie across the table-for-two and past the single candle flame that almost interrupted his line of sight, and she stared back at him.

"What's the matter, Floyd?" she replied, almost acting uncomfortable.

"I'm just contemplating my pal Harry's stupidity."

Debbie looked amused. "What?"

"Why in the world did he break up with you?" Floyd wondered.

"Oh, that. It's a long story, but the short version is that about the first week of February I got a letter from him out of the blue saying that he'd become a Christian and had decided that our relationship could not continue because I was not a Christian."

Floyd grinned out of the corner of his mouth. "That sounds like something he'd say."

"The only reason I understood at all was because my younger brother had 'gotten saved,' as they say, at one of those big revival meetings a few years ago, and he'd started quoting the Bible and telling my parents and my other brother and me that we're going to hell, and all that nonsense."

"Did Harry say any of those things?"

"He did, but he was at least gentle about it. Terry, my brother, got all riled up one night. Dad got so flustered he had to take a walk. Didn't come back until two in the morning. Anyway," she shrugged as she reached for her wine glass, "I was disappointed in Harry, but it wasn't the end of the world. I decided if he was going to be like my brother I didn't want him anyway."

"That's kind of harsh, isn't it?" Floyd asked.

"Well, that's what I was thinking then. I've softened on both of them now, and if Harry had asked me to eat with him tonight, I would have."

"What about your brother? What made you change your feelings about him?"

Debbie got very quiet and waited a few moments before responding. "Terry's a naval officer, too, and his ship got sunk back in February or March. He's a prisoner of war now."

"Oh," Floyd replied simply. "I'm sorry to hear about that."

"Yes, so was I. It changed a lot and made me realize how much I do love him, despite his crazy religion."

"I've never really thought of Christianity as crazy," Floyd commented. "It's pretty popular where I come from."

"And where do you come from, Floyd?" Debbie asked, placing her right elbow on the table and resting her chin on her fist. "You look like a city man to me."

Floyd laughed. "If you believe that, then why don't you try to guess where I'm from?"

"Well, you're not from New York. You don't have that accent. I think you're from the South, and I'd guess Atlanta."

Floyd shook his head. "Nope."

"New Orleans."

"Getting closer."

"Well, what else is over there?!"

Floyd chuckled. "I'm from a small town in Arkansas named Springdale."

"Arkansas?" she bellowed. "You're joking, right?"

"Not at all. Is that a problem? Harry's from Idaho, so if you were okay with him, I hope you're okay with me."

"No, in fact I think you're very charming and sophisticated for a man from the hills."

"Springdale's not exactly in the hills, but I know what you mean. Where are you from?"

"Born and raised near Los Angeles, destined to be an actress from age three, or so my mother tells me," she related with that wry grin.

"Tell me about this movie you're making."

"It's a romance about an Army pilot and an Army nurse based here on the island. It's going to be called *North Shore Sunrise.*"

"I assume you're the leading lady."

"Ha-ha, oh, no!" Debbie cackled. "I'm one of the other nurses. I'm in a grand total of three scenes, but one of them is set on a sugar plantation, and California's just a little short of those, so that's how I got to come on this trip."

"Well, you got a date with the assistant director. That counts for something."

Debbie dismissed the comment with a scornful wave. "Oh, he's such a cad. I'd bet my next paycheck that at this minute he's two blocks away from here eating dinner with the leading lady herself. He probably set up the date with me just to make her jealous."

"Make her jealous of a rookie actress, right?"

"Right! I'm so sick of men like him."

"Are all the men in your company like that?"

"The production staff is either all married or all uninterested in a nobody like me."

Floyd grinned at this self-effacing statement.

Debbie noticed his reaction and interrupted herself. "What? I know my place, and I'm not too proud to admit it. Anyway, I have no chance with the older men, and most of the younger men on the crew and in the cast have such enormous crushes on me that they're scared to speak to me. All the other girls in the small roles are church mice, so I'm the only one looking for male company, and none of the men are looking back."

"Except to set themselves up for bigger dates," Floyd filled in.

Debbie's eyes shone. "Exactly!"

"Well, I hope my company is adequate consolation to you."

"It definitely is. I'm so glad we ran into each other, Floyd."

"So am I," he replied with a smile. "I'm looking forward to getting to know you. We don't head to sea again for a couple of more weeks, you think we'll be able to see each other again?"

"Floyd, we haven't even eaten yet and you're already asking me out again?"

"Yeah, I know, I just want to take care of this early so I can relax," he explained.

"You have nothing to worry about. I think I can find the time to see you again."

Floyd smiled back with satisfaction but said nothing in reply as the waiter delivered their meal.

On the drive back to Kaneohe, Giles noticed Floyd in a better mood than he had been in months. "I gather you and Debbie hit it off, huh?" he offered.

That simple, intentionally naive question, unleashed from Floyd an excited narrative of his dinner with Debbie Galloway. "She's got so much class, Harry, she puts all the other women I've dated to shame. She's amazing! I'm sure glad you got saved or whatever you did, pal, because she's a winner if I've ever seen one."

Giles allowed himself to grin courteously but kept his eyes on the road ahead. "I'm glad you had a good time," he replied, not really meaning it.

CHAPTER TWENTY-SIX

Phil Brown's strategic placement as a lawyer in the Navy Department put him in no greater position to know of his missing son's whereabouts than if he had worked in the White House itself. He learned of the Batavia radio broadcast the same way he learned of everything else regarding Preston, through letters and telegrams sent from his daughter-in-law in Australia. That she knew so much thanks to a friendly intelligence officer assigned to the Submarine Force Southwest Pacific while the captains and admirals in Washington knew nothing rankled him. It was almost as if the Navy Department had forgotten *Houston* had ever existed.

It was true that the sinking had received major press coverage when it had finally been confirmed, but with the exception of the city of Houston, that interest had died down since Memorial Day. The city had made quite a production out of having 1,000 volunteers inducted into the Navy in a grand ceremony attended by the cruiser's former American task force commander. Each recruit was supposed to replace one of *Houston*'s sailors, and the original idea gave the impression that they were to man a new cruiser of the same name. Two elements undermined this gesture. First, plans called for the new cruiser to be named *Vicksburg*, and old Navy hands believed in decades of superstition that said that changing a ship's name once her keel had been laid was bad luck. The new *Houston* might not be any more fortunate than the old one, and therefore, might have been more useful to the war effort as *Vicksburg*. Second, the Navy would not allow all 1,000 volunteers to serve aboard a single ship, so the gesture reverted to symbolism. Still, though, the patriotic spirit of those inspired by the old cruiser's loss would now benefit the entire fleet.

But of course, after all the pomp and circumstance surrounding Houston's Memorial Day remembrances — including the reading of a special letter from *Houston*'s most special passenger, President Franklin D. Roosevelt — the ship and her men faded into memory, blending with the thousands of dead and captured souls of Bataan, Corregidor, and Wake. Since *Houston*'s men and the soldiers of the Second Battalion, 131st Field Artillery — known as the "Lost Battalion" — had been lost on Java and not on American soil, their absence was not as noticeably felt.

So as Phil Brown resigned himself to the fact that his only son had been swallowed by the enormous tidal wave that was this world war, he refused to resign himself to being a minor player in it. Filling a staff judge advocate position and being charged with reviewing American prisoner-of-war policies was not what Phil had had in mind when he called Capt. Theodore Bonner at the Bureau of Personnel back in March. It was exactly what Bonner had had in mind for his old shipmate, however. Phil chafed at the assignment, but accepted it because he had no other options. Still, though, he wanted to skipper a ship, not a desk. He had needled Bonner on and off throughout the month of April, but Bonner had started to ignore him. They hadn't spoken to each other in two months, and now, with the news that Preston was more than likely still alive, Phil experienced a new surge of indignation. He headed to Bonner's office, determined to get transferred out of Washington or get court-martialed trying.

Ted Bonner was an Annapolis man who had stayed in the full-time Navy, unlike Phil, and had always been a step ahead of the career reservist. The two had met aboard the destroyer *Boggs* when Phil was an ensign and Bonner was a lieutenant (junior grade). They had been friends ever since, but Bonner had clearly become part of the Navy bureaucracy. After serving as a destroyer commander and an executive officer on a cruiser, he had transferred ashore and worked his way into the Bureau of Personnel. He had not been to sea since 1938, something Phil liked to point out every time Bonner made an issue of Phil's lack of recent seagoing experience.

Phil surprised Bonner by walking straight past his sputtering yeoman in the outer office and entering his inner office unannounced. Phil presumptively took a seat and declared his presence to Bonner.

"Good morning, Ted," Phil greeted his friend in a manner matching that of his entry and not that of a junior officer.

"Phil, I haven't seen you in weeks," the captain replied with surprise. "To what do I owe this rude visit, or do I know already?"

"You know," Phil replied simply.

Bonner gave an exasperated sigh. "I thought you had forgotten about that, but then again, folks have always accused me of being hopelessly naive."

"You wouldn't know a crooked attorney if he walked up and sued you for those stripes on your sleeves."

Bonner didn't miss a beat. "And you would, which is why Secretary Knox wants lawyers like you managing the regulations for the wartime tribunals. Some German spies just got picked up in New York a few days ago. A U-boat dropped them off on Long Island. If there are any American citizens out there who helped them, and we find them, we sure don't want them becoming those crooked attorneys' next clients."

"If I actually got assigned to prosecute a tribunal or a court-martial, I might be a little more encouraged, Ted, but all I'm doing now is sifting paperwork while my son's sitting in Jap prison."

Bonner held up his hands. "And how is that my fault?"

"It's not," Phil replied. "I just want you to do me the biggest favor you could ever possibly do, and that is use whatever influence and weight your 25 years and four stripes have earned you to get me out of the States."

"Are you still demanding a sea command?" Bonner asked him with a hint of weariness in his voice.

"That would be ideal. Surely there's an opening somewhere, if not on a destroyer then on a minesweeper."

"You'd take a minesweeper?"

"What, is the work too lowly for me?" Phil challenged. "My ambitions aren't as high as yours. I know you've got your heart set on getting one of those new battlewagons we're building. I just want to actually fight the war. I can do all the lawyering I want back in Little Rock."

"Your pestering is almost making me wish you were back in Little Rock now, Phil," Bonner remarked with a wry grin.

"Get me a ship and I'll be out of your hair faster than you can say 'all ahead full.'"

Bonner chuckled and shook his head. "Phil, it's a wonder you've never served time for contempt-of-court. You are the most obnoxious person I know, and that includes several admirals, a host of civilian suits, and my sister-in-law. I'll have an answer for you in a few days, I promise."

Bonner looked at Phil for acknowledgment, but the lawyer was glancing quickly around the room.

Puzzled, Bonner inquired, "Looking for something?"

"Just a Bible," Phil responded, making eye contact again. "I think I want to hear that again under oath."

Bonner lowered his head, toughened his gaze, and said, "Get out of my office, Phil, before I accidentally get you reassigned to Guantánamo Bay."

Phil grinned and stood. "I knew I could count on you, Ted."

"Yes, well, whatever happens, don't say I never did anything for you."

"I won't," Phil promised.

"I'll be seeing you."

Phil tucked his cap under one arm and said, "Have a good day, Cap'n," before heading back through the door and telling the rigidly standing yeoman to stand at ease as he left the office.

Four days later a sealed envelope arrived at Phil's office in Washington. Inside he found what he had been waiting for. They were his orders to pack immediately and be in San Francisco by June 30. He would be flown from there to Pearl Harbor and then on to Auckland, New Zealand, where he would join the staff of Vice Adm. Robert Ghormley, the commander of the U.S. Navy's South Pacific Force. It was not the assignment he coveted, but it was at least located within a theater of operations.

Three days after receiving the assignment, Phil was back in Little Rock, packing his belongings and preparing for an indefinite deployment. His wife Olivia carried a stack of white undershirts across the bedroom and laid them in his open sea bag, which he had wondered if he would ever again have a chance to use.

"You're determined to make me a childless widow, aren't you, Phil?" Olivia commented glumly. She had not been pleased with his overseas assignment and was not showing very many signs of support.

"You're not childless, dear," Phil replied calmly and confidently. "Carolyn's safe in Fayetteville; Preston's still out there somewhere; and nothing can happen to me as long as I have a staff position in New Zealand."

"Don't tell me that," she retorted. "You expect me to believe that admirals never go to sea or see combat?"

"It's not likely. Ghormley's command isn't a tactical one. He's responsible for an entire area, not just a task force or two. I imagine I'll spend most of the war in New Zealand or some place like it."

"Well, it's too far away for my liking, and I know you'll pull every string you can to get a command. And then I'll wind up losing you, too."

Phil straightened up from packing and looked at her. "Livvy, darling, have some faith, please. Having my own command is a dream of mine, you know that. If I get the chance to fulfill that dream, I'm going to take it. I'm not trying to hurt you; I'm trying to do my duty. Our only son risked everything trying to do his duty, but I believe he will come home alive. I will come home alive, too, but I have a job to do first."

"Until this spring your job only required you to spend eight hours per day in your office or in a courtroom," Olivia countered.

"Yes, and then the world changed," Phil replied. "I'm not going to spend the war fighting court cases while Preston is fighting for his life in a prison camp. And if I have to fight court cases, I'd might as well do it in uniform."

Olivia fell silent, and Phil returned to his packing. "Well, this obsession you've always had with the Navy is why Preston's gone anyway," she said abruptly. "He could have gone to any university in the country, but you convinced him to go to the Naval Academy."

"You're not going to hang that albatross on my neck," Phil insisted, feeling his blood pressure begin to rise. "The only people who deserve blame for where Preston is right now are the Japanese. They started this war. We did not ask for it, and Preston did not ask for it, but they gave it to us anyway. Life will not return to normal until we defeat them."

"But it's not just the Japanese we have to defeat, Phil. We have to beat the Germans and the Italians, too, and the way Roosevelt's talking, the Japanese are the smallest priority. If Preston is still alive, how long am I going to have to wait to get him back?"

Phil shook his head. "I don't know, I really don't. But we will win. I have faith that we will, and that Preston will be fine."

Olivia stared at him sadly. "I wish I had that kind of faith."

Phil had run out of things to say. The conversation was proceeding poorly enough without him telling her that she was self-centered. Olivia always had been a materialistic woman. She was a Christian and had raised their son and their daughter well, but she had never been impressed by the military. Phil and Olivia had met during the first war, and she had been all too glad for him to leave active duty. He was grateful she had at least tolerated his periodic reserve assignments during their marriage. Her mood had begun to sour about five years earlier when Preston had been accepted into the Academy. His ambition to be a naval officer like his father had fallen short of her expectations, and now that war threatened both Preston's and Phil's lives, Olivia's impatience was beginning to show itself in a big way.

"I wish you had faith, too," Phil finally said. "I wish you could say you believed in me and would pray for me."

A pained expression crossed her face as she shook her head. "You underestimate me. I *will* pray for you," she said as she approached him and gave him a hug. "I am simply afraid that God will see fit to allow you to get lost in this war just like Preston did."

Phil held her tight and spoke directly into her ear. "Preston's not lost. The Lord knows exactly where he is, and He will know exactly where I will be, too. Please, be strong for us. Be strong like Elaine is being strong."

Olivia pulled away from him and looked him in the eye.

"Our daughter-in-law is putting you to shame, dear," Phil told Olivia frankly. "At least you didn't think Preston was too good for her."

Olivia nodded with a sad expression in her eyes. "Elaine's an incredible young woman. And you're right — she is putting me to shame."

"Then do something about it," Phil said and leaned forward to encourage her with a kiss on the forehead.

"I'll do my best," she replied softly.

"Can you do it before you drop me off at the train station?"

"Yes," she replied, not sounding very confident.

"Then let's not let this disagreement be the last memory we'll have of each other while I'm gone."

"All right," she said and stepped forward to kiss him.

As Phil Brown's war was just beginning, Preston Brown's was entering a new phase. It was the Fourth of July at Bicycle Camp, and the loyalty oath the Japanese had unsuccessfully tried to force upon the prisoners the previous month resurfaced again. This time, the Japanese were more determined to make the men sign it.

Preston had gone out to the dockyard with a *kumi* that day, and as he led it back into the camp, he noticed all of the prisoners already present lined up outside the commandant's office.

"Detail, halt!" he ordered in cadence, and the marching column came to a stop.

A Japanese NCO approached and called out to Preston in Japanese using a few words Preston had become accustomed to. Preston left his men and followed the sergeant into the guardhouse. Another guard met them inside and presented Preston with a note that read in English, *"If you do not sign the oath, your life will not be guaranteed."*

Preston knew immediately that this was a repeat of the June attempt to secure the prisoners' obedience, and he had no more intention of signing in July than he had the month before.

The second guard motioned Preston toward the back room, the door to which was opened by the first guard. Preston stepped inside and saw the rest of the Allied officers standing at attention against the wall. The Japanese officer pushed him toward the group, and Preston squeezed in between Terry Galloway and Jake Dunn. There he stood with the others with nothing to do but stare at the Japanese, who did nothing but stare back.

After an agonizing 45 minutes, the guards finally signaled the prisoners to follow them out of the guard house. They marched across the camp to the Japanese zone, where the guards directed them into a garage. The Japanese officers were waiting.

The door shut behind the prisoners, locking them inside the dimly lit, musty room that smelled of motor oil and mildew. There was a cacophony of clattering metal, and Preston looked around to see the guards loading and cocking their rifles and then casually holding them at their hips in the direction of the prisoners. A guard approached displaying a sign bearing the same message that Preston had read on the note: *"If you do not sign the oath, we do not guarantee your lives."*

When Galloway whispered, "It looks like the jokers are serious this time," Preston thought it would all end right there.

No reply was necessary, and Preston remained silent, barely inhaling the tense, damp air. It certainly appeared that the Japanese intended to either extract their signatures or extract their lives. This was the moment of truth they all had feared. Preston cautiously searched the faces of his fellow officers, waiting for one to make the first move. Nobody budged, except the guards, who wrapped their fingers a little tighter around their rifle triggers. Preston figured he'd reached the end of God's plan for his life, and breathed a prayer and closed his eyes, fully expecting to never open them again on Earth. Then he thought of Elaine and prayed that someone would take care of her.

COMING SOON

Chaos Dark, the sequel to *Peril on the Sea*...

With her husband Preston still a prison-er-of-war in Java, Elaine Brown waits in Australia for more news of his condition as American and Australian forces take the offensive against the Japanese to capture an obscure island called Guadalcanal. Among the men bound for combat are naval aviator Floyd Craven and his buddy Harry Giles, Elaine's sailor brother Danny and his Marine best friends, twins Mike and Matt Mayfield, and Aussie sailor Tony Fraser. Meanwhile, Preston's father Phil and naval intelligence officer Stan Townsend find their own places in history working alongside the admirals directing the campaign. Elaine must fight her own battle to hold onto the men she has left in her life as they encounter the gruesome realities of war and death and as she continues to face the prospect that Preston may never return to her.

Chaos Dark is the second novel in a series detailing the War in the Pacific.

GLOSSARY

U.S. Navy Officer Ranks & Abbreviations

Admiral	Adm.
Vice Admiral	Vice Adm.
Rear Admiral	Rear Adm.
Captain	Capt.
Commander	Cdr.
Lieutenant Commander	Lt. Cdr.
Lieutenant	Lt.
Lieutenant (junior grade)	Lt. (j.g.)
Ensign	Ens.

ABOUT THE AUTHOR

Jonathan D. VerHoeven

Jonathan D. VerHoeven developed a deep affection for naval history at a young age. A postcard of the U.S.S. *Arizona* Memorial sparked an interest in the Pearl Harbor attack at the time of its 50th anniversary, and by age 6 he had begun checking out episodes of the classic World War II documentary series *Victory at Sea* from his local library. By age 10 he had discovered the writings of Samuel Eliot Morison and begun hand-writing one-page summaries of World War II sea battles. Had the skeptical librarians guessed that nearly twenty years later he would be a published author, they might have approved more visibly of the home-schooled boy and his fascination with war. As a history major at John Brown University, he wrote his senior honors thesis on the battle for Leyte Gulf and read Alfred Thayer Mahan's *The Influence of Sea Power Upon History* for fun. Later, while pursuing his master's degree, he placed runner-up in a white paper contest sponsored by the Maritime Security Expo. *Peril on the Sea* is his first published novel, and he plans several sequels telling the stories of the Pacific War for a generation that has seldom heard them.

www.ingramcontent.com/pod-product-compliance
Lightning Source LLC
LaVergne TN
LVHW091026080826
845145LV00002B/373

9781935986027